No More Dying

David Roberts

W F HOWES LTD

This large print edition published in 2009 by
W F Howes Ltd
Unit 4, Rearsby Business Park, Gaddesby Lane,
Rearsby, Leicester LE7 4YH

1 3 5 7 9 10 8 6 4 2

First published in the United Kingdom in 2008
by Constable

A CIP catalogue record for this book is available
from the British Library

ISBN 978 1 40743 571 8

Typeset by Palimpsest Book Production Limited,
Grangemouth, Stirlingshire
Printed and bound in Great Britain
by MPG Books Ltd, Bodmin, Cornwall

FSC
Mixed Sources
Product group from well-managed
forests and other controlled sources

Cert no. SGS-COC-2953
www.fsc.org
© 1996 Forest Stewardship Council

For the two Georges

I am most grateful to Lord Brabazon of
Tara and Gary Lowe for instructing me in the
mysteries of the Cresta Run. Philip Truett
knows everything there is to know about
Huntercombe Golf Club, and I must also
thank Nicholas Courtney who is knowledgeable
on a whole range of abstruse subjects.

So shalt thou feed on Death, that feeds on men,
And Death once dead, there's no more dying then.

Shakespeare, *Sonnet 146*

It cannot be but he was murder'd here;
The least of all these signs were probable.

Shakespeare, *Henry VI*

FEBRUARY AND MARCH 1939

CHAPTER 1

In the thick fog – a 'pea-souper', they called it – Verity Browne nosed her way down unfamiliar streets, her handkerchief to her mouth, dodging the cars and buses which loomed, yellow-eyed and sinister, out of the Stygian gloom. She was looking for Ransom Street, which she knew to be in the maze of narrow alleys behind Warren Street underground station. She strained to see the street names, half-tempted to give it up and return home. The doctor had warned her not to go out in fog as she was not yet fully recovered from tuberculosis and her lungs were still sensitive to polluted air. She had been lucky. It had not been a serious infection but she knew it was foolish to take chances. She asked herself wryly why she had left her gas mask behind.

It was an indication of the dangerous political situation in Europe that, despite Prime Minister Neville Chamberlain's every effort to appease Hitler, Sir John Anderson who was in charge of Air Raid Precautions – the ARP – had begun to issue gas masks in anticipation of poisonous gas attacks from the air. Trenches were being dug in

3

the Royal Parks, anti-aircraft gun emplacements hurriedly constructed against the anticipated bombardment by the Luftwaffe's supposedly invincible planes. Primitive bomb protection shelters, six feet by four, made from six curved sheets of corrugated iron, were being distributed to any house with a back or front garden into which a shelter could be buried. Londoners were resigned to their fate, only asking that the strain of waiting and imagining the unimaginable should at last be over.

Verity's goal was a branch or 'group' meeting of the Communist Party and she felt nervous, like a lapsed Catholic seeking out a mass against her better judgement. She retained only a residual loyalty to the Party. It was no longer the 'band of brothers' she had joined in a state of almost religious fervour in 1934. Then she had anticipated becoming an unimportant foot soldier in an army of like-minded seekers after truth, attempting to hold back an inexorable wave of Fascist terror. Spain's democratically elected government was facing an army in rebellion, supported by the Roman Catholic Church. The International Brigade had been raised to fight for the Republican cause – volunteers drawn mostly, but not exclusively, from the working classes of many countries rallying to the aid of their oppressed Spanish brothers. It had been a logical and thrilling extension of the Party's defiance of Fascism.

They had been defeated. That was bitter enough. Only a few nights ago she had been at Victoria station to welcome back the pathetic remnants of that proud army of idealists, but the worst of it was that she had seen the Party turn on itself, gnawing at its own entrails. It had been betrayed by its leaders – the cause subverted by devious and unprincipled apparatchiks. The International Brigade, which had gone to Spain to fight for justice and liberty, had been a chaotic amalgam of Communists, socialists, Trotskyists, anarchists and trades unionists. The Communists, on the orders of their paymasters in Moscow, had rejected this communion. They had 'purified' the Party of 'dissident elements' with the grim determination of the religious extremist. Anyone who refused to accept unquestioning obedience to Moscow was 'liquidated'.

Verity had never counted obedience among her virtues, preferring independence of thought and action, so she had gradually, though reluctantly, distanced herself from the movement she had joined with such high hopes. She still counted herself a Communist but was seriously thinking of turning in her Party card. However, if anything of the original Party remained, it was to be found in these local meetings where fifteen or twenty comrades gathered together to hear the word preached to them.

She had three special reasons for braving the fog and bitter chill. In the first place she liked and admired the District Secretary, George Castle, a locomotive driver, and his wife Mary. It was in their house that the meeting was being held and this was the first time Verity had visited their new home. When they had first been married, they had lodged in a stinking tenement near the railway line but, painfully slowly, they had saved enough money to rent their new respectable, rat-free abode.

In the second place she had been asked – no, ordered – to be there by David Griffiths-Jones. He was a senior Party figure and had once, briefly, years before, been her lover; in fact, she smiled apologetically to herself, he had been her *first* lover. He had deflowered her, as she had so much wanted, seeing virginity as one of those 'bourgeois' shackles she was determined to discard as she fought clear of what she saw as suffocating middle-class morality. Neither she nor David had pretended to be in love with one another but, as a lover, he had been efficient to the point of brutality. He was pragmatic in everything he did and had discarded her without a word of apology or regret as soon as it suited him.

She had not seen him for many months – not since just before the destruction of the Basque city of Guernica by German bombers in April 1937 – and she was curious to see how he had weathered the political storms which had followed that disaster. She suspected that he had been forewarned of what was to happen to the peaceful, undefended town and had deliberately refrained from alerting the authorities. There was evidence to suggest that Guernica had been sacrificed in a last desperate bid to generate international sympathy for the Republican cause. If it were true, Verity swore she would never forgive him or the Party.

And, finally, there was the reason that David had given her. The guest speaker was to be an old friend of hers – Fernando Ruffino, a young Italian Communist who had joined the International Brigade and fought in Spain against Franco and his German and Italian Fascist allies. Mussolini, desperate to ingratiate himself with Hitler and eager for a share of the spoils, had sent troops and, more importantly, Camproni bombers to Spain to help in the war against godless Communism.

She had liked and admired Fernando, and there had been a moment when they had almost become lovers, but he had been wounded on the Aragon front and hospitalized in France. He had not returned to Spain and was rumoured to be fighting Fascism in Italy. She had heard that he was now married with a child. She knew nothing of Italian Fascism – she had never even been to Italy – and she was looking forward to hearing what he had to say about it.

A policeman materialized out of the fog and, gratefully, she asked him for directions. He was kind enough to walk with her to Ransom Street and waved his bull's-eye lamp down towards the end of the road.

'Number nine's on the left, miss, by the second lamp post. Was it George Castle you was looking for?'

'Yes, it is, constable. How did you know?'

'He's a respected figure hereabouts. There's folk who owe him a lot. Leastways, that's what I hear, and that's despite the company he keeps.'

'The company he keeps?' Verity felt rather insulted.

'No offence, miss, but it's all politics nowadays and working people has no need of politics. If I may say so, miss, you'd do better not to wander round here, lost like, in your pretty hat and that bag of yours hanging on your arm so tempting. You'd as likely as not lose it on a night like this, if you understand me. Goodnight, miss.'

He touched his helmet respectfully and disappeared into the fog. Verity felt justly rebuked but was angry with herself for not remonstrating with him on the democratic duty of everyone to stand up and be counted. Of course it was all politics nowadays because no good citizen should stand by without protest and watch his country turned into a fascist state. She sighed and then coughed as the fog filled her lungs. She feared that the British – or at least the English – were not a politically aware people.

She turned to knock on the door of number nine. The constable was right about one thing, she admitted to herself. It had been stupid to put on that silly hat – the one she had bought in Bond

Street the day before – to pay a visit in this neighbourhood. She saw how it might appear a challenge to the local youths, asking to be knocked off her head. Furthermore, it was not suitable for a Party meeting. Even now, she still had time to tear it off her head and throw it in the gutter, but she did not. Instead, she stuck out her chin in a way her friends would have recognized. Why should she pretend to be what she was not? It was a beautiful hat. '*Très jolie*,' the assistant had said as she had packed it in its box. But who had made it – a girl sewing herself blind in some dingy sweatshop for a starvation wage? At least she *had* work. Verity was unable to deal with the contradictions in her life. Perhaps she was unsuitable company for George Castle, as the constable had hinted, but, take it or leave it, she could not, would not, change.

She was late and the tiny parlour was already tightly packed. Castle welcomed her warmly and introduced her. There was David, of course, so tall and good-looking that he seemed to fill the room all by himself. He did not kiss her – that would not have been suitable in a gathering of comrades – but shook her by the hand and seemed genuinely pleased she had come. He had his arm round a girl who hardly took her eyes off him. He, in turn was defensive, even rather awkward as he introduced her to Verity.

'Lucinda Arbuthnot-Grey,' he mumbled. 'I've told you about Verity Browne, haven't I, Lulu?'

Lulu! Verity repressed a giggle. She seemed utterly uninterested in Verity and without so much as a 'hello' dragged him away. 'I'm dying for a ciggie, dahling. Whatever that stuff was we were drinking last night, it's given me the most ghastly headache.'

'Shall I put you in a taxi? There's no need for you to stay.' To Verity's astonishment, David was positively oozing concern.

'Are there taxis in this place?' she replied in a voice which made even David wince.

'There's usually taxis in Charlotte Street,' George Castle interjected politely, 'though in this fog . . .'

'Oh, I know I'm being a bore but would you be a dahling . . . ?'

'Of course,' Castle said, seeming unmoved at being so addressed. 'I tell you what, young Leonard Baskin will take you.'

An underfed, spotty youth of about nineteen who was making sheep's eyes at a pretty girl in her twenties called Alice Paling, who had recently joined the Party, turned at the sound of his name and blushed scarlet. He was clearly not used to escorting girls like Lucinda Arbuthnot-Grey, but an order from George Castle was not to be questioned and he got his donkey jacket and donned his cloth cap while David helped Lucinda into her expensive-looking fur coat.

'Tomorrow then, dahling? Kiss, kiss.' She pursed her lips to David, appearing to demand that he

10

acknowledge their relationship. As George Castle held open the front door, allowing a cold, dank swirl of fog to chill the atmosphere, David, as nearly embarrassed as Verity had ever seen him, kissed the girl and put something in her coat pocket – perhaps something with which to pay the taxi, she thought uncharitably.

Lulu – Lucinda Arbuthnot-Grey – was so obviously out of place in this gathering that Verity was puzzled. Why had David brought her and why was he now so happy to be rid of her? He had friends – or at least acquaintances – among the aristocracy and would, without a second thought, have brought one of them to a local party meeting if it suited him but he never did anything without a reason. On the face of it, Lulu was straight out of Mayfair – but that was it! She had finally put her finger on what had been worrying her – Lulu wasn't real. There was something about the way she pronounced her vowels which made Verity suspect she had been born within the sound of Bow Bells. And her make-up – her lipstick, in particular, had been applied too thickly and her scent was cheap and nasty. And then it came to her. Of course! Lucinda Arbuthnot-Grey was a whore and her real name was probably something without a hyphen. Verity grimaced. She was a snob, she upbraided herself, but, truly, it wasn't Lulu's class she objected to – far from it. It wasn't even her trade. It was her affectation. It always made her grit her teeth when someone pretended to be something they weren't.

11

She grinned and David asked her sharply what she was smiling about.

'Nothing – nothing at all. Or rather, tell me, David, would I be right in thinking you wanted me to meet your girlfriend for a reason?'

He smiled but wouldn't meet her eye. 'Well yes, but I'll tell you about it later.'

Of the fifteen people at the meeting, she knew half a dozen. Danny O'Rourke, a fiery public speaker committed to the class struggle, was one. She did not like or trust him and she knew the dislike was mutual. There seemed to be a threat behind everything he said. To disguise her true feelings, she was effusive and he looked unconvinced and embarrassed. The treasurer, Harold Knight, a solid, loyal party man, asked after her health. She brushed aside his concern too hastily, saying – which was true – that it had been a very light bout of TB, and, less truthfully, that she was now fully recovered.

Everyone, except David, looked at her with, if not sympathy, then at least interest tinged with disapproval. She was quite beyond their day-to-day experience – an exotic bird, a celebrity, a woman with a 'past'. They had read her reports from Spain and Vienna in the *New Gazette*. She also wrote a monthly column on foreign affairs – of which, Danny often joked, she had had many – for the *Daily Worker*, the official publication of the Communist Party. It was almost unheard of for a woman to be a foreign correspondent for a national newspaper and, since most working-class men and women had never been abroad, she was admired and envied. Castle considered it a distinct feather in his cap to have her as a member of the group. True, she had not attended many meetings – that was hardly surprising given her other commitments – but she was here now. Furthermore, the presence of David Griffiths-Jones, a party high-up, signified that this was by no means a routine gathering.

Fernando Ruffino appeared from the kitchen with Mary Castle bearing sandwiches – meat paste and sardine – and a large brown teapot. As soon as he saw Verity, he put down the tray he was carrying and came over to kiss her. He drew back to look at her properly and told her she was too thin but more beautiful than ever. 'If *mamma* saw you, *cara*, she would say you needed feeding. Is it true that you have been ill? *Merda!* But you are better now, *Bella?* Tell me you are better.'

His eyes were moist and she remembered his infectious sympathy for whomever he was addressing and the delightful *ragù* he made of English and Italian. She tapped him on the wrist and told him he was being silly but her sparkling eyes told another story. He was not handsome in a conventional way – he was rather plump and no taller than she – but he had that indefinable 'something' which made him attractive to women.

'Did I hear you were getting married to that man of yours, Lord Edward Corinth?' David spoke his name with barely concealed contempt.

'You are *fidanzata* – betrothed, *cara*? I am *stravolto* – how do you say? – distraught. You ought to have asked my permission and I would not have given it.' Fernando clutched her hand and, for a moment, she thought he was going down on one knee. '*Tristezza, tristezza*,' he intoned. 'My heart breaks.'

'Please, Fernando! You're embarrassing me,' Verity protested, trying to disengage herself. 'Did I not hear that you were married with a child?'

'Si, Basilio. Two years old and the apple of his mother's eye.' He looked at her from underneath long eyelashes and whispered, loud enough for everyone to hear, a few words of Dante, '"*Amor mi mosse, che mi fa parlare*"' – 'As love has willed, so have I spoken.'

George Castle hurriedly brought the meeting to order. He had a way of referring to members of the group as brothers rather than comrades that Verity liked but of which she was sure David disapproved. He spoke warmly of Fernando and then, with head bowed, recalled the fall of Barcelona in January and dramatically held up an enlarged photograph which had recently appeared in *Our Fight*, the International Brigade's weekly paper, of refugees laden with belongings heading towards the French border and the refugee camps in the Pyrénées Orientales. It was a portrait of abject misery – innocent civilians driven from their homes by a terror they did not begin to understand. Although this was a scene with which she

14

was all too familiar, it still made Verity choke with emotion.

A phrase from a song the men used to chant before going up to the line came to her. It compared love of the Republic with the love of a woman – '*Mi corazón estaba helado, y ardía*' – 'My heart was frozen and it burned.'

Castle was repeating like a mantra, 'Bombs on Barcelona today, bombs on London tomorrow.' Verity's eyes pricked as she recognized the photograph he held up like a religious icon as being by her friend, André Kavan. They had been together at the bombing of Guernica when his girlfriend Gerda Meyer had been killed at her side.

Then Fernando stood up. He threw off any hint of the comic Italian and spoke with impressive authority of Fascist Italy – its brutality and venality. He could not deny that Mussolini was popular with the majority and that the opposition was fragmented, riven by political rivalry and infiltrated by the OVRA, the secret police. He turned to the plight of the Jews. In 1932, Mussolini had publicly spoken out against German anti-Semitism and many Jews had sought refuge in Italy from Nazi persecution. However, in July 1938, Mussolini had published his Manifesto on Race which prohibited Italians from marrying Jews, forbade Jews from entering the country and ordered the expulsion of those already in Italy.

As Verity watched Fernando tell of the desperate struggle to fight back against an authoritarian government which had been in power since 1922, she was reminded – no doubt blasphemously – of Christ preaching to the disciples. There were not enough chairs to go round so the younger comrades lay or squatted on the floor. Every face was concentrated on the Italian.

He had fought the good fight. He had been jailed in Milan, shot at in Turin, beaten up in Rome. He had started and distributed an anti-Fascist newspaper which had survived for three issues. He spoke modestly and with humour, but the ever-present danger in which he lived and worked was apparent to all his listeners. Verity could almost hear everyone in the room ask themselves if they would have the courage to do the same should England ever become a Fascist state.

He poured scorn on Neville Chamberlain and Lord Halifax who had visited Mussolini in January believing, wrongly, that the Italian dictator could influence Hitler, seeming not to realize that Hitler despised and ignored his partner in crime. As Mussolini complained, 'Every time Hitler occupies a country he sends me a message.'

The meeting broke up soon after Fernando had finished speaking, as though discussion of mundane party matters was inappropriate. Castle thanked him for providing 'leadership in our great fight' and went on to say that membership of the Communist Party in London had risen from 4,562 in April 1938 to 7,084, and the Young Communist League had more than trebled its membership to

8,000. He added that London sales of the *Daily Worker* had increased from an average of 27,000 to 51,000 on weekdays, and to 72,000 on Saturdays. He hoped they would reach 100,000 before the end of the year.

Fernando was spending the night with the Castles before going on a tour of cities in England and Scotland to address meetings and ask for financial and moral support. Unwilling to let Verity go, he suggested walking round to the Kardomah in the Tottenham Court Road for coffee.

'I have so much to say to you, *cara mia*. I want to hear how you are. You must tell me about your English lord. He must be a good man if you love him but has not David told you that you are betraying your class and the Party? But when the heart speaks, we must answer, *non è vero*?'

He had said what she knew everyone was thinking but so teasingly that she could not be angry. She blushed, however, and replied – hoping to annoy him – 'Yes, let's *all* go round to the Kardomah.'

Fernando scowled, as she had guessed he would.

'You youngsters go,' Castle said. 'Harold and I have some business to sort out and we need a bit of peace and quiet. David will shepherd you.'

The fog was very bad and they struggled to find their way across Fitzroy Street and into the Tottenham Court Road. '*Nacht und Nebel*, as the Germans say,' David coughed, wrapping his scarf

17

round his mouth as they narrowly avoided being run down by a bus.

The glow through the Kardomah's art deco windows guided them to a haven of warmth and steam-cleaned air. A man brushed past her, a woollen scarf wrapped about his neck and a hat pulled down over his face. He was clutching a little girl dressed in a thin-looking blue coat with a tam-o'-shanter on her head and Verity thought how wrong it was that the child should be out in such weather. Then she remembered the hundreds – possibly thousands – of children who, in this prosperous country, lived on the streets or in cellars – mere holes in the ground – cold and hungry, and once again she felt the fire of indignation which had led her to join the Communist Party. They breathed in the heady aroma of coffee beans. The gurgles and hiss from the shiny stainless steel coffee machines lifted their spirits as they took off their coats and pulled two tables together, greeting the waiters like old friends. Fernando passed round a packet of Nazionali and was amused when Verity said she had given up smoking.

After they had ordered, the conversation turned naturally to the recent demonstrations by the unemployed. The National Unemployed Workers Union had organized two highly successful 'actions' at Christmas. In one, two hundred people lay down in Oxford Street, disrupting the traffic and making the point to shoppers that in many industrial towns children would be receiving few, if any, presents. And, on New Year's Eve, another group of unemployed carried a coffin into Trafalgar Square bearing the message 'Unemployment – No Appeasement'. Then, just a week earlier, Danny O'Rourke had been one of the hundred who had gone to the Ritz Hotel to order tea and cause chaos in what was, to many of them, a symbol of the social divide. The newspapers had devoted many pages and photographs to the protests so the Communist Party, which had been behind the demonstrations and claimed to represent the unemployed more effectively than the Labour Party, boasted of a splendid victory.

Verity noted that very little was said about the Munich Agreement, which the Prime Minister had signed three months earlier. Hitler had already broken the solemn promises he had made to respect Czechoslovakia's independence, and Chamberlain's desperate but successful attempt to stave off war had divided the country. He was said to have received forty thousand messages of congratulation for bringing home 'peace with honour' but there were many, like Verity, who saw it as a humiliating defeat and a betrayal which in the end would have to be paid for. However, it could not be denied that it was pleasant still to be able to walk around London in safety. It had been drummed into everyone that there was no defence against the bomber and that the Luftwaffe would reduce London to rubble the moment war broke out.

Verity asked David what he thought of the Munich Agreement but he refused to be drawn except to say that the Soviet Union had sent part of its air force to its borders in order to protect the Czechs if asked to do so.

Fernando was affectionate but, to her relief, did not renew his protestation of undying love. She enjoyed flirting but was now focused on her impending marriage. She and Edward had officially announced their engagement to un-surprised friends and family at Christmas, which they had spent at Mersham Castle. Edward's brother, the Duke of Mersham, disliked Verity. He did his best to hide his distaste for the marriage but the Duchess had been warm in her welcome, telling Verity how glad she was to have her as a sister-in-law.

'I truly believe no other woman could make Ned happy,' Connie had said when she had got Verity alone in her boudoir. 'There will be people who will do their best to be unpleasant to you because you are different from the kind of woman they expected him to marry but you must take no notice. His closest friends and even my husband understand that he is a remarkable man and that he needs a remarkable woman by his side.'

Verity's eyes had filled with tears and she had been unable to respond except by embracing her.

Edward's nephew, Frank, was also engaged – to a delightful Indian girl, Sunita, the daughter of a friend of his, the Maharaja of Batiala. The wedding would be a grand affair but Verity and Edward were determined that *their* unlikely conjunction should be the quietest celebration possible. They had decided on a registry office in London a few days before Frank and Sunita were married in Winchester Cathedral so that, with any luck, no one would notice. Sunita, brought up a Hindu, had decided to convert to Christianity, much to the Duke's relief. There was to be a grand party at Mersham, of course, mainly for Frank and Sunita, but to which Edward and Verity would also invite their friends.

The Christmas celebrations had been heartfelt but subdued as everyone present knew that this would be the last before the European war they had been anticipating for so long. On New Year's Eve they had raised their glasses, but their toast to 1939 had been muted. Verity had seen Connie look at her son with fear and longing. He had been accepted by the Royal Navy and was to begin training in earnest the following week. Where would he be, she must be wondering, a year from now?

Fortunately, there were still a hundred or more refugee children at the castle, waiting to be allocated places with English families, and they needed feeding and entertaining. Many of them were missing their parents and had to be reassured and comforted. Even though Jewish children could not be expected to celebrate the birth of Christ, they could at least give thanks for their preservation and

21

pray for those they had left behind. Their presence gave meaning to what otherwise might have been a hollow festival.

But who, if any, of her friends *would* she invite to her wedding? Verity looked round the little group of Communists, their faces pink in the warmth of the Kardomah. She had a sudden vision of her fellow Party workers turning up at Mersham Castle and being scandalized by its magnificence. She knew that, because of her love for Edward, she was going against her most deeply held principles and breaking faith with everything the Party stood for. She did not believe in marriage as an institution but she *was* getting married. She believed in destroying the class system, which she held to be divisive and absurd, yet she was marrying the younger son of a duke. How could she have known that love would make a nonsense of everything in which she thought she believed?

Fernando had transferred his attention to Alice Paling. She clearly worshipped him and Verity suppressed a twinge of jealousy as she watched him take her hand and whisper something in her ear. Then she caught sight of Leonard Baskin wearing the unmistakable look of a rejected lover and wondered if Fernando knew or cared how many hearts he broke.

Fernando saw her looking at him and, almost shyly she thought, came over and sat beside her.

'You're not a Catholic, are you?' Verity asked.

'I mean, I know you're a Communist but aren't all Italians Catholic?'

'I was brought up a Catholic, of course, but I no longer go to mass.'

'Because the Catholic Church supports Franco in Spain?'

'Yes, although many poor priests in Spain and in Italy side with the people. But I say *e ce freghiamo*! To hell with the lot of them! I mean the bosses.' He became conspiratorial. 'Cardinals, generals, Party bosses – what is there to choose between them? They use us, suck us dry and then, when we have nothing more to offer, throw us aside.'

'David would say you are cynical.'

'I know what I'm talking about.' Fernando shrugged. 'If I was made to choose between black and red, I would of course choose red. I *have* chosen red. But it's not the colour of the man that matters – not the *colore* but the *volore*, so to speak.' He chuckled. 'In these days, we need men of courage – courage to tell the truth. Prejudice, bigotry, cruelty, I despise. Pride, independence, common sense, an honest heart and, yes, courage, I admire.'

Verity was impressed. 'How often do you find what you admire?'

'More often than you might think among ordinary people who know that to stand up to evil means putting themselves and their families in danger.' He looked gloomy and depressed.

She was distracted by David who had come up behind her, perhaps curious to know what she and Fernando were talking about so earnestly. Doing his best to be offensive, he asked what she hoped to gain by marrying Edward. He had always hated him, though he would have denied that it was jealousy. She replied sharply that she did not expect to gain anything. 'I don't suppose you can understand,' she added with all the indignation of the guilty, 'but if you love someone, you don't make a list of what you expect to lose and what you expect to gain.'

She was quite pleased with her answer despite having an uncomfortable feeling that she had once made just such a list. David was a Party man through and through and, though he might enjoy sex, he could never contemplate marriage. The Bolsheviks despised family life. For the selfless revolutionary, nothing should be private – everything was political. Individualism had to be eradicated. David lived for his work and dispensed with anything which might get in the way of it or make demands on his time or emotions. Verity guessed that he considered love to be a bourgeois luxury.

'I've got a little job for you,' he said with a thin smile. 'If you have time before your wedding, of course.'

'A job . . . ?' Verity echoed uncertainly.

'Don't worry – nothing too difficult. I just want you to get to know the American Ambassador.'

'Joseph Kennedy? Why . . . ? How could I possibly do that?'

'Your friend Kay Stammers teaches his children tennis. Ask her to introduce you.'

'But why?'

'I can't tell you that yet. As you know, Mr Kennedy is an admirer of Herr Hitler and will do his utmost to stop Britain declaring war on Germany. If he is unsuccessful, he will do everything possible to prevent President Roosevelt from bringing America in on our side. It is our patriotic duty to do what we can to make him change his mind. It would be useful for the Party to have someone in his inner circle who can report on his thinking and how far Roosevelt is under his influence.'

Verity looked at him suspiciously. She had never thought of David as a patriot though she acknowledged that, in theory at least, there ought to be no conflict between loyalty to the Party and to one's country. As a Communist, she abhorred the political system and wanted to change it to make England a better place in which to live. But still . . . where exactly did David's loyalties lie?

As though he had read her mind, David, who was always quick to lecture her, continued, 'You recall what Georgi Dimitrov said at the Seventh Comintern Congress in 1935? "We Communists are the irreconcilable opponents of bourgeois nationalism in all its forms but we are not supporters of national nihilism. The task of educating the workers in the spirit of proletarian internationalism is one of the Communist Party's fundamental tasks but that does not permit the Communist Party member to sneer at the national sentiments of the mass of working people."'

As far as Verity could understand, this seemed to mean that national sentiment could be encouraged as long as it was directed at the bourgeoisie but was to be condemned as soon as it conflicted with the interests of the Communist movement or of the Soviet Union.

'Even if I were introduced to Mr Kennedy,' she objected, 'is he likely to take any notice of a not very important journalist and a Communist at that?'

'Not likely, no, but we may have something to give him – a message, perhaps – and it would be useful to have someone who can meet him socially without attracting attention.'

Verity looked doubtful. 'I'll see what I can do,' she said slowly. 'As it happens, I *can* ask someone to introduce me, apart from Kay. Harold Laski is one of my father's oldest friends and, for some odd reason, Kennedy chose to send his eldest boys, Joe Jr and Jack, to be educated by him at the LSE. I gather their father – rather unexpectedly – had the imagination to want them to hear the other side of the argument.'

Danny O'Rourke, who had overheard the last few words, broke in, 'Joe Kennedy Sr is no aristocrat. He's Boston Irish and Roman Catholic. To get where he has with those disadvantages makes him a hero to some of us. Last year, when he visited Ireland, de Valera called him a true son of Ireland and Kennedy called his journey to Dublin a pilgrimage. It was a moving occasion. I know because I was there.'

'He's also a capitalist profiteer who hates Jews, blacks and Communists,' David responded drily.

'Even so, we can forgive him anything because he's Irish,' O'Rourke said, turning away.

'Harold Laski – yes, I should have thought of him,' David said. 'Your father's abroad, isn't he?'

'Yes, but I've met Laski several times. I'll telephone him tomorrow, but I still don't understand what you want me to do if I manage to meet Kennedy.'

'Don't worry about that. You'll get your orders in good time.'

Verity winced. She did not like taking orders from anyone but, she supposed, as long as she remained a member of the Party, she had to abide by its discipline.

As though he could read her mind, David said, 'I've had to speak to you before about discipline. The Party can achieve nothing without it. You will remember that Lenin wrote: "Organization and discipline are the proletariat's only weapons." We no longer see revolution as a spontaneous mass uprising but as a war of manoeuvre directed from above. There's no room for egotism and amateurism. Fernando will tell you that the great Antonio Gramsci – who helped found the Italian Communist Party and who died two years ago – likened the Communist International to a worldwide engineering factory. Lenin called us revolutionary realists. We must submit ourselves to the great plan.'

As always when Verity was lectured at, she wanted to argue but she knew David too well. He was not susceptible to argument and it was better just to nod and pretend to agree.

'You were going to tell me why you wanted me to meet your new girl?' Her scorn was a little too evident and David bridled.

'She's not my girl but she's useful. You'll meet her again and, when you do, be polite.'

As they were leaving the Kardomah, blue flashing lights appeared and disappeared in the fog. The muffled but still strident bells of police cars warned them something was afoot. Fernando embraced her. 'Good luck, *cara* – as we say back home, "*in bocca al lupo*".'

'In the mouth of the wolf?' she guessed.

'It means "good luck" and you should answer "*crepi il lupo*" – kill the wolf. If your man does not want you, come back to me and I'll teach you *il linguo d'amore*. Promise me.'

'Thank you, Fernando, but he does love me.'

He shrugged, unconvinced, and let her go.

Making their way towards Tottenham Court Road underground station, she and David were stopped by a police constable. Apparently a bomb had gone off in the left luggage office and another one had gone off at Leicester Square. The constable thought that it was an IRA outrage similar to the explosions in Coventry. Verity – the journalist in her coming to the fore – started to say that she ought to go and see what was happening but she discovered that she had come out without her press card. Very reluctantly, she was dissuaded from trying to get behind the police barrier. David told her not to be a fool. It was not her job and she certainly shouldn't stay out any longer in the fog than absolutely necessary. Ignoring her protests, he stopped a passing taxi and, giving the driver the address of her flat in Cranmer Court, pushed her into it. As a reporter, it was against all her instincts to turn away from a news story. She was quite well, she told herself, coughing into her handkerchief.

CHAPTER 2

Lord Edward Corinth swung the Lagonda across the gravel and pulled up in front of the elegant eighteenth-century wooden door. As he was shown into the surprisingly narrow hall, he thought, as he always did, how modest a home Chartwell was for a man who had been a leading political figure before Edward was born. And yet he knew from what Churchill had told him that, unpretentious though it might be, its upkeep was a constant struggle financially. Churchill had bought it in 1924 for £5000 but he had spent four times that amount on remodelling it and it was still far from perfect. Waiting in the drawing-room, he shivered despite the fire in the grate. As Mrs Churchill complained, the house was draughty even when the weather was warm.

Above him, he heard the unmistakable grumble of the owner of the house and his heavy footsteps as the great man paced up and down in his study. Edward knew he was at work on his *History of the English-Speaking Peoples*. Somehow, Churchill found time to read and write about the Wars of the Roses after the long hours spent on his political work. He had told Edward that he seldom went to sleep before three in the morning.

Edward had been waiting ten minutes when the door of the drawing-room opened and Guy Liddell was shown in. He greeted Edward with a firm handshake.

'I had no idea you were to be here, sir,' Edward responded. 'I had a summons to attend an urgent meeting but I had no hint as to what it concerned.'

'How is your knee, Corinth?' Liddell said, not giving anything away. 'And how is Miss Browne?'

Guy Liddell was the head of MI5, an organization so secret that its existence was unknown to the public and denied even by its political masters. Its task was to counter the activities of foreign agents in Britain. In just a few months it had doubled in size as war became a certainty but, even now, it was understaffed and Liddell found himself using odd characters like Edward when the need arose.

Only a few months earlier, in the summer of 1938, Edward had killed a German agent, officially an assistant secretary at the German Embassy in London but unofficially the controller of a network of spies and traitors. Edward had hurt his leg in the struggle but, as he told Liddell, he was now 'Right as rain and Miss Browne is well on the way to recovery. The doc gave her a clean bill of health but she has to be checked every six months as, apparently, TB can never be

completely cured but remains dormant, sometimes for years.'

'Well, we must hope for the best,' Liddell
responded, breezily. 'And I believe I may congratulate you on your engagement.' His cold eyes could
almost be said to smile. It was a standing joke
among Edward's friends and acquaintances that
Verity had proved almost impossible to drag to
the altar or rather – since she was an atheist and
would never agree to a church wedding – to
Caxton Hall.

'Thank you,' Edward said, attempting to look
unconcerned. 'We're hoping to get married next
month when the weather improves. Just a small
wedding, you understand, immediate family and
close friends.' Then, wondering if he sounded
rude, he added, 'But we are having a party at
Mersham Castle and would be delighted if you
were able to be there, though perhaps . . .'

Edward thought that Liddell – given his position – would not wish to join a large party but,
to his surprise, he said he would be delighted to
come. 'I have often heard Mersham described as
one of England's most beautiful houses and would
very much like to see it and, of course, to wish
you and Miss Browne good luck in your life
together.'

Their conversation was interrupted by a familiar
growl of greeting and Churchill appeared, cigar
in hand as usual. Edward could hardly ever
remember seeing him without one of his favourite

Romeo y Julietas. On a previous visit to Chartwell, Churchill had shown him the small room between his study and his bedroom in which he stored over two thousand cigars. They sat in boxes on shelves labelled 'wrapped', 'naked' and 'large'. He never used a cigar cutter, preferring to pierce his cigar with a match. He had told Edward that, when he had complained of painful indigestion a couple of years earlier, his doctor had ordered him to cut down on his smoking but he had taken no notice. It occurred to Edward that one way of assassinating Churchill might be to present him with a box of poisoned cigars. He had once been involved with a murder case in which a man had been poisoned by the cigarettes he smoked. He shuddered inwardly. How did you go about protecting a man like Churchill?

Edward noted, as he always did when he had not seen him for some time, how small Churchill was, although, after a few moments, his considerable presence made one forget his lack of height.

'Forgive me, gentlemen, for keeping you waiting,' he said, shaking hands, 'but I just wanted to complete a description of the battle of Towton.'

'1461,' Liddell volunteered.

Churchill pretended not to hear him. 'Palm Sunday, 29th March. It was bitter weather. The Yorkist vanguard under young William Nevill advanced on the Lancastrian position. His archers took advantage of the snow which blew in his enemies' faces. In savage hand-to-hand fighting the two armies tried their strength. Late in the afternoon, the Lancastrian line of battle collapsed. Many were drowned in the Cock River and many more were cut down near the town of Tadcaster. The slaughter was immense.' He looked round to see the effect of his peroration on his visitors and then added, 'Warfare used to be cruel but magnificent but has now become cruel and squalid.'

Churchill's eyes blazed and Edward felt his great love for England and its history. He was comforted that, in the new and horrible war that was about to break over them, this man would be at the helm. Edward simply could not believe that, in the event of war, Chamberlain would survive long as Prime Minister and, then, who else was there? 'Writing a book,' Churchill continued, 'is an adventure to begin with, then it becomes a mistress, then a master and finally a tyrant.'

Liddell broke in rather impatiently, knowing Churchill's habit of trying out speeches and apothegms on any captive audience. 'Forgive me, Mr Churchill, but I have to get back to town for a meeting at two o'clock. Might we . . . ?'

'Of course!' Churchill was immediately penitent. 'I shouldn't have brought you out to Chartwell but . . .'

Turning to Edward, Liddell said, 'The fact of the matter is that Mr Churchill refuses to take me seriously when I say that there is a threat against his life.'

Edward was horrified. 'You mean an assassination attempt? But who . . . ?'

'You must not alarm yourself.' Churchill spoke as though the threat was against Edward's life rather than his own. 'There are always lunatics vowing death to any of us with a measure of public notoriety. It's just words.'

'I beg to differ, sir,' Liddell said with icy courtesy. 'This particular threat has to be taken seriously. My source is unimpeachable . . . This time we're not dealing with some lunatic but a deliberate, carefully planned plot. Our information is that a professional assassin has been hired to deprive us of you when the country needs you most.' He smiled his most wintry smile. 'That is not something we can allow to happen.'

'But it is all so vague . . .' Churchill protested. Then his face cleared. 'I have a bottle of champagne on ice. Will you excuse me one moment?'

Edward understood that he did not wish to listen as Liddell outlined the nature of the threat against him.

'He drinks too much,' Liddell grunted after Churchill had closed the door behind him.

'I think he drinks when he's bored but I've never seen him the worse for wear. I have had dinner with him when he's consumed the best part of a magnum of Pol Roger but normally he keeps to weak whisky.'

'I know. And I've seen him add soda water to

his claret, God help us! Still, whatever his eccen-tricities when it comes to his alcohol intake, he's the best man we've got.'

'The only man,' Edward echoed. 'But who would want to assassinate him?' he asked again.

'Nobody or everybody. We're particularly worried by the IRA threat. Despite everything he has done to bring peace to Ireland, including shaking the hand of Michael Collins . . . That stuck in my gullet, I must say. When half the police in Ireland were looking to arrest him, he was taking tea at 10 Downing Street. Despite that, the Irish hate Mr Churchill. Did you know that in 1921 Sinn Fein tried to kidnap him and Mr Lloyd George? That plot was foiled by the Yard, thank goodness, but there have been plenty more.'

'I never knew that.'

'They managed to keep it dark.'

'Was that at the time of the Black and Tans?' Edward had not approved of Churchill's decision to send those battle-hardened troops to Ireland to suppress the IRA. Their brutality had created many martyrs among the ordinary Irish. As a result, even moderate Republicans were persuaded to support the 'armed struggle' to rid Ireland of the British, whatever the cost in human lives.

Liddell hurried on. 'On his recent American tour, Mr Churchill received over seven hundred letters containing death threats, many of them from Indians. The Ghada Party, an Indian secret society, has threatened to kill him because of his opposition to Indian independence. And then, of course, there are the Nazis. If there is a war, Hitler would prefer to be facing a British prime minister like Mr Chamberlain rather than Mr Churchill. I could go on but I expect you get the idea.'

'I'm afraid I must be very naive,' Edward confessed. 'It never crossed my mind that there could be any real danger of . . . I mean, dash it, it's so un-English. Surely no public figure has been assassinated since . . . since Spencer Perceval in 1812?'

'You forget that the London Brigade of the so-called Irish Republican Army shot Sir Henry Wilson dead on his doorstep in June 1922 . . . in Eaton Square, no less.'

Edward grunted. A thought struck him. 'Liddell, is Mr Churchill in more danger than other public figures?'

'I'm afraid the answer is in the affirmative. He says what he thinks and his profile is much higher than even the Prime Minister's. Only the other day Mr Chamberlain called him Number One Bogeyman, and for many people that's precisely what he is. Scarcely a week goes by when there isn't an article in a daily paper by him or about him. Have you seen *Truth* recently?'

'It's a ridiculous magazine!'

'Ridiculous maybe but week after week it ridicules Mr Churchill and warns against his "pseudo-Napoleonic" antics. This week there's an article by Sir Joseph Ball who, I am ashamed to say, was my predecessor at MI5 saying that on no account must he be brought into the government. Ball now runs intelligence for Conservative Central Office and, we have discovered, secretly gained control of *Truth* to use it against Mr Churchill. He's a close friend of Mr Chamberlain and has acted as an unofficial go-between with Mussolini. The two of them – I mean Ball and the Prime Minister – went on a fly-fishing holiday when Hitler invaded Czechoslovakia last October.

'Abroad, particularly in America, Mr Churchill is listened to when Mr Chamberlain is not and he is often thought by foreigners who should know better to be speaking for the British Government.'

Churchill re-entered the room carrying an ice bucket with a bottle of champagne bobbing about in it. He put it on a table and took off the foil without speaking. The cork shot out with a satis-factory pop. As he gave them each a glass, he said, 'You're getting me a Special Branch officer, I gather, Liddell?'

'Yes, Walter Thompson. You know him.'

'He's a good man.' Churchill nodded and sipped his champagne contemplatively. 'He's looked after me before,' he explained to Edward, 'but I still don't fancy being followed about by a nursemaid.'

'Why is this threat different from all the others you mention, Liddell, and what can I do?' Edward asked. 'I imagine you have experts in this sort of thing?'

'Indeed. We are working day and night to iden-tify the would-be assassin.' Edward thought

38

Liddell was trying to make Churchill understand the danger he was in by using words like assassin but, on the surface at least, Churchill appeared unmoved. 'There's a particular job I need you to do, Corinth. Let me explain,' he went on before Edward could say anything. 'The information comes from our people in Berlin. They have heard from three different sources that Hitler wants Mr Churchill dead. There used to be an unwritten agreement that heads of state did not authorize assassination attempts on the lives of other heads of state or prominent figures.'

'Not cricket?' Edward said, imagining Verity's scorn had she heard Liddell's remark.

'As you described it earlier, un-English,' Liddell agreed drily. 'The Nazis, we now know, are little better than gangsters. Hitler has killed many of his own people – think of "the night of the long knives". Ernst Röhm thought he was too close to Hitler to be in any danger but he and the other SA leaders were murdered *en masse*. There have been dozens since.'

'*Sola mors tyrannicida* – Death is the only way to get rid of tyrants, as Thomas More put it.' Edward could almost hear Verity begging him to stop quoting, particularly in Latin.

Churchill, not to be outdone, quoted Hazlitt. 'Words are the only things that last for ever.'

'Not just tyrants get assassinated. That's our problem,' Liddell corrected Edward, ignoring Churchill's interjection.

'But why would they want to kill Mr Churchill? He isn't even in the cabinet.'

'I've told you,' Liddell said irritably, 'he is the voice of opposition to German Fascism. Isn't that enough?'

'I'm flattered,' Churchill growled, 'to be so hated by that gang of hoodlums. It's the English-speaking nations almost alone who keep alight the torch of freedom.'

'So the threat comes from Germany – not any of the other secret societies or whatever that you mentioned?' Edward asked Liddell.

'Yes, but don't imagine all we have to do is to look for thugs speaking with marked German accents and wearing jackboots and a swastika. They are just as likely to use a disaffected Irishman or even an Indian to do their dirty work for them.'

'So what can we do? We can't just wait for it to happen!'

'I'd certainly prefer it, Guy, if you could put a spoke in these fellas' wheel. Call me selfish but I've got a few things to do before I go to meet my maker,' Churchill put in mildly.

'Well, as I say, we're following up leads but one thing our people in Berlin have been telling us is that the assassin may be attached in some way to the American Embassy.'

'Attached to the embassy? Surely the Americans don't employ just anyone?' Edward asked in astonishment. 'Don't they look into their backgrounds . . . that sort of thing?'

'You'd think so, wouldn't you?' Liddell replied. 'And of course they do up to a point but, unfortunately, it's all rather more complicated. After the war, the United States abolished its intelligence service. President Wilson hated the whole idea of spying and being spied on. Apparently, he told those who objected to his decision that "gentlemen don't read each other's mail". He thought it undemocratic and un-American. President Roosevelt has now seen the error of his predecessor's ways and the service is being reformed but it's a slow business and at the moment it's pretty chaotic. Every branch of their armed services has its own agents and none of them talk to the FBI.' Liddell suddenly seemed to realize that he might be speaking rather too freely. 'I need hardly tell you, Corinth, that this is absolutely secret and what I tell you must never be repeated. The point is that you can't start up a new intelligence service overnight and expect it to be effective. It takes months – probably years. We are trying to teach them a little of how we do things over here but mistakes will be made. It's inevitable.'

'So the American Embassy . . . ?'

'God knows who is employed there.' Liddell sounded exasperated. 'In any case, the person we're looking for might not be someone actually working in the embassy. He might be a friend of the Ambassador's or even his children. We just don't know.'

'But hang on a minute,' Edward expostulated,

41

'the Americans are . . . if not our allies, then friendly to us. Surely, if there is something they know about a threat to Mr Churchill, you only have to alert the Ambassador and he'll pull out all the stops to find out who it is?'

'That's another problem. Mr Kennedy is not enamoured of Mr Churchill. In fact, he regards him as a danger to world peace. The Ambassador backs Mr Chamberlain's policy of appeasing Hitler. He distrusts Mr Churchill and believes that, if war breaks out between Britain and Germany, we would be defeated in weeks, if not days.'

'Not without reason,' Churchill opined.

'But surely the American Ambassador would never be a party to an assassination attempt on Mr Churchill?' Edward was scandalized.

'No, of course not but, equally, Mr Kennedy's in no hurry to investigate. He has been apprised of the threat to Mr Churchill but he's inclined to pooh-pooh it.'

Edward scratched his chin. What was it that Walsingham was supposed to have said? 'There is nothing more dangerous than security.' It had been true in the time of Queen Elizabeth and it was even more so today. 'So what can I do? I need hardly say I'll do whatever you ask of me.'

'Good man!' Liddell responded with chilly geniality.

'What have your people heard?' Churchill asked, without appearing to be very much concerned.

'Something . . . not much. Little more than gossip, in fact . . . a name.'

'What name?'

'A name to make us sit up and take notice. Nest Bremen.'

'What's that? A German bird-watching outfit?' Edward asked facetiously.

'I see I need to explain how the German secret service works. It's not that efficiently organized, surprisingly. There are two overlapping organizations. As you know, the Abwehr is the German High Command's intelligence service. It's divided into three basic groups. Abt I is concerned with offensive intelligence and espionage, Abt III with counter-intelligence and security. We are concerned with Abt II which is responsible for sabotage and subversion. They have *Nebenstellen* or nests – small groups controlled from Berlin but based wherever they can be effective.'

'Did Major Stille work for the Abwehr?' Edward asked. Stille was the German spymaster he had killed the previous summer.

'No, he was an officer of the Sicherheitsdienst.'

'I'm confused. Who or what is the Sicher . . . whatever you called it?'

'The SD is the security and intelligence service of the Nazi Party. It is in competition with the Abwehr and, as far as we can see, will eventually take it over. The Abwehr has not had any real success here or in America. We know all its agents and watch them like hawks.'

'So the Abwehr isn't a real threat?'

'Quite the contrary. If it is to fight off the SD, it needs some dramatic successes which will impress Hitler. Our belief is that it has decided that killing Mr Churchill is just the sort of coup to show the world and the organization's political masters what it is capable of.'

Edward was silent for a minute or two as he considered this. 'Is this all guesswork or have you any evidence?'

'Our girl in the American Embassy happened to hear the Ambassador mention a name before he closed his office door . . .'

'*Our girl*? We have a spy in the American Embassy?' Edward was dumbfounded.

'We need to know exactly what the Americans are thinking,' Churchill explained. 'We need the Americans to come in on our side as soon as war breaks out. Without them we have no hope. My aim is to persuade President Roosevelt that we *will* stand up to Hitler, that we *will* fight, despite anything Mr Kennedy tells him.'

Liddell interrupted him. 'So you see, Corinth, we need to know who is winning the battle of words. Information is power. Never forget that.'

'So what is the name your girl heard, Liddell? Nest Bremen?'

'No, the name was Der Adler.'

'The eagle?'

'Der Adler is the name of their top assassin. We know he has killed at least four important

44

political leaders who were seen as a threat by the Nazis.'

'Such as . . . ?'

'Such as the Austrian Chancellor, Dollfuss. You will remember that he was killed by the Nazis in his own chancellery in 1934. His death led inevitably to the *Anschluss*.'

'Do we know his real name?'

'Der Adler? No. We know almost nothing about him. There are no photographs, no descriptions. He may even be dead. We thought we'd killed him in Buda last year but maybe not. Perhaps they've given the same code name to someone else in order to confuse us. We must never think we know anything about him because that might prevent us from recognizing him or her.'

'Her? Surely not?'

'Nothing can be ruled out,' Liddell warned.

Edward puzzled over the paradox, murmuring to himself Prometheus's stoic remark, *"'Il faut avoir un aigle."'* He had recently been reading Gide's *Le Prométhée mal enchaîné* and his blistering attack on Communism, *Retour de l'U.R.S.S.*

'What are you talking about?' Liddell asked irascibly.

'Sorry, I was thinking. So tell me again – exactly what do you want me to do?'

'Get the Ambassador's confidence. Find out whatever he knows . . . whatever there is to know. If we want to keep Mr Churchill safe, we have to get this man and to do that we have to know who he is.'

'It's a tall order,' Edward sighed. 'Why don't you ask him yourself, sir?'

'Can't stand the man,' Churchill replied truculently. 'I won't be beholden to anyone who prays for the demise of the British Empire.'

'Well, why don't you put in an official request, Liddell?'

'There's no future in that. We'd just get a "sorry, can't help you". We don't want to embarrass ourselves or the Americans. You can imagine what would happen if it got into the press that we suspected the American Embassy of harbouring political assassins . . . You've proved you have a gift for getting on with tricky characters. Why, even the Duke of Windsor ended up thanking you . . . We have other agents following up other leads and other sources of information. We're not asking for miracles but my hunch is that Joe Kennedy knows who Der Adler is or at least could find out. He may even be over here already.'

'So how am I going to meet Mr Kennedy?'

'Your brother knows him.'

Edward frowned. 'I'm not involving my brother in this.'

The Duke was a long-standing friend of Lord Lothian, one of Kennedy's closest friends in England, and was occasionally to be seen at Cliveden, the country seat of Lord and Lady Astor. The Duke had been introduced to Kennedy but had not taken to him. 'He tried to flatter me,

Ned,' the Duke had said scornfully. 'I don't want flattering by a crooked Boston racketeer.'

'Stop making those faces, Corinth,' Liddell laughed. 'In our business, we have to mingle with people we don't like. We have to get our hands dirty to catch our fish. Lady Astor is having a lunch for the Ambassador in St James's Square on Tuesday. You will receive an invitation which you will accept. Is that understood?'

'Is Lady Astor a friend of yours, sir?' Edward asked Churchill, genuinely curious.

'I have known her a very long time. Yes, I'd say we were friends though I don't expect she has forgiven me for opposing her election as a Member of Parliament.'

'Why were you opposed to her becoming an MP?'

'Call me reactionary, my boy, but I've never believed women should take part in the hurly-burly of politics.'

'Yes, I remember it was one of Verity's – Miss Browne's – grouses that you did your best to stop women getting the vote.'

'Well, I'm not foolish enough to think that was my finest moment,' Churchill said with something approaching an apology, 'but, if the truth be told, I am still not convinced that women belong in the so-called Mother of Parliaments, but there we are . . .'

'And Lady Astor? What of her in particular?' Edward persisted.

'She is in very many ways a remarkable woman. It takes more than money to be the first woman to take a seat in the House of Commons. Our prejudices against women and foreigners were swept aside and she was escorted to her seat by Mr Balfour and Mr Lloyd George. She has a kindly heart and a wagging tongue which some-times gets her into trouble. She is not, I am sure, anti-Semitic but she comes out with ill-considered comments which can be taken as insults by Jews with sensitive skins. She hates Catholics even more, which makes it all the more amusing that she has made such a friend of Joe Kennedy. I believe she calls herself a Christian Scientist but I doubt she understands its tenets.'

'And her great friend, Lord Lothian – isn't he a Catholic?'

Churchill shrugged. 'Like most women, she's not consistent. She went to Russia with that very silly man George Bernard Shaw and accepted Communist hospitality and flattery. Commissar Litvinoff organized a sumptuous banquet for these two innocents who were, perhaps, unaware of the food queues in the back streets of Moscow. Stalin took an hour or two off from signing death warrants to offer this arch-capitalist every compli-ment he could think of. She came back praising his new order while at the same time seeming to find much to admire in Herr Hitler. It would be comical if it were not a touch obscene.'

'Perhaps Stalin and Hitler are not as far apart

as we tend to believe,' Liddell said drily. 'Lady Astor is a very rich American with powerful friends on both sides of the Atlantic and is a danger to world peace.'

Edward shook his head bemusedly. He wondered what Verity would say when he told her where he was lunching and with whom. 'How long have we got to find Der Adler?' he said at last.

'We don't know. A few days, a week, a month . . . ? We're working hard at the German end but, in the meantime, get yourself into Kennedy's good graces. Get to know the children. I understand that Kathleen – "Kick", I believe they call her – is enchanting. Get to know the people they know.'

Edward again shook his head. 'I really can't see how I, a complete stranger, can find out anything. Is it likely Kennedy is going to say, "Let me tell you about the secret information we have received about this German agent"?'

'I tell you what, my boy,' Churchill broke in, 'I think you underestimate yourself. You have a way of getting hold of the truth – untangling a spider's web – which I have come to admire. I think you can do it.'

Edward sighed. 'If you ask me to, sir, of course I will try my best but . . .'

'Thank you,' Churchill responded simply, holding out his hand.

'Good chap,' Liddell said, patting Edward on the shoulder. 'Oh, by the way, there's a friend of yours at the embassy – a man called Casey Bishop. I gather he was up at Cambridge with you.'

'Casey! Why, I haven't seen him for years. What's he doing over here?'

'He's setting up their intelligence service network. We're teaching him a bit about how we work.'

'So he's the man to tell you everything you want to know about this assassination threat,' Edward said, his face clearing.

'I did put the word out but he says he doesn't know anything about it. I think he's lying. You'll make him talk though.'

CHAPTER 3

Harold Laski, now in his mid-forties, was a formidable figure. An economist and political philosopher, he knew everybody worth knowing and was listened to by politicians on both sides of the divide. Both Churchill and President Roosevelt respected him without always agreeing with his diagnosis of what caused the economic collapse in 1929. He counted himself a Marxist but was a supporter of Roosevelt's 'New Deal'. He had taught at Yale and Harvard but had been lured back to England to co-found the London School of Economics. He was a charismatic speaker and teacher.

Verity was nervous as she was shown into his office in the Old Building in Houghton Street off the Aldwych. She knew that this busy man had only consented to see her because of the respect and affection he felt for her father, a leading left-wing lawyer. They had both been members of the Fabian Society but Verity's father had gone on to become a Communist – even though he could not join the Party if he wanted to practise at the Bar. Laski had become a leading light in the

Labour Party. Whereas the Communist Party preached that Communism was a revolutionary movement – the entire structure of society must be changed and this cannot be achieved by peaceful means – Laski preached 'non-violent revolution'. He believed that economic and political change was necessary if Britain was to survive and he held that capitalist democracy was a fraud. 'No state,' he had written, 'had been able to change its class basis without revolution.' But could England be the exception? He spent his life trying to achieve what Marx had called 'revolution by consent'.

'Sit down, my dear,' he said, getting up from behind a desk piled high with papers. He moved with all the neatness and delicacy of a bird.

'I'm so sorry to interrupt you,' Verity said, surveying the paper mountains. 'I know how busy you must be.'

'Oh, you mean this?' Laski indicated his desk with a wave of his hand. 'Don't worry about it. I don't, so why should you? I only arrived back from the States last week and you know how things pile up. Now, what can I do for you and how is your father?'

He spoke in a penetrating monotone – not superficially attractive but effective when he wanted to put over a point. He was a small man with a big head and very bright eyes which shone behind enormous black-framed glasses. His intelligence and the confidence it gave him almost dazzled

Verity and, though she had not seen him for some years, she recalled the fascination her father's friend had always had for her as a child. She had loved him then and the sweetness of his smile behind his moustache made her smile too.

'My father's very well, as far as I know, but to tell the truth, I hardly ever see him. He's so busy and almost always abroad . . .'

She must have looked wistful because Laski broke in hurriedly. 'He must be very proud of you. I have read your reports from Spain in the *New Gazette* but I have just remembered . . . They told me you had been ill . . .'

'I've had a bout of TB but I'm fully recovered,' Verity lied. 'I'm not yet quite ready to go abroad but I'm still doing political stories for Lord Weaver.'

'That old scoundrel,' Laski laughed.

'In fact, that's why I asked to see you. I want to do a piece on Joe Kennedy and his support for Mr Chamberlain. I think he is backing the wrong horse . . .' she added lamely, 'and Mr Churchill is our only hope.'

Laski looked at her sharply. 'Yes, there is a story there and I'm inclined to agree with you but I'm surprised to hear you speak well of my friend Winston. You are still a member of the Communist Party?'

If Laski had a fault it was that he always claimed to be a close friend of any famous person who came up in conversation. It was hardly vanity as he did know many of them although perhaps not as well as he might have liked.

'Yes, I'm still a Party member though, to be frank, I was rather disillusioned by some of the things I saw in Spain.'

'I think I understand you.' He was silent for a moment and then seemed to come to some sort of a decision. 'You must come to dinner one night. Frieda would so like to see you again. She said so when I told her we were meeting today. I want to hear all about your experiences in that unhappy country.'

'I'd like that. But Mr Kennedy . . . would you be able to help me?'

'Yes, indeed, I know him well. He sent his sons, Joe Jr and Jack, to "sit at my feet".' Laski spoke ironically but he was obviously flattered that an anti-Semitic, Irish capitalist should entrust his boys to a left-wing Jewish intellectual.

'I know. That's why I came to you. If it's embarrassing . . . me being a Communist . . .'

Wondering what her real motives were for wanting to meet the Ambassador, he asked, 'Why don't you simply telephone the embassy and ask for an interview?'

'His people will know I'm a Communist. I don't think he'll talk to me without an introduction from someone he trusts.'

Laski looked pleased and then doubtful. 'You won't – now, what was the phrase I learnt when I was in New York? – stitch him up? You can disagree with him but if you mock him it won't do much for Anglo-American relations. He's very prickly. He's tough but he's got a thin skin like so many of these self-made millionaires. By the way, didn't I hear that you are engaged to an aristocrat of some kind? I hope you are not going over to the other side. You mustn't be misled by what my friend Beatrice Webb calls the "aristocratic embrace". We cannot live with the aristocracy and avoid their ways of thought.'

Verity blushed and stammered, 'I . . . love him.'

'Well then,' Laski responded benignly, 'that's all there is to say about it. I hope you'll be very happy. He must be something special to make you want to marry him. As a child you always swore never to marry.'

'Don't rub it in,' she said with a smile. 'I tried not to fall in love with him but in the end I just couldn't stop myself. We're not getting married in a church or any of that rot,' she continued, trying to regain some points. 'And I'll go on working, of course.'

'What is his name?'

'Lord Edward Corinth. He's the younger brother of the Duke of Mersham.' She stuck out her chin defiantly. She wasn't going to be ashamed of Edward. He was what he was and there was no point in pretending otherwise.

'Of course!' Verity wondered if Laski was going to claim to be a friend of the Duke, which she knew would be an impossibility. Instead he said,

'You persuaded the Duke to turn over the castle into a reception centre for refugee children, didn't you? I read about it in the *New Gazette* and intended to write and congratulate you. Here at the LSE, we are doing our best to bring over our Jewish friends from German universities, but,' he sighed, 'it's not enough . . . it's never enough. The fight against Fascism is the great struggle of our times and history will judge each one of us on what we did or didn't do.' He glanced at his watch. 'Oh dear, I'm late for a meeting. I love the teaching but the administration gets me down. With regard to Joe Kennedy, I'll do what I can. It was good to see you, my dear. Do you see anything of Harry? I've rather lost touch with him.'

'Mr Pollitt?' Harry Pollitt was the secretary of the Communist Party. 'I have only met him once.'

'Only once! I must tell him about you. Yes, I must get the two of you together over dinner. A dear friend . . .'

Verity left, feeling that she had been in the presence of someone with as much personality and intellectual strength as Churchill. Like all such men, he had his weaknesses and vanity but she was still inclined to think he was a great man.

'You're *what?*'

'I'm going to lunch with Lady Astor. No harm in that, surely?' Edward repeated truculently

'Of course there's harm in being seen with that

band of . . .' Verity hesitated as she searched for the telling phrase, 'that band of Fascist conspirators.'

'Oh please, V, don't exaggerate. I don't pretend they share my vision of the world but . . .'

'Share your vision . . .' She was incandescent. 'They are friends of Hitler. Their poisonous tentacles stretch across banking, journalism and industry, and it's all politics.'

'Lady Astor has been MP for Plymouth since the war and Major Astor has represented Dover since 1922. Nothing wrong with that.'

'And William Astor has been MP for East Fulham since 1935 and the Astors', son-in-law is MP for Rutland . . . I could go on,' Verity said icily.

'They have a lot of influence,' Edward conceded.

'Edward! Who is chairman of *The Times*? Major Astor. Who owns the *Observer*? Lord Astor. In the hands of these two brothers lie the newspapers who consistently put over Hitler's policies to the British people.'

'You're being silly.' Edward was rapidly losing his temper. The trouble was that he couldn't tell Verity why he had all of a sudden accepted an invitation to dinner from the so-called Cliveden Set and that made him feel guilty.

Claud Cockburn, a colleague of Verity's at the *Daily Worker* and a committed Communist, had coined the phrase 'the Cliveden Set' to describe the Astors and their friends. In a leaflet he had published the year before, he had demonized them as a conspiracy of powerful politicians and industrialists who wanted some sort of agreement with Germany whatever the cost. Cockburn was unscrupulous and happy to distort the truth to serve the Party, but Edward was forced to agree that the Astors had surrounded themselves with a powerful group of like-minded, influential figures which included the Governor of the Bank of England, Sir Montagu Norman, Sir Harry McGowen, chairman of Imperial Chemical Industries, Geoffrey Dawson, editor of *The Times* and Sir John Simon, the Chancellor of the Exchequer. Most significantly, the Prime Minister frequently dined at the Astors' magnificent house in St James's Square

'You know how the family became so wealthy?' Verity demanded. 'Selling liquor to poor negroes in America,' she answered for him but, seeing him look ever more gloomy, she calmed down. She had no wish to precipitate a row and it occurred to her that Edward must have a reason for accepting the invitation.

'So who's going to be at this lunch of yours?' she said in a normal voice.

'How should I know?' Edward tried to sound breezy and Verity was immediately suspicious.

'You *do* know! Confess. Who's going to be there?'

'The usual crowd, I suppose. Lord Lothian, Lord Londonderry . . .' Edward thought he might as well be hanged for a sheep as a lamb. Lothian was one of the figures most excoriated by the political left. He was a close friend of the previous German Ambassador, von Ribbentrop, and had seemed to welcome Hitler's invasion of Austria. He had met Hitler on several occasions and claimed to admire him. Londonderry was, if possible, even more hated by the left. His huge wealth was based on the family coal-mines and, though he treated his workers better than some, he was still regarded as a prime example of a capitalist exploiter.

'Londonderry!' Verity was scandalized. 'You do know that his miners get *less* than a shilling for each ton mined while Londonderry, who does nothing more than own the land under which the coal lies, receives *more* than a shilling for every ton mined? Londonderry is paid more than two million pounds a year for doing nothing!'

'And the American Ambassador, Joe Kennedy,' Edward soldiered on, pretending he had not heard her.

He looked up in surprise. The diatribe had stopped.

'You're lunching with Joe Kennedy?' Verity asked in quite a different tone of voice. 'I suppose you couldn't get me invited, could you? No, of course you couldn't. What am I thinking about? A Communist journalist among that pack of hounds! I'd be torn to shreds.'

'Why are you suddenly so keen to meet Kennedy?' It was Edward's turn to be suspicious.

'I suppose I'd better tell you. I never was much

59

good at keeping secrets. The fact is David Griffiths-Jones wants me to get to know him.'

'Why on earth . . . ?'

'I really don't know. He says the Party wants to know what Kennedy's up to and, in particular, what he's telling President Roosevelt. There! I've told you and you can "shop" me if you want.'

'But how did David think you would be able to meet Kennedy?'

'Well, as it happens, my father is a great friend of Harold Laski and Kennedy sent his two sons to be taught by him at the London School of Economics. I've just been to see Laski as a matter of fact.' Verity tried to sound nonchalant. 'And, if that doesn't work, Kay Stammers teaches his children tennis.'

'I see,' Edward said meditatively. He grimaced and then came to a decision. 'Since you've been frank with me, I suppose I ought to be honest with you although I swore not to tell anyone . . .'

'Especially me!' Verity interjected.

'Specially you,' he agreed, 'but, damn it, I really can't go on with this unless you're in on it. So, please, this is not to be repeated to anyone, least of all David.'

'As if I would.' She was genuinely hurt.

'They've had information that there's going to be an attack on Mr Churchill. They don't know where it will come from or who will make the attempt but they believe it may be someone working in the American Embassy or a friend of Kennedy's or at least someone known to him.'

'They?'

'Special Branch,' Edward prevaricated. He really didn't dare tell Verity about MI5. She knew about Special Branch but believed it was mainly concerned with persecuting the Communist Party.

'Golly! You mean someone's going to try and kill Mr Churchill – a Nazi?'

'A Nazi or a Communist . . .'

'Don't joke, Edward. No Communist would stoop so low.'

Edward wasn't so sure about that but let it pass. 'It might be the IRA or an Indian extremist . . . the Nazis may use someone else so they can distance themselves, especially if it doesn't succeed. That's why I'm going to lunch with the Astors.'

'I see. That explains everything. For a moment, I thought you had gone off your chump.'

Shortly after they married, the Astors had bought a magnificent eighteenth-century house on the east side of St James's Square. Although their country house, Cliveden, was where they were most at ease and did most of their entertaining, St James's Square – particularly when the House was sitting – was a focal point for those who supported the government. In reality, Lady Astor probably exerted much less political influence than she was given credit for but the perception among her enemies was that it was at St James's Square that conspiracies were hatched and government policy made.

Leaving his cab, Edward was rather taken aback to find a small group of photographers and reporters barring the way to the Astors' door. A constable stepped forward to make a path for him and, before he could even knock, the door swung open and Edward was admitted, but flashbulbs had popped and his name had been written down in half a dozen notebooks. It was ridiculous, he knew, but he had been unprepared for the journalists and his heart sank at the idea of being numbered among Lady Astor's coterie.

On Tuesdays Lord Astor had 'committees' in the House of Commons and, in his absence, his wife held lunch parties for her own close friends. As Edward was ushered into the drawing-room Lady Astor came up to him and was charming. She asked after his brother and described him as one of the most honourable men she knew and Mersham as the most beautiful house in England, 'after our dear Cliveden, of course'. She insisted that he call her Nancy and treated him with a delicacy and tact which seemed to make nonsense of her reputation for blunt speaking and insensitivity. There were no women, apart from his hostess, and only six other men in the room. Two of them he knew. He had met Lord Lothian at Mersham and had not liked him, finding him supercilious and uninterested in anyone but himself. However, on this occasion, he could not have been more gracious.

'I was talking to Van the other day and he was singing your praises,' Lothian began. Vansittart had been Permanent Under-Secretary at the Foreign Office when Edward had undertaken a delicate investigation for him and was now the government's Chief Diplomatic Adviser.

'That's very kind of him,' Edward replied and, wanting to change the subject, said, 'I gather you have just returned from Washington?'

'Yes, Mr Kennedy and I returned to England together on the *Queen Mary* two weeks ago.'

'Did you have an opportunity of meeting the President?'

'Indeed I did,' Lothian said, his face lighting up. 'I had an hour with Mr Roosevelt and I found his views entirely sound. He will stand with us against the dictators.'

Edward pretended to be unaware that – contrary to what he was now being told – the President had found Lothian exasperating. Vansittart had told him just a few days earlier that Roosevelt had been disgusted by his defeatism after Lothian had apparently expressed the view that there was no possibility of Britain opposing Hitler or Mussolini and it was up to the Americans to 'take up the torch of civilization from our drooping fingers'. According to Van, the President had gone for him and told him that, if Britain took that line, America would not offer one iota of help.

'And did you find support for Mr Chamberlain in America?' Edward asked innocently.

'Except among radicals, Jews and academics, I did,' Lothian replied without a moment's hesitation.

What a crew, Edward thought – Ribbentrop, Joe Kennedy and Lothian. Hitler used anyone who could help him get his way. Ribbentrop, he knew from what Vansittart had told him, considered Lothian to be Germany's most important ally in Britain.

Nancy soon swept Edward away to meet Lord Londonderry – whom she referred to as 'Charlie'. In other circumstances, he would have been very interested to meet him. The Londonderrys were a match even for the Astors in wealth and influence and their annual reception for the Opening of Parliament was regarded as one of the major events of the London season. As with Lothian, Londonderry's pro-German tendencies and frequent meetings with Hitler had made him something of a figure of ridicule and he was lampooned in the popular press as 'Londonderry Herr'.

Geoffrey Dawson came over to join them bringing with him Joe Kennedy and his good-looking sons. Edward had first met Dawson at one of Lord Weaver's parties and had taken to the great man although he deplored his political views. Dawson, like Lord Lothian, had been in South Africa as a young man and had come under the influence of that arch-imperialist Lord Milner. Milner had collected around him a 'kindergarten' of bright young men including Leo Amery, the author John Buchan, and Lothian, all of whom were taught that the British Empire was civilization's highest achievement and they owed it to the world to embrace the whole of Africa, if that were possible, within its kindly arms. There was a certain irony that so many of these men now seemed happy to see the British Empire fall under the sway of the German Reich. Edward assumed they mistook Hitler's brutal regime for the strong hand that Milner had offered as a solution to Africa's tribal chaos.

Dawson had been editor of *The Times* when it was owned by Lord Northcliffe but had resigned in 1919, not approving of his boss's political views. After Northcliffe died and *The Times* was bought by Jacob Astor in 1923, Dawson was reappointed editor. He sincerely believed that it was in Britain's interests to placate Hitler and had become a close friend of Neville Chamberlain. Verity had long complained that *The Times* refused to report what was really happening in Germany for fear of annoying Hitler. Like Lothian, Dawson was a friend of Ribbentrop's and was Churchill's most virulent critic in the press.

Dawson was all smiles. 'Ambassador, I would like to introduce you to a most interesting young man. I'm very glad to see you here, Corinth. I thought it would not be too long before you saw

65

the light and joined those of us who believe that war can still be averted if we satisfy Germany's legitimate demands.'

'Glad to meet you,' the Ambassador said, shaking Edward's hand and sounding very American among cut-glass English accents. Edward realized with a grin that everyone in the room apart from their hostess, the Kennedys and Grindlay, the Astors' butler, had been educated at Eton. He was not certain it did the school much credit but it certainly bore out something about which Verity always teased him. Much as she liked some Etonians, she thoroughly objected to the fact that the British Empire appeared to be the personal fiefdom of Eton past and present.

Before Edward had time to say anything intelligent which might justify Dawson's good opinion, Grindlay announced that luncheon was served and, led by their hostess and Ambassador Kennedy, they obediently trooped out of the drawing-room. Edward, as befitting the least important guest, lagged behind and found himself beside Joe Kennedy Jr, a young man with a ready smile whom Edward liked at first sight.

'Are there always this many lords, Lord Corinth?'

'Always,' Edward grinned.

'Is that what I should call you – "Lord Corinth"?'

Edward had no wish to correct him and to have to explain the vagaries of English titles so he merely said, trusting in Americans' liking for immediate intimacy, 'I hope you will call me Edward.' It was not an invitation he would normally extend to a stranger and one much younger than himself but he thought that, if ever there was an occasion to make an exception, this was it.

'Why, thank you, Edward. And you must call me Joe. To tell the truth, I've not yet figured out your English titles. In the same family, you seem to have different names. My father says he has met your brother and he's the Duke of Mersham. It's not so grand or so complicated where I come from. By the way, we were talking about you this morning.'

Edward laughed. 'We? Who's "we"? Should I be worried?'

'Not at all. I guess you know Kay Stammers. She's been helping me and my sister Kathleen – "Kick", we call her – to improve our tennis.'

'Kay, yes indeed. You couldn't be in better hands.'

'She told me you were marrying a Communist,' Joe said with a grin, hoping for a reaction.

Edward had prepared himself for this. His engagement to Verity had been commented on in the gossip columns and he was resigned to a degree of ribbing.

'Miss Browne's a Communist but she's not yet converted me. I'm afraid what I have seen of the Party doesn't convince me that Stalin is much to be preferred to Hitler.'

67

'But do you believe . . . ?'

Fortunately, perhaps, the young Kennedy was unable to complete his question. Nancy was directing them to their places around a table bright with silver. Edward, to his embarrassment, found himself sitting next to the guest of honour, Ambassador Kennedy. These great men must surely wonder why he was so favoured. As though reading his thoughts Nancy said, 'I decided, Ambassador, that you should meet some of our younger men. You already know all the stuffed shirts . . .' She beamed at Lothian and Londonderry who looked less than pleased at being so described. Edward now understood why his hostess could cause so much offence with her little jokes.

'Lord Edward is one of Mr Churchill's bright young men.' Now it was his turn to frown at her description. Kennedy looked at him with interest.

'Indeed? I have had the pleasure of meeting Mr Churchill but I have to tell you that I was less than impressed. Forgive me for saying so, Lord Edward, but I found him full of wind. He blusters about the menace posed by Herr Hitler but he has nothing to offer in exchange except posturing and empty threats – mere sabre rattling and that's always to be avoided when one's scabbard is empty.' He was obviously pleased with his remark even if it didn't bear close examination. 'He wanted me to convey to my friend, Mr Roosevelt, England's determination to fight.

68

Well, I had to laugh. I gave him some statistics about Germany's armed forces and asked him if England had anything comparable. He had to confess that she did not. I think his reputation is overblown by his acolytes. As Mr Chamberlain put it, rather amusingly I thought, "Winston's success is going from failure to failure without losing enthusiasm."'

Edward thought angrily of how this smug American must have delighted in rubbing Churchill's nose in these 'statistics'. As if Churchill didn't realize how weak the Royal Air Force was. Had no one told Kennedy that he was in possession of more accurate figures on British and German armaments than even the Prime Minister as a result of the constant flow of secret information he received from so many quarters? However, Edward checked the impulse to say as much knowing that it was his disagreeable task to ingratiate himself with this man – not antagonize him.

He muttered some words which might have been taken as agreement and sank back in his chair. The footman – there was one standing behind each guest – was offering him wine and this gave him the opportunity to pull himself together. If he was to do his job he must be circumspect and, as so often, the thought of Verity's disgust at the company he was keeping brought a smile to his lips.

As soon as the soup was served, Lord Lothian

began to praise a book he had been reading by a friend of his, Viscount Lymington, entitled *Famine in England*. As it happened, Edward had been reading a review of it a week or so earlier in *The Criterion* so, when Lothian asked him what he thought of it, he was not completely at a loss.

'I haven't read the book but I gather from the reviews that it is anti-Semitic, is it not?' he risked, speaking as mildly as he could.

'Not at all,' Lothian replied. 'Lymington argues for an agricultural revival, the stockpiling of a year's food and the abolition of death duties on land – anything which will make us self-sufficient and able to avoid starvation in the event of war.'

'But doesn't he denounce the "foreign invasion" of London – meaning, I suppose, Jewish refugees from Nazi Germany?'

'And why should that be anti-Semitic?' Lothian asked frostily. 'Lymington believes that England's heart and strength is to be found in the country-side, in its great estates rather than in deracinated towns.'

Edward could not resist one last shot. 'I believe he quotes with approval from Arthur Lane's *The Alien Menace* – a text dear to all anti-Semites.'

An embarrassed silence fell over the table, broken at last by Nancy at her coolest. 'We are not anti-Semites, Edward, but it's true I don't like Jews.'

Edward was strongly tempted to stand up, throw his napkin to the ground and flounce out. Instead

70

he said calmly, 'I know no one at this table countenances what is happening to the Jews in Germany. Isn't that right, Ambassador?'

Kennedy took a mouthful of soup and laid down his spoon with some care. 'Indeed not, Lord Edward, but I do sometimes think that the Jews bring misfortune upon themselves. In my country they exert too much influence. Their money buys political power . . .'

Before he could enlarge on his views Joe Jr broke in. 'I have many Jewish friends, Edward. I would hate you to think that as a family or as a nation we approve of any kind of discrimination. We Irish have had to fight for generations against just such prejudice and that is why I am so proud of my father for achieving what no Irishman has ever done before in politics and business.'

The young Kennedy's words were greeted with a murmur of appreciation in which Edward joined. His instinctive liking for the young man strengthened. He had stuck up for his father and deftly turned the conversation away from dangerous shoals.

'Have any of you been to the television exhibition at Selfridge's?' Nancy asked brightly.

'I have,' Lothian replied. 'My wife wanted to see this new marvel.'

'And what did you think? Was it marvellous?' Nancy asked.

'It was certainly interesting but I doubt it will ever attract a significant audience. Sir John Reith was telling me how much he hated it. He says it will bring unpleasantness into the home and I think he's right.'

'But what did you see?' Nancy insisted, turning back to Lothian.

'They were showing some film but really, the screen was so small and the image so blurred one could hardly make it out. Why on earth would someone prefer television to the cinema with all its gaudy colours?'

'Anyway, it will always be too expensive for the working class,' Londonderry said comfortably.

'And if there's a war?' Nancy asked.

'The BBC will close it down. Apparently it uses metals – I confess, I don't quite understand the technical details – which we'd need in wartime for weapons,' Lothian said firmly.

After lunch they returned to the drawing-room. Edward wondered how he was to get an invitation to meet the Ambassador again but the problem was solved by Joe Jr. In the course of a conversation about tennis, he said, 'You know what you were saying about the Jews, Edward? When I went to Germany in 1934 with my friend Aubrey Whitelaw, I have to admit we were impressed – maybe I mean dazzled – by what we saw – the pageantry, the marching, the new-found pride of the German people. They marched everywhere. The children marched to school singing songs and raised their arms in the Hitler salute. Everyone said *Heil Hitler* instead of hello. It was almost comical.

'My view then was that they had tried liberalism and it had failed. They had become despondent, divorced from hope, and then Hitler came along. He had to find a common enemy – someone to be cast out. It was good psychology and it was too bad it had to be the Jews. That was what I thought and, of course, now I kick myself for being so wrong-headed. I was completely deceived about the real nature of Nazism. I believed the Jews had risen to dominate law and big business – and all credit to them for having managed it – but they hadn't been too scrupulous in getting where they were and now had to pay the price. I was only nineteen and naive but I fear my father still thinks that way. We have the most terrible arguments about it. I wish we didn't but we do.'

'A lot has happened in five years,' Edward said. 'I don't see how any right-minded person could not be sickened by what the Nazis are doing to Jews and Communists . . .'

'Talking of Communists,' Joe Jr broke in, 'I'd sure like to meet Miss Browne. Kay says she's a humdinger, if you'll excuse the expression.'

'And I know she would like to meet you,' Edward smiled.

'That's fixed then. I'll invite you over to our place. It's "frightfully grand", you know,' he said, grinning as he imitated an upper-class English accent – rather well, Edward was forced to admit.

When he left St James's Square, Edward thanked his hostess for a most interesting luncheon. 'So

73

you don't think we are the enemy after all?' Nancy said, holding his hand in hers. 'You must come to Cliveden and bring that young lady of yours. In fact, why not come next weekend? It'll only be ourselves and the Kennedys. I can see the boys have really taken to you.'

'Are you sure?' Edward said, rather taken aback.

'It's awfully short notice, I know, but my husband would very much like to meet you and Miss Browne. Well, talk it over with her and telephone me. You would be doing me a favour. I'm afraid the Kennedy young will be awfully bored with just us.'

'Miss Browne – Verity – is very argumentative,' Edward said, doubtfully. 'What the French call an *agitateuse*.'

'Never mind that. I say what I think and I like other people who do. I'm not afraid of an argument. In fact, it stops me being bored.'

The photographers were still there as he stepped into the square and they once again took his photograph, as though, he thought, he might have sprouted horns while he was inside.

CHAPTER 4

The following morning, Verity had a telephone call from the American Embassy. The Ambassador had half an hour to spare that very afternoon if she cared to come to Grosvenor Square. She put down the receiver with a whoop of joy. Harold Laski had done what he had promised. She spent some time deciding what to wear, discarding one dress after another. She wanted to appear serious but not frumpy. She had heard that the Ambassador was a womanizer – he had owned a film studio and was believed to have bedded many would-be actresses and several genuine stars, most notably Gloria Swanson – but she did not want to be seduced. She gave a little shiver of horror at the thought. In the end, she chose a severe tailored suit with wide shoulder pads Schiaparelli had made for her. Not wanting to look too serious, she selected one of Schiaparelli's perky hats complete with feather which she had bought in a fit of extravagance when she was feeling ill and needed cheering up.

Although she had a notebook and a list of questions, she decided not to plan too much but see how the interview went. Her object, after all, was not simply to make the most of this one interview but to develop some form of relationship with a man she expected to distrust and dislike. It was more than likely that he would throw her out when he realized she was a Communist and in some ways that would be a relief. She did not like dissembling and was not good at it. However, she had thought about what David Griffiths-Jones had asked her to do and come to the conclusion that there was nothing intrinsically immoral about it.

The American Embassy in Grosvenor Square was a palatial building given to the United States by the financier J.P. Morgan. As instructed, she asked for Eamon Farrell, the Ambassador's press secretary. He had sounded more Irish than American on the telephone but, when he appeared at her elbow, she saw that he was indeed American. He was dressed informally with a highly coloured tie loose around his neck and he was chewing gum. He had a soft, silky moustache and was, she supposed, about forty-five.

'Miss Browne?' he said with studied lack of interest. 'If you'll come with me, the Ambassador is running a little late but I'm sure you won't mind waiting.' He showed her into a small ante-room where she cooled her heels for twenty minutes. If the Ambassador really did have only half an hour to give her, she'd be lucky to get ten minutes, she thought.

It was another twenty minutes before Verity was

shown into his office. It was huge, rather over-decorated, dominated by a magnificent desk upon which the Ambassador was resting his feet. He did not rise when she came into the room or apologize for keeping her waiting. He motioned her to a chair and looked at her challengingly. 'Mr Laski said you wanted to interview me. Well, fire away.'

Verity was well aware she was being tested. Kennedy was being as rude as possible. He was even, like his press secretary, chewing gum. She decided to be as sweet as pie.

'It's very good of you to see me, Ambassador,' she began.

'I sure don't know why I am,' he interrupted. 'You're a Commie and you'll make me out to be some kinda monster, I guess.'

'Why should you think that? Although it's true that I am a Communist, this interview is for the *New Gazette* and Lord Weaver supports everything you are trying to do in England. He certainly would not publish a hostile article about you or the United States.'

'Is that so?' Kennedy inquired, still bellicose. He did, however, take his feet off the desk. 'Well, ask away. By the way, I met that fiancé of yours yesterday. Seemed a nice enough guy.'

'I know. I talked to him on the telephone when I knew I was coming to see you,' she said with a smile, 'and he was complimentary about you too, Ambassador.' This wasn't strictly true but Verity could hardly say otherwise. 'He very much liked your son, Joe.'

'Little Joe,' the Ambassador's voice filled with pride. 'I trust my son's judgement, Miss Browne, and he told me your guy wasn't like some of these tight-arsed English lords.'

'Perhaps you can guess my feelings on that subject,' she replied gravely. 'I'm not much enamoured of aristocrats myself.'

'Then why marry one?'

'I suppose it's because I love him,' she said calmly.

Kennedy frowned at her and then his frown became a smile. 'Is that a fact? Hmm. And you Communistic. Still, I guess that's the right answer. I've loved my Rose since we were children together and I married her despite her father doing his best to stop me. Thirty years ago she was the belle of Irish Boston – as pretty a girl as you ever did see. Her father Mayor Fitzgerald – "Honey Fitz", we called him – had some Harvard-educated Democrat he wanted her to marry. But I guess I was the kind of guy who, if I wanted something bad enough, would get it and to tell the truth, young lady, I didn't much care *how* I got it. I've got money, lots of fuckin' money, but it don't make much difference to a man without he loves his family. I tell you this for nothing, Miss Browne . . .'

She didn't doubt he was sincere – that his love for his children was genuine – but she wondered how he squared his womanizing with his avowed devotion to Rose. She had met men before – Lord Weaver came to mind – with a strong sex drive and the wherewithal to indulge it, who took the view that sex had nothing to do with marriage. It was a weakness, she decided, that so many American men placed their wives on pedestals. Edward had explained to her that the American wife and mother was sacred, inviolate and boring. It was not just that she could not satisfy her man's animal needs but that he would have been shocked if she had. There were other women he did not respect or value who would do that for him. How Edward knew this she had not liked to ask.

'Please call me Verity,' she said breathlessly. Kennedy had a vigour and a ruthlessness she found both repellent and attractive. She had heard that he was foul-mouthed and coarse but she had never expected him to open up to her in this way. She hated his casual use of that sexual swearword. Even in Spain, under the most difficult conditions, she had noticed the men had rarely used bad language in front of her. She didn't think she was a prig but she was still shocked. Or was this another test?

'My boys are the light of my life. Say, I'd like you to meet them. I guess Laski was right. He said you had spunk. He said you'd argue with me but you'd play fair.'

Verity felt rather uneasy. Was she playing fair?

'You were in Spain backing the wrong side, I'm

told. Joe Jr went and took a look back in '34. He'd be interested in your view of that conflict.'

'I was on the right side,' Verity snapped, forgetting herself for a moment.

'There! Got you. I like a woman with passion. Now what do you want to ask me?'

Verity hesitated and then decided to go in with guns blazing.

'Some say you're a Fascist, Mr Ambassador. It's also said you want Hitler to win – that you're anti-Semitic. Is there any truth in that?'

'Who says it?' Kennedy demanded angrily. 'Where do they get that idea? It's true I have a low opinion of some Jews in public office and in private life. That doesn't mean I hate all Jews and believe they should be persecuted. I don't. I do business with Jews – have done for years. They're all right.'

'So you support the fight against anti-Semitism?'

'Anti-Semitism is *their* fight. Anti-Irishism is *my* fight.'

'But, going through the press-cuttings, I haven't been able to find you denouncing anti-Semitism.'

'What good would that do? If the Jews would spend less time advertising their racial problem and more time solving it, the whole thing would recede into its proper perspective. It's entirely out of focus now and that's their fault.'

Verity was disgusted but had to admire his frankness. Indeed, she thought, his candour would have been admirable if he had anything worthwhile to say.

When the interview was over, she glanced at her watch and was amazed to find that she had been with the Ambassador for almost two hours.

'You're not going to print all this, are you, Miss Browne?' He sounded a trifle apprehensive. 'My press secretary would kill me if he knew everything I've said to you.'

'On the eve of world war, Ambassador, there's no way my paper would ever portray you as anything other than a friend and a statesman,' she said almost ruefully. 'You've been very kind giving me so much of your time. You don't have to worry that I'll twist anything you said against you.' Easy though that would be, she thought to herself.

'I'd like to read what you've written before it goes in the *New Gazette*.'

'You can read it and, obviously, I am happy to correct any factual errors but I won't agree to change anything just because you don't like it.'

'That's my girl!' Kennedy said unexpectedly. 'You've got what it takes. You can have a job with me any time you like. Laski was right. He said you would amuse me.'

'Amuse you?' Verity was affronted.

'Hey, don't look like that. I meant he thought you would stimulate me. Stop me being bored. I guess I'm surrounded by people saying "Yes, sir, up my arse, sir, you're dead right, sir," and I never know whether they mean it. That's why I like to have Joe Jr with me. I need one honest man beside me. Look, tell you what, why don't you and your

81

Lord Edward Corinth come and have dinner with us tomorrow night. Just a family affair, you understand. I can read your article and you can meet my boys.'

'I'd enjoy that,' Verity said and was surprised to find that she meant what she said.

That evening, when they were talking over Nancy's invitation to Cliveden in his rooms in Albany, Edward asked if she had liked Kennedy.

'Of course I didn't like him,' Verity replied, 'but I liked his style. He's so much less formal than any of our people would have been. I liked it when he said all that debutante business was too stupid. Apparently, he's annoyed all the toffs back home by refusing to introduce their daughters to the King and Queen. I didn't know about it but he says there's this presentation ceremony for American girls over here to get them into society. Sounds mad to me. Oh, and he really uses the press. He's got a press secretary, a publicist and a speechwriter. He was quite open about it.

'I asked him what he wanted to be when he stopped being Ambassador and he said President of the United States but he told me I couldn't quote him. I think he wants me to sort of imply it. He thinks we British are decadent and that it's natural justice Germany should have its turn to rule the world.'

'That's a real scoop, V. Congratulations.'

'It is and isn't,' she said, wrinkling her brow.

'I've been struggling with it ever since I got back from the embassy. It's difficult to get the tone right. I don't want Kennedy to think I've made a fool of him. In fact, I more or less promised him I wouldn't. On the other hand, I don't want to sound sycophantic. Anyway, Joe Weaver wouldn't allow me to write the whole truth.'

'So David's pleased with you?' Edward asked snidely.

Verity ignored him. 'I want to tell the truth but not the whole truth – not yet, anyway. I couldn't even if I wanted to. If I did, he'd sue for libel or buy the newspaper or something.'

'But if it's true . . . I mean about him wanting to be President . . . ?'

'He could always deny it. There was no one else in the room. That was flattering, by the way.'

'Or else the press secretary didn't take you seriously.'

'Don't be so mean. I did get a scoop. It's just that at this moment in our history when we need America – isn't that what you are always telling me Mr Churchill says? – we can't afford to insult its representative at the Court of St James.'

'Yes, I know. Sorry. I suppose I was just jealous. Shall we go out to dinner?'

'Not possible, I'm afraid. I've got to go back to the flat and take the receiver off the hook and hammer out this article. I promised him he could read it tomorrow evening.'

'I wonder who'll be there,' Edward mused.

'He said it was just a family affair. Not Mrs Kennedy, apparently. He told me she's in Paris buying from all the fashion houses in order to look good when she dines with the King and Queen. The boys will be there and Kathleen, of course. Everyone seems to love her.'

'You'll like Joe Jr His father calls him Little Joe and is immensely proud of him.'

'So I gather but, still, I don't envy him. He's hardly more than his father's secretary at the moment. One thing Kennedy said which made me feel for his children was "I don't want any losers around me. In this family we want winners. My children won't be second best." Something like that anyway. He's very much leader of the pack. If he doesn't become President, then he's determined Joe Jr will.'

'Hmm. I wonder what Freud would have to say,' Edward mused. 'How often do the children of these sort of men ever amount to much? More likely they break under the strain. I gather from what I read in the newspapers that Jack, Joe's younger brother, is a sickly boy. I can't see him ever becoming President. What do you think it costs the old man to support an expensive wife, nine children, several mistresses and entertain on the scale he does?'

'I did some digging and discovered that officially he's only paid a pittance – something like eighteen thousand dollars a year with another five thousand for "expenses". Not a lot if you're spending two hundred and fifty thousand dollars, which is what I hear he spends.'

'Don't worry about the old man,' Edward snorted. 'He's as rich as Croesus. Never forget he's a gangster. He was a friend of Al Capone. And this is his apotheosis. This is where he becomes respectable. He wants to go down in history as a great man and, next to being President – which I very much doubt he ever will be – being Ambassador over here is the most important position he's ever likely to hold. Doesn't it make you feel queasy to think that this man who ought to be in jail is representing his country at a time when there should be someone of the highest calibre over here?'

'Golly! You sound even more censorious than me. Well, we're doing what's been asked of us in getting to know the man. We'll just have to see what happens. Do you think we're hypocrites?'

'They say that ambassadors are sent abroad to lie for their country. I expect if we have to lie a bit in a good cause, we'll be forgiven. I say, what are you going to do tomorrow?' he added hopefully.

'Working,' Verity replied virtuously. 'What about you? Lazing about like all you decadent aristocrats, I suppose.'

'I'm having a tennis lesson with Kay in the morning. Lunch at the club and then a snooze. I want to be on top form for our dinner. Shall I pick you up about seven?'

'Yes, and don't forget it's informal – a dinner jacket, nothing more.'

Verity was just reading over what she had typed when there was a knock on her door. She looked at her watch. It was two o'clock and she was hungry, not having broken for lunch.

'Yes? Who is it?' She thought it absurd but Edward had persuaded her not to open the door of her flat without first knowing who was on the other side. 'You've made some pretty ugly enemies in your career so far,' he told her. 'It makes sense to take a bit of care. I don't want to have my girl hit over the head or something before I've had a chance of doing it myself.' His joke was feeble but his concern was genuine.

'Miss Browne. It's me – Tom Wintringham. Let me in, will you?'

'Tom? Of course, hold on a moment.'

Tom Wintringham had been war correspondent on the *Daily Worker* and had joined the International Brigade as soon as it was formed. Verity had met him first in Spain and had liked him. He was a Balliol man but Oxford hadn't suited him and he had come down without a degree. He became a committed Communist, to the chagrin of his father who was a vicar. In his late thirties, he was slim, almost weedy-looking, with steel-framed spectacles, a high-domed head and an academic stoop.

'Tom!' Verity said, kissing him. 'So it *was* you

the other night. Come in. You look awful,' she added, seeing him properly. 'What on earth have you been up to?'

'You recognized me, then?'

'Outside the Kardomah? Certainly I did but I had a feeling you didn't want me to show it.'

'That's right. Megan and I . . .'

'The little girl? Is she your daughter?'

'Yes, she's mine. Just five,' he added proudly.

'I was worried in that fog that she might be cold.'

'She's a tough child but her mother was cross with me for being out so long. The thing was, I saw who you were with.'

'David Griffiths-Jones?'

'Yes, and O'Rourke.'

'You know Danny, then?'

'Yes, I do. Do you remember when we were in Spain there was that Irishman in my battalion – Liam MacDade?'

'I do. He'd been in the IRA, hadn't he? I didn't like him and I know he didn't like me.'

'He hated you.'

Verity blenched. 'But he was killed on the Jarama River, wasn't he? That was what I heard.'

'He was wounded but survived. He's here in London now. I've seen him with O'Rourke.'

'You aren't saying they are behind this bombing campaign, are you?'

'I haven't got any proof but I believe so. The thing is, if anything were to happen to me, I wanted someone to know . . .'

'Nothing's going to happen, Tom. Even the IRA don't go around murdering people – at least not in England,' Verity added, suddenly doubtful. 'When did you see them together?'

'There's an Irish pub – the Spread Eagle – in the docks. As you know, most of the dockers are Irish.'

'Nothing wrong with that.'

'No, but I saw O'Rourke, MacDade and that other fellow who was in Spain with us – "Bomber" Kelly.'

'The one who blew up bridges?'

'Yes.'

'I see.' Verity hesitated. 'You didn't hear what they were talking about?'

'No. I didn't want to get too close to them. I've got a wife and daughter.'

'You could go to the police.'

'I told you – I have a wife and daughter. I don't want to die quite yet.' Tom's smile was thin. 'Anyway, think about it – we Communists aren't too popular with the forces of law and order. I go into the police station and ask to see the duty sergeant. He's probably Irish but, even if he isn't, all I can say is that I saw three Irishmen talking together in an Irish pub. Sounds like a bad joke. He'd kick me out as soon as look at me.'

'I don't know – not with these bombs in underground stations. I believe in Irish independence. I think what the Black and Tans did in Ireland was unforgivable and we'll go on paying for it for generations. On the other hand, killing innocent people on the Tube or anywhere else for that matter is not . . .'

'Anyway, it wasn't O'Rourke I came to talk to you about.'

'No? Who was it then?' Verity looked meaningfully at her typewriter.

'Sorry, you're busy.'

'I have this article to write. But go ahead. You wanted to talk to me about . . . ?'

'About Griffiths-Jones.'

'David?' She was surprised.

'Yes, David.'

'I didn't know you knew him.'

'I know him all right. In fact, I've been following him.'

'I don't understand. You've been following David? Why?'

'Because I don't trust him.'

'He's a senior figure in the Party. He's your superior. You oughtn't to say such things about him.'

'I know but . . . well, I first watched him in Spain. I was what you might call his ADC for a few months. I got to know him pretty well. You know him well too. Surely you can see what I see?'

Verity began to be irritated. 'Look, I'm sorry, Tom, but I really don't know what you're talking about. If you've got something to say, please say it, otherwise I must get back to work.'

He hesitated. 'Another time. I can see I'm being

a bore. How are you, by the way? I heard you've had TB.'

'Yes, but I was lucky. I'm better now.'

'You don't look better,' he said bluntly.

'Well, I am,' she replied crossly.

'And you are getting married. Congratulations.'

'Thanks,' she said abruptly.

'Well, I'll be going now. I'm glad I've warned you.'

'About the IRA?'

'And about David.'

'There's nothing about David I don't know. He puts the Party first and people second. I've known that for a long time.'

'Yes, well, be careful. That's all I can say.'

Verity felt uncomfortable. She longed for Tom to leave. For some ridiculous reason she felt guilty but about what she could not say. She knew he was right about David but she didn't want to admit it. It seemed disloyal to allow anyone to criticize him in front of her.

'Why did you tell me about Danny O'Rourke?'

'Because I trust you,' he said, and then spoilt it by adding, 'and you know important people – people in authority. They'll listen to you.'

Informal dress was easy enough for Edward but it took Verity almost as long to decide what to wear as it had to write her article. She wanted to be smart and attractive but not too showy. She had an idea that she shouldn't make Kathleen

Kennedy look dowdy by comparison. In the end, she chose a simple, tight-waisted, full-skirted dress by Lucien Lelong which Edward had bought her as a birthday present when she had been ill. She hadn't worn it before and she knew it would please him if she wore it now.

When he came to pick her up in the Lagonda – his valet, Fenton, acting as chauffeur – Edward told her she looked beautiful. She refused to let him kiss her because, unusually for her, she had put on make-up and had no wish to arrive with her lipstick smeared.

He pretended to be disgruntled. 'Now you've recovered and I'm allowed to kiss you, you won't let me.' He looked at her more closely and brightened up. 'Isn't that the dress we bought together? You look . . . well, you look good enough to eat. I warn you that, if that nasty old man puts his hand on your knee during dinner, I may have to punch him.'

'You won't *see* if he puts his hand on my knee but you don't have to worry. He wouldn't try anything with his children present. Mind you, he can be pretty rude when he wants to be, so don't rise. And he swears like a navvy.'

When they arrived at the American Embassy residence in Prince's Gate – another of J.P. Morgan's gifts to a grateful nation – they were greeted by a cloud of flunkeys and taken up to the drawing-room. It was a beautiful room but rather stifled by ornate French Empire style furniture and heavy velvet curtains. Whether this was the taste of the previous Ambassador, Robert Worth Bingham, or Kennedy's own, Verity never discovered but she found it oppressive.

Far from being hostile, Kennedy could not have been more friendly. Edward thought he was about to kiss Verity but, in the end, he remembered that he hardly knew her and contented himself with shaking her hand and then forgetting to let go of it as he introduced her to his children.

'I hope you don't mind,' he said, 'but this is just a family party. I get fed up entertaining a lot of old men my age even if they are English lords. My apologies, Lord Edward, but I find when you've met one English lord, you've met them all.'

Edward turned away what might have been meant as a jibe with an easy shrug of his shoulders. 'I recall Lord Halifax –' Halifax was the Foreign Secretary – 'saying he felt the same way about ambassadors.'

'*Touché*!' Joe Jr said with a laugh. 'So, Edward, aren't you going to introduce us properly? I gather you gave my father a hard time yesterday, Miss Browne,' he went on, not waiting for Edward to respond.

'She's one tough lady. Have you brought that article for me to read?' The Ambassador seemed genial enough but Edward suspected that, if Verity had not brought it with her, he would have shown his displeasure.

'Yes, Ambassador,' she said, taking it out of her handbag.

'Thank you. If you'll excuse me, I'll go and read it over while you kids get to know one another. Come with me, will you, Eamon?'

Eamon Farrell, the Ambassador's press secretary, waved apologetically at them and followed Kennedy out of the room. Edward, rather startled at being labelled one of the kids, said to Verity in mock alarm, 'If you've got something wrong, we'll probably not be allowed to sit down to dinner.'

Joe Jr laughed. 'Now, Miss Browne, who amongst this grisly crew haven't you yet met?'

'Please, you must call me Verity or I'll begin to feel left out.'

'Right! Verity it is. Now, this is Kathleen, my sister, whom everyone calls Kick . . .'

It was easy to see why Kick was so popular in London society. She wasn't exactly pretty – her hair was mousy and her figure a little too full – but she had bright blue eyes and a delightful smile so that it was almost impossible not to smile back at her. She was just nineteen and had what Verity had seen described in the popular press as 'sex appeal'. Bags of it. She looked – as the French say – *bien dans sa peau* and Verity noticed that Edward had that smile on his face she had seen before when he liked the look of a woman.

'Miss Browne, I've been longing to meet you. Everyone's been so kind and hospitable but I only

93

seem to meet . . . well, you know, girls doing the "season". They're all young and they haven't done anything yet. You must tell me about Spain and Austria. Joe's been all over Europe but I've seen nothing.'

She bubbled away but, behind her loquacity, Verity sensed a shy girl who did not perhaps wholly believe in the success she was enjoying. Verity did not, as a rule, read the gossip columns but she had been unable to avoid them altogether and knew that Kick was invited to all the grandest houses and had danced with everyone from Prince Leopold and the Duke of Kent to 'Billy' Cavendish, the Marquess of Hartington who would one day be the Duke of Devonshire. *Queen* had devoted a double-page spread to 'America's Most Important Debutante'. Her triumph was all the more remarkable because the English aristocracy did not normally take kindly to interlopers, especially Irish-American Catholics.

'And this is my younger brother, Jack,' Joe continued, ruffling the hair of a handsome, fresh-faced boy. 'So now you've met us all, Edward, what do you think?'

Fortunately, Edward was spared having to answer by the entry of his Cambridge friend, Casey Bishop.

'Edward – great to see you! It's been so long.' He gripped Edward's hand and looked him up and down with a trace of mockery in his eyes. 'Sorry to be late. And this must be Miss Browne.

I'm delighted to meet you. The Old Man seems to have taken rather a shine to you.' The voice was slow and easy. It had served him well with the English girls who had flocked round him when Edward had first known him at Cambridge. To his chagrin, he hardly looked a day older. 'So you're marrying Edward? Well, well . . . He always was a lucky guy.'

Edward smiled weakly and Verity's grin broadened. As he watched her take in this good-looking man with his perfect teeth and thick fair hair, he felt distinctly worn about the edges.

'It's very good to see you too, Casey. It's been too long. I'd heard you were in London and have been meaning to look you up.'

'You've forgiven me, then?' Casey's smile was impish.

'Forgiven you?'

'That girl – what was her name? Phoebe something.'

'Oh, yes, of course.' Edward was embarrassed. 'It was all so long ago.'

'You two know each other?' Kick was surprised.

'We were at Cambridge together,' Casey replied. 'I was up at Trinity for a year in . . . when was it?' He looked at Edward interrogatively.

'Too long ago to calculate,' he replied hurriedly. He felt Verity seething with curiosity beside him.

'You must tell me about this Phoebe,' she said with a laugh. 'It's the first I've heard of her and I thought I knew all his sins.'

Edward was beginning to enjoy introducing Verity as his fiancée but the moment was spoiled for him by her rather too frank appreciation of his friend.

'Never think you know all a man's sins,' Casey said with mock gravity. 'Probably even he doesn't know them.'

'And Phoebe was one of them?' she inquired.

'Edward accused me of stealing her but, if you ask me, I did him a good turn,' he smiled back. 'She was "orflly nice" and all that but, when she introduced me to "Mummy", I knew it was time to make myself scarce. But that's all old history. I'm so pleased to meet you at last. You know the Old Man hasn't stopped talking about you since you interviewed him yesterday. By the way, may I say that I read your articles in the *New Gazette* with considerable interest, Miss Browne, and, though I sometimes disagree with your conclusions, I am always impressed by the clarity of your exposition and the reasoning behind it. You have witnessed history being made, which I envy.'

'You call it history but I'd call it tragedy if it weren't so squalid. Betrayal, cowardice and moral bankruptcy . . .'

Verity's face was flushed and Edward looked at her with alarm. He hoped she wasn't going to embark on one of her lectures. Catching his eye, she hesitated. 'But I won't bore you.'

'Please, you won't bore me. When I was in New York, they announced that the theme of the World

Fair was to be "The World of Tomorrow". I thought you might appreciate the irony. It assumes there will be a tomorrow. If England were to go under . . .'

'Why do all you Americans love England so much?' Verity said, suddenly angry. 'Our slums are the worst in Europe and our rich are for the most part quite careless – I mean uncaring – of the misery at the back door. Our foreign policy – if you can call it a policy – is based on cowardice and betrayal. This country is literally and metaphorically bankrupt.'

'For all that, I love England. Often I wish it were entirely inhabited by Americans,' Casey answered her lightly. 'Couldn't you take New England in exchange? We would drain the swamps, redeem the slums and make it the Garden of Eden of our imagination. We could be England's future if you would permit it.'

Verity laughed, disarmed by his ability to be light-hearted and serious at the same time. 'Not possible, I'm afraid. We must make do with the present – with today. We know our future and it has to be endured. No doubt America will have a tomorrow and if we slip into the darkness, perhaps you will have *our* tomorrow. It would serve you right.'

'You really think things are that bad?'

'Don't you, Mr Bishop?'

'Please call me Casey. Look, I guess you'll think it forward of me but may I invite you to lunch

97

one day and we can have a good – what do you English call it? – a good chinwag.'

Verity smiled. 'I don't know yet if I'll ever be allowed in again. It all depends whether the Ambassador approves of my article.'

At that moment the door of the drawing-room opened and Kennedy reappeared, his face wreathed in smiles.

'Very good, Miss Browne. I have made . . . suggested, I should say, just a few alterations. Did I really say, "I expect, with great regret, to write the obituary of the British Empire"?'

'You did, Ambassador.'

'Well, if I did, I was wrong and I regret saying it. You will remove it, won't you? I'm sure Lord Weaver would agree that this isn't the moment to cause friction between our two countries.'

Verity smiled wanly. He was correct, of course. Weaver would never print such a statement from the American Ambassador. It was too inflammatory.

At dinner she sat between the Ambassador and Eamon Farrell and was subjected to a barrage of questions about the war in Spain and what it meant to be a Communist now that worrying stories of Stalin's repressive regime were being reported on a daily basis. The Ambassador was, unsurprisingly, a fervent admirer of General Franco and it was only with a considerable effort of will that Verity managed to keep her temper. She was exhausted by the end of the meal and glad to get away and play backgammon with Joe Jr.

Edward was seated between Kick and Casey Bishop. He took the opportunity of asking Casey for help in identifying Churchill's would-be assassin. 'Our sources indicate that there may be some connection with the embassy,' he finished up, 'and we need your help.'

Casey was dismissive – almost suspiciously unwilling to co-operate. 'I'm sorry, Edward, but as I said to your people when this rumour was first mentioned to me, I don't believe it. It is just a rumour with no basis in fact. Now, don't let's spoil our dinner with a discussion of absurd gossip.'

Edward could do nothing but accept the brush-off and they went on to talk of old Cambridge friends and memories of times past.

Kick told him all about being presented to the King and Queen and how she had had to learn how to curtsey at Miss Vacani's School of Dancing – no easy matter wearing a long dress and tight shoes. She regaled him with all the social blunders she had made which seemed mostly to consist of her being relaxed and informal instead of stiff and reserved. She told him about her morning ride in Rotten Row and playing tennis with Kay Stammers.

'She's just adorable,' Kick enthused. 'I love her to bits. She says I might be quite good if only I practised harder.' And in whispers – so that her father could not hear – she told him of her liking for 'Billy' Cavendish. 'I know it can't come to

99

anything,' she said sadly. 'For one thing, there's this religious business. Apparently the Dukes of Devonshire were famous for hating Catholics and I don't know what my father would say if I told him I was going to marry a Protestant. Anyway, what am I talking about? Billy's family is about the grandest in England. He's got to marry someone like a princess.' She put her hand on his arm. 'Please, Lord Edward, you won't repeat any of this, will you? I don't know why I'm confiding in you. I think it must be because you are marrying Miss Browne. I don't suppose that went down very well with your family. I mean, I think she's just great but . . .' She giggled and looked to see if he was annoyed. 'There I go, being tactless again.'

Edward smiled. 'No, you're quite right. My brother doesn't approve of Verity but I do believe one ought to marry for love unless . . . he hesitated, 'it's your duty to sacrifice yourself for the greater good.'

'You mean like the Duke of Windsor and Mrs Simpson?'

'I suppose I do. Fortunately neither of us has to choose between the person we love and serving our country.'

Kick pursed her lips. 'I'm not sure Billy would agree with you, Lord Edward. If things get very bad for me, may I come to you for advice?'

'I would be honoured,' he said, touched by her naive trust in him.

'Did my father tell you that we've been invited to Cliveden this weekend? Nancy – she insists I call her Nancy which is so sweet of her – says you and Miss Browne will be there too. That'll be such fun. I like Cliveden. Papa's happy talking to all his political friends and we lesser mortals can fool around. There's always dancing after dinner or charades and, of course, in the summer there's the pool and tennis . . . One can relax there. They don't allow newspapermen anywhere near the house. I don't mind having my picture taken but it's nice being out of the limelight sometimes, isn't it?'

'Will he be there?'

'Billy? No, sadly not. I'll just have to find someone else to flirt with, won't I? There's always Casey and Eamon. Which do you think is the better looking? Casey, I suppose.' She put her finger to her chin as though she were a little girl trying to choose between two dolls. 'But he has that lean and hungry look which rather scares me. No, I think, he's more Miss Browne's type. She could tame him. Now, don't look like that. I was only joking.'

'I'm used to being jealous, Miss Kennedy.'

'Please call me Kick. Everyone does.'

'Eamon's good-looking,' Edward said, trying to match her mood.

'He is rather but of course one mustn't flirt with the hired help.' Once again she saw she had gone a little too far and added quickly, 'I'm still joking.

101

Eamon is almost one of the family. You can tell him what I said if you like. I've called him much worse.'

'Will they both be at Cliveden too?'

'Oh yes. Father never goes anywhere without them.'

'If I may say so, the best-looking man in this room is your brother.'

'Joe?'

'He is very good-looking, but I meant Jack.'

To Edward's embarrassment she leant across the table and said, 'Do you hear that, Jack? Lord Edward thinks you are more handsome than Joe.'

Jack, who had said very little during dinner, looked at Edward with sleepy eyes and raised his wineglass in an ironic toast.

'He's been very silent tonight,' Kick remarked. 'I think his back must be paining him.' She spoke quietly but her brother must have guessed they were talking about him because, with a muttered word of apology, he pushed back his chair and left the room.

'He has a bad back? An accident or . . . ?'

'No, not an accident. Although he looks strong, he's been plagued by illness from when he was a child, poor boy. Will you excuse me? I had better go and see if he needs anything.'

'Of course, anyway it's time we were going,' Edward said, rising. 'I have so much enjoyed talking to you, Kick, and I much look forward to seeing you again at Cliveden.'

'Me too,' she responded with a smile that lit up her face. 'I feel we shall be great friends.'

'I very much hope so,' he replied, quite sincerely

When Edward dropped Verity off at Cranmer Court, he could see she was very tired but in high spirits. She kissed him on the mouth.

'Thanks for being there,' she said, touching his face with her hand. 'I couldn't have managed without you.'

'You were very restrained, and the Kennedy young loved you.'

'Do you think it's a good idea us going to Cliveden? What if I say something awful and disgrace you?'

'You won't. And if you do, what does it matter? Nancy says exactly what she thinks and gets away with it.'

'I'll talk to you tomorrow. If I'm honest, I still don't have quite the energy I used to before I was ill.'

'You're getting stronger every day. You can't expect to be back to normal yet.'

'Thank goodness, I hear you say.' She smiled wryly. 'Now go. We've kept Fenton up long enough. Goodnight, Fenton. Keep him out of trouble, will you?'

'I'll do my best miss,' he replied with a theatrical sigh.

In the car Edward said, 'I have this terrible fear she'll have a relapse. The doctor warned it could happen.'

Fenton made no comment. He knew his master well and the last thing he needed was facile re-assurance. 'Shall you wish me to drive you and Miss Browne to Cliveden?'

'No, I'll drive. You take the train with the luggage.'

'Very good, my lord.'

CHAPTER 5

The following day, Verity tried to find Danny O'Rourke. She telephoned George Castle. He was at work but Mary said they hadn't seen him, adding in a stage whisper that she was relieved because she did not like him.

Verity wanted to ask if she thought Danny was involved in the IRA bombings but David Griffiths-Jones had drummed into her that the telephone was insecure and might even be tapped. She tried a few other people she thought might know where he was but without much success, although Harold Knight had heard a rumour that he had been arrested – a rumour David confirmed when he telephoned her to arrange a meeting.

She hesitated to ring him because, whenever she did, he so often seemed to have another job for her and all David's jobs were at best embarrassing – making use of friends and contacts to gain information – or at worst frightening. More often than not she found herself using that word when she thought about him. He had always been something of a bully and his ill-disguised contempt for Edward and her life in general had made him even less easy to talk to than when she had first known him. That must have been what had made her impatient with Tom Wintringham when he had put into words what she was thinking.

She and David met in a pub off the Strand and for once he seemed to be in a good mood. He was pleased with her and said so. He explained that the main objective of any political organization or security service was to place someone as near the top of a rival organization as possible.

'To have eyes and ears so close to Kennedy is a bit of a coup. I gather you are driving down to Cliveden this afternoon?' Verity nodded. 'Very good. You may meet someone you know there.'

'Lulu?' she guessed.

'Best to pretend not to know her.'

Verity was uncomfortable with the idea that she was a spy and a hypocrite but she couldn't think of any way to justify her behaviour so she kept quiet and accepted his praise with as much grace as her queasy stomach would allow. She did not ask why Lulu was at Cliveden because she thought she could guess.

'Incidentally, O'Rourke and MacDade are being questioned by the police but they'll have to let them go as they have no evidence to link them to the bombings.'

Verity heard the satisfaction in David's voice and wondered if, in the Soviet Union, suspects could count on being released when there was no evidence that they had committed a crime. It was at that precise moment she decided to resign from the Party but she said nothing.

When she discussed it with Edward later, as they drove down to Cliveden, she confessed that she had been unable to bring herself to tell David she was leaving the Party. Edward refused her comfort, merely quoting his school friend, Eric Blair, who now wrote under the name of George Orwell, 'In a time of universal deceit, telling the truth is a revolutionary act.' 'I have come to the conclusion, V, that Lord Acton was wrong when he said power tends to corrupt. I think fear corrupts – corrupts us all.'

Cliveden was approached down a long drive, the far end of which was marked by an ornate Italian fountain in the form of a shell being viewed by a puzzled-looking sylph or naiad which Verity remarked would put her off oysters. It was not a 'great' house like Chatsworth or Blenheim but it was in a perfect position. The original house had been built by Charles II's favourite, the Duke of Buckingham, in the late 1660s. He had sited it dramatically on a cliff with long views over the River Thames snaking its way through woodland towards Henley. That house had been destroyed by fire, as was the one that succeeded it. The house the American millionaire, William Waldorf, 1st Viscount Astor, bought in 1893 was mainly the work of Charles Barry who had also designed the new Houses of Parliament. Astor bought it for his wife, Mary, but she died a year later. He continued to restore and improve the house but his heart was no longer in it and he gave it to his son and daughter-in-law as a wedding present in 1906.

Nancy, one of the famously beautiful Langhorne sisters from Virginia, had met Waldorf in England where she was recovering from a brief, disastrous marriage and subsequent divorce. Bernard Shaw called her a volcano and she had certainly turned Cliveden upside down. She had thrown out much of the dark Victorian decorations and furniture, banishing what she called the 'splendid gloom' which had suited her father-in-law. She set out to make the house the centre of English political and cultural life.

With over a hundred staff, each guest was treated like royalty. It was just after four when Edward brought the Lagonda to a halt outside the elegant but rather oppressive entrance. They were immediately surrounded by footmen. Their bags were taken away almost before they stepped out of the car and it was driven away to be garaged. As they were ushered into the house, Edward looked at Verity with concern. She had been uncharacteristically silent on the journey and he guessed that she might be worried about her reception, whether she would find the Astors overwhelming and Nancy, in particular, too much the *grande dame*. Mr Lee, the Astors' famous butler – he had also been butler to Waldorf's father – welcomed them to Cliveden with courteous dignity and escorted them into the hall where Nancy met them with her usual ebullience.

'Now Verity, my dear – I may call you Verity, mayn't I? – you mustn't believe everything you hear about us. This is not a nest of spies or anything of that kind.'

'Oh, please don't worry, Lady Astor. You must remember that I work for the newspapers so I know not to believe a single word they say. But,' she added hurriedly, 'I promise I'm off duty this weekend. My friend, Professor Laski, says you are his favourite Conservative.'

'He's a dear, dear man.'

'And Ellen Wilkinson, who I first met on the Jarrow March, told me when I said you had been kind enough to invite me to Cliveden – now, how did she put it? "Lady Astor knows a good deal more than most of her critics about political affairs. Her biggest political drawback is that nothing can prevent her laughing at pompous fools."'

'Ellen and I may be on opposite sides of the House but we stick together as we women have to. It's not easy being women in what Winston once told me was a gentlemen's club. You must remind me to tell you about the only lavatory we are allowed to use.'

Changing the subject, Verity remarked on the vases of lilies that stood on pedestals on either side of the front door.

'I'm so glad you like them. It's a little fad of

mine – one that Waldo indulges. I have lilies here all year round – from our hothouses, you know. This is so exciting.' She clapped her hands together. 'I can see we are going to be great friends and I do like to make new friends. How clever of you, Edward, to have found her – or did she find you? Now, I don't know why I'm keeping you standing here in the hall. Let's go into the drawing-room. I'm sure you must both be dying for a cup of tea.'

Edward had stood in silent amazement as what might have been an embarrassing meeting between two strong-minded but very different women turned into a show of mutual admiration. He supposed that Nancy – or rather Mr Lee – had welcomed so many statesmen and celebrities to Cliveden that his arrival with his fiancée, a notorious Communist and journalist, did not merit a raised eyebrow.

For Nancy, this was not a large party – the Kennedys and their entourage including Casey Bishop and Eamon Farrell, without whom they seemed unable to exist, and her special friend Philip Kerr, Lord Lothian. Casey, Eamon and the three Kennedy children were out, Nancy said, exploring Cliveden's gardens.

'I think you know one another, don't you?' she said as Lothian rose from his armchair, putting aside a copy of *The Times*.

'Yes, indeed. How nice to see you again, Lord

Edward, but I haven't had the pleasure of meeting Miss Browne.' Lothian held out his hand and Verity took it, contenting herself with a neutral smile, trying not to see him as the epitome of everything she disapproved of about the so-called 'Cliveden Set'.

Lothian was one of Nancy's oldest and dearest friends. He was calm and quiet but was always ready to listen to her chattering away on subjects about which she knew nothing. She liked to tell stories against herself and one she told over tea and crumpets concerned Gandhi to whom Lothian had introduced her.

'When he came over to England in 1931 for the Indian Round Table Conference, Philip brought him to Cliveden. I must say I thought the Indians were very fortunate to be part of the British Empire and I told him so, probably at too great a length. I remember I called him a humbug and told him his policy of non-violent opposition to the British authorities in India was destructive.

'How I dared, I really can't think, but I did. He listened quietly to everything I had to say and then asked me whether I would like to listen to him or go on talking. Of course I apologized and promised to listen to him without interrupting. He then told me the whole story of the national movement in India and I was immediately converted. It's one of the things Winston and I quarrel about most often – giving India independence. He's such an old imperialist that he

111

won't hear of anything which smacks of surrendering the British Empire.'

'You know Mr Churchill has had death threats from Indian nationalists?' Edward put in. 'I wondered, Lord Lothian, whether you thought he ought to take them seriously?'

'I don't think so,' Lothian replied easily. 'Now the IRA . . . I would take threats from those brigands seriously.'

Kennedy disagreed. 'Naw! The Nazis or the Commies will get him first. Sorry, Miss Browne, I don't mean your polite kind of Commie. I mean those guys that did for Trotsky.'

'Did you know –' Nancy turned to Verity – 'that Karl Marx wrote a pamphlet about Lady Sutherland who lived here at the beginning of the last century?'

'No, I didn't,' she replied, intrigued.

'Well,' Nancy went on, 'she had great estates in the Highlands of Scotland and these were "improved", which meant the wholesale removal of the impoverished population – mostly subsistence farmers – to new settlements on the coast. Many died or emigrated and Marx wrote *Sutherland and Slavery* in 1853. There's a copy in the library if you'd like to see it.'

'I would indeed,' Verity said, already contemplating writing an article on the subject for the *Daily Worker*.

At that moment, they heard shouting in the hall and Kick Kennedy came in, looking wild-eyed and very much not the cool, sophisticated young woman Edward had met in London.

'I say, you folks,' she said, breathlessly, 'I've just told Mr Lee to telephone for the police. We've found a body in the – what do you call it? – the Blenheim Pavilion.'

'A body in the Blenheim Pavilion?' Nancy repeated. 'Whose body?'

'I don't know whose body,' Kick said with a touch of irritation.

'A man or a woman?' Lord Astor barked, getting up from his armchair.

'A man – a young man. Not a tramp.'

'Well, we had better go and look. You stay here, Nancy. We won't be long but if it's a member of staff . . .'

'May I come with you?' Edward asked. 'I have had some experience of dead bodies.'

'Of course.'

'And I'll come too,' Kennedy said with almost too much enthusiasm. 'I have had no experience of dead bodies but I guess that's all going to change.'

Carrying torches, as it was now quite dark, and dressed for the cold, damp air, the little party approached the pavilion.

'Joe,' Kennedy called. 'Are you OK?'

'That you, Dad?' It was Jack's voice. 'We're OK but this poor fellow isn't.'

The two boys made way for their father and

Lord Astor. Eamon and Casey were kneeling over the body but moved to one side when Edward asked to examine the victim. He lay flat on his back, almost formal like a marble funerary monument, except that his eyes were open and staring.

'He's dead all right,' Edward said, feeling for a pulse. 'Quite cold. Has anyone moved him?'

'We haven't but someone must have. He didn't die here. He must have had a jacket or coat but we can't find anything,' Eamon remarked. 'I wonder who he is?'

They all stared at the dead man. He was about thirty-five with black, wiry hair. His clothes – a white Aertex shirt and slacks as though he was dressed for tennis – were in disarray but there was no evidence of a fight and no sign of blood. He was not much physically. His shoulders were rounded and his narrow chest suggested that he might be consumptive.

'Has he had a heart attack?' Joe Jr asked doubtfully.

Gingerly, Edward lifted the dead man's head and gave a snort of surprise. The shaft of a thin knife – what he thought of as a poniard – was protruding from the side of his neck. Gently, he lowered the head and stood up.

'We should leave now and not touch anything,' he said decisively. 'This young man has been murdered.'

'Murdered! But that's not possible,' Lord Astor exclaimed.

'I'm afraid it is,' Edward replied. 'Is he known to you?'

'I've never seen him before in my life.'

'I know who he is,' Verity said in a small voice from the doorway.

'Verity! What are you doing here? I thought you had stayed with Nancy.'

'No, you know me. I tagged along,' she replied miserably.

'Well, who is he then?' Kennedy demanded.

'He's a man called Tom Wintringham. He's a . . . he was a journalist I knew in Spain.'

'But what's he doing here?' Lord Astor asked irritably.

'He may have been coming to see me,' she said unwillingly.

'You had an appointment with him . . . here?'

'No, I had no idea he was here. He came to see me in London. He wanted to warn me . . . he wanted me to know . . . if anything happened to him . . .'

'Know what?' Lord Astor demanded.

'He believed he knew who was behind the IRA plot to bomb London.'

'Did you tell the police?' Lord Astor asked sharply.

'I didn't. I told him he should but he said he didn't dare . . . as a married man.'

'As a married man? What does that mean?' Kennedy demanded.

'He feared for his life if the IRA got to know he

had informed on one of their men,' Verity explained. 'He said he had seen someone called Danny O'Rourke talking to two men he recognized down at the docks – Liam MacDade and a man called "Bomber" Kelly. They are all IRA and Danny's a Communist.'

'O'Rourke!' Kennedy exclaimed. Edward thought he was going to say something more but lapsed into silence. However, he gave Eamon a look and there was no doubt in Edward's mind that he recognized the name. 'Did you know these men too, Miss Browne?' Kennedy suddenly demanded.

'No!' Verity was on the defensive. 'Or rather,' she added, 'I knew Kelly in Spain. He used to blow up bridges.'

There was a stunned silence. Then Edward said dubiously, 'Well, one thing, Lord Astor, as Mr Farrell says, Wintringham – if that's who our corpse is – didn't die here. Do you see? There's no blood, no nothing – just the body. But why on earth did they dump him here?'

'His spectacles,' Verity said, wanting to close the staring eyes. 'Where are his spectacles?'

'And where is his coat or jacket?' Edward murmured. 'It's a cold night to be out in just a shirt.'

Verity looked at the frail, hunched body of her friend and felt as though she might be sick. He had come to her for help and she had not given it. She swore to herself that she would find

116

O'Rourke and accuse him of murder. Surely, it had to be one of the three IRA men who had killed him – unless, of course, they had the perfect alibi and were in police custody.

'Ah, that sounds like a police car,' Lord Astor said.

'That's all I know, Inspector.' Verity was weary and depressed. It was the following morning and she had been at the police station for over an hour. Would she be arrested and, if so, for what? She had gone over her story three times and Inspector Voss still seemed unconvinced. He was a tall, ungainly man with a lazy eye which somehow made his expression difficult to read.

'Of course, Inspector,' Edward ventured, 'we cannot be sure that Wintringham was going to see Miss Browne. You didn't tell him you were spending the weekend at Cliveden, did you, Verity?'

'No,' she agreed, 'but who else might he have wanted to see?'

'Lord Astor, Mr Kennedy . . . who knows?'

'You've informed his wife?' Edward asked the Inspector.

'We have.'

'Presumably she knew nothing about why he was here?'

'No,' the Inspector answered shortly. He obviously had no intention of sharing his thoughts with them.

'Poor little Megan,' Verity sighed. An image of the little girl in her blue coat, hand in hand with her father in the fog outside the Kardomah, came vividly to mind.

'You never met his wife?' the Inspector asked.

'No, I told you. I hardly knew Tom. I didn't even know he was back from Spain until I saw him that evening. I never even talked to his daughter. I just . . .'

She gulped. It was against her principles to cry but, really, this was the last thing she needed. She felt she was in some undefined way to blame for his death. As she knew he would be, the Inspector had been highly suspicious that she had met O'Rourke at a Communist 'cell' meeting, as he called it. He had made a telephone call and confirmed – sounding rather disappointed – that O'Rourke was still being questioned by the police but MacDade had been released and Kelly had not yet been found. The combination of the IRA and Communism was as if she had admitted to meeting Guy Fawkes just before he blew up the Houses of Parliament. She knew that, if Edward had not stood at her side throughout her interrogation, she might have been given an even rougher ride.

And now she was worried that she might get into trouble with David Griffiths-Jones and George Castle. They would probably assume that she had turned informer. For a few days she had been so happy. Was it now all turning sour? She glanced at Edward. His expression was stern but watchful, like a bird of prey protecting its young.

'Thank you, Miss Browne,' Voss said at last, 'and you, too, Lord Edward. I don't think I have any reason to detain you longer. I gather you are staying with the Astors until Monday morning?'

'That is correct, Inspector, and if you need us after that you have our addresses.'

Verity wondered if Lord Astor would want her out of the house before Monday. She knew she wanted to go. After this, it was going to be a hundred times worse than she had ever imagined.

When they were back in the Lagonda, Edward said, 'You know something, V? When we gave the Inspector our addresses, it occurred to me that we haven't given any thought to where we are going to live after we are married. You have a flat hardly big enough to swing the proverbial cat and I have rooms in Albany, a bachelor establishment if ever there was one. Poor Fenton has to lurk in a small room in the attic which has always embarrassed me. We must buy a house. Shall we live in London, do you think, or would you prefer a country life? Somewhere for Basil.'

Basil was Verity's curly-coated retriever who currently lived at Mersham where there was plenty of room for him and to whom both the Duke and the Duchess were devoted.

'I don't think we would want to live at Mersham, do you?' he went on. 'I know Gerald would give us a house on the estate but I don't think we would want him breathing down our necks.' Edward was well aware that his brother did not approve of his future wife and, while Connie would do everything in her power to make it work, living close to the castle would be difficult for all of them.

Verity looked at him with a smile of gratitude. She knew that talking about where they would live was his way of reassuring her that Wintringham's death and her contacts – with what the Inspector no doubt considered 'enemies of the state' – did not make him regret asking her to marry him. He had not reproached her with either word or look for failing to tell him about Tom's visit and his warning about the IRA threat. She knew that Edward put up with a lot of criticism – silent and not so silent – about his choice of wife and this was just the sort of thing that made people say 'I told you so.' There had been a poisonous, unsigned article in the *Mail* insinuating that he had been trapped into marriage by a scheming harpy. When he had shown it to her – he would never have pretended not to have seen it – they had both laughed and counted it a compliment. But still the drip, drip of – if not abuse, certainly dis-approval – was wearing.

'I've been meaning to tell you,' she said. 'I had a letter from Adrian and Charlotte. They say there is a house just near their cottage which they think would suit us. I thought – when this is all over – we might spend a weekend with them and look at it. You know they've been pressing us to stay for months.'

'Good idea!' Edward said. 'We'll do that. I say, about Megan and Wintringham's wife or rather his widow. I can see you are really cut up about what it will do to them. Shall we try and find them and see what we can do to help?'

'Would you mind?' Verity said, a flood of relief making her feel once again that she might cry. 'I would really like to. I don't understand exactly why but I can't get the image of the little girl out of my mind. I feel responsible even though I know I'm not.'

'Good, that's settled then. Now let's get back to Cliveden. I know we would both rather turn tail and run for home but that's not our way, is it? We've got to see this through, haven't we?'

Verity stuck out her chin and nodded in agreement but in her heart she wasn't sure she could hold out.

Nancy did her best to ensure that the body in the pavilion did not cast too great a gloom over the company. She decided not to cancel arrangements for dinner that evening which included guests from nearby. Dr Channing, Lord Astor told them, had a cottage on the estate. In exchange for treating any of the household who might fall ill, Dr Channing had, rent free, a delightful cottage and use of Cliveden's gardens, swimming pool and tennis courts.

There was something bogus about Channing which struck both Edward and Verity as soon as they were introduced to him. He was altogether too full of himself. He smiled and rubbed his hands and bowed until Edward was reminded of the bumptious clergyman, Mr Collins, in *Pride and Prejudice*. He professed a belief in the fashionable evangelical Christianity preached by Frank Buchman, an American Lutheran priest whose 'Oxford Group' – so-called because it had many adherents at the university – had recently changed its name to Moral Re-Armament. It purported to provide an alternative to the other kind of rearmament and strove to attract those, like Edward, who rejected both Fascism and Communism. In fact, Edward saw it as at best a delusion and at worst a distraction from the fight against Hitler. The Astors, on the other hand, were attracted to it. Buchman – like Lothian – believed he could mediate between the dictators and the democracies, but calling Hitler the 'front line of defence' against Communism, as he had done recently, had lost him credibility. Moral Re-Armament appealed to outdoor types, such as Kay Stammers' friend, the tennis player Bunny Austin who thought it was just 'common sense', but, as far as Verity could see, it was simply another anti-Communist pressure group.

Dr Channing had brought with him two girls, one of whom Verity was dismayed but not surprised to find she knew. It was Lulu – Lucinda

Arbuthnot-Grey – to whom David had introduced her at the meeting in Ransom Street. She recalled David hinting that she might come across her at Cliveden and, if they did meet, she was to pretend not to know her.

Lulu smiled sweetly at Verity and allowed herself to be introduced as though they had never met before. Clearly, Lulu too had her orders and Verity – unwillingly – allowed herself to be drawn into the conspiracy. There had been enough said already in front of the Astors about her Communist connections, and she thought they might rebel if it was brought to their attention that another of her dubious acquaintances had turned up at Cliveden in the company of their tenant.

Fortunately, Lulu then ignored her and concentrated her attentions on the Ambassador. Although, as Christian Scientists, the Astors were teetotal, they did not inflict their views on their guests. To Verity's disgust, Kennedy drank with all the enthusiasm of a confirmed drunkard. The champagne caused him to drop his guard and he made it obvious that he found Lulu to his taste. She stroked his hand and played up to him, revealing too much cleavage. Dr Channing seemed to find the whole charade amusing and even encouraged the old man. Edward wondered how this squared with his professed belief in moral probity. Verity was interested to see the different reactions of Kennedy's two sons. Joe Jr made an effort to steer his father away from the girl and the bottle, his embarrassment at his father's behaviour painful to watch. Jack's expression was less easy to read. He, too, seemed to find Lulu attractive but he did not paw her like his father, though Edward rather fancied she was not unaware of his interest. Kick, at the other end of the table, talked to Edward and Lothian, ignoring her father's antics.

Verity felt sick having to dine with people she despised, Tom so recently dead, murdered perhaps by the IRA but just possibly by someone round the table, all of whom were his natural enemies. She saw Edward looking at her anxiously and tried to be brave. To her relief, Channing took his girls away after dinner, inviting them all to visit his 'humble cottage' for drinks before Sunday lunch. It seemed to be an accepted ritual that Dr Channing and his guests had Saturday dinner and Sunday lunch with the Astors in the main house.

Nancy had tactfully put Edward and Verity in adjoining rooms. When he tapped on her bedroom door just after midnight, he heard a muffled 'Come in.' Unsure of his welcome and finding the room in darkness, he was about to retire when the unmistakable sound of sobbing made him change his mind.

'Darling V, are you all right?' he asked, meaning 'Would you like me to comfort you?'

She sat up in bed and he put his arms round

her and stroked her hair. 'Oh Edward, it's been so horrible. I've tried not to let it get to me but – I don't know – I'm just so tired and I'm so disgusted with myself.'

'You mean about poor Wintringham?'

'Yes, and those awful people tonight – that horrible doctor and Mr Kennedy leering over that little tart. The worst of it is I know her.'

'You know her?' Edward stopped stroking her head in surprise.

She told him how David Griffiths-Jones had introduced her to Lulu before the Ransom Street meeting. 'I knew then that she was little better than a prostitute.'

'You think David's using her to get at Kennedy?'

'That's what it looked like to me.'

'Maybe he's planning to blackmail the old man.' Edward chewed his lip thoughtfully. 'Kennedy's pretty tough though. He'd just get one of his people to pay her off. By the way, did you notice that both Kennedy and Eamon Farrell knew O'Rourke, or at least recognized his name?'

'I didn't and I don't care! I can't think what I'm doing here with all these horrible people. They all hate me and I hate them. Not Nancy, I mean, but Channing and Kennedy. I ought to have known better. Can we go away from here in the morning? I want to find Megan and her mother and see if they are all right.' Seeing his face, she added, 'You stay here. Put me on a train.'

'Hey, darling, don't take on so. I've never seen

you like this. Of course you can leave tomorrow. The Astors will understand. I'd better stay until after lunch. Now, get some rest. Would you like me to leave you to sleep?'

'No! Don't go. Hold me, just hold me. I feel so cold. Maybe it's that beastly TB. I thought I was over it but I still feel so weak sometimes. I mustn't give it to you though.'

'You won't give it to me. Remember, the doctor said you were better but it would take time to recover your strength.'

He slipped off his dressing-gown and climbed into the bed beside her. Her feet were cold and, when he took her in his arms, he felt her silently weeping. About ten minutes later she was asleep.

The following morning, Verity tapped on Nancy's door – she had her breakfast in bed – and asked if she might have a word. She explained that she was still not herself after her illness and the shock of seeing Tom Wintringham's body in the pavilion had made her decide she would like to go home and rest. Nancy was genuinely concerned, saying she quite understood and, if Edward wished to stay, she would have her chauffeur drive Verity back to town. She was grateful but said she did not want to be more of a nuisance than necessary and would take the train.

She and Edward breakfasted alone in the dining-room. Lee, the butler, informed them that the Kennedys and their party had gone to early mass.

126

Verity was glad not to have to say a lot of embarrassing goodbyes.

Walking in the gardens smoking a cigarette after he returned from the station, Edward got talking to one of the gardeners. Despite its being Sunday there were always staff at work. Nancy had told him they employed fifty outdoor staff. Of course, the gardener had heard of the murder – everyone had. Edward had noted a small gaggle of journalists held in check by a solid-looking police constable as he sped through the gates in the Lagonda. Fortunately the news had filtered through too late for the Sunday papers, but he dreaded that his and Verity's photographs might appear the following day. He even caught himself hoping that some new international crisis would sweep this grubby little story off the front pages.

'I was trying to clear up round the pavilion,' the gardener was saying as he leant on his spade. 'The police had made such a mess of the grass.' He shook his head mournfully. 'I counted the marks of at least four cars.'

Edward's brow furrowed as he considered the gardener's words. 'You mean three cars. There were two police cars and the ambulance.'

'No, there was another car – a heavy one, I believe, because the tyres had dug deep into the grass.'

'Can you show me?'

The gardener looked dubious. 'I cleaned most of it up best as I could but maybe you can still see what I mean.'

127

They strolled down the drive towards the shell fountain and then over rough grass to Giacomo Leoni's elegant little folly. It had been built in 1727 for Lord Orkney, one of the Duke of Marlborough's generals, who had then owned Cliveden. Edward told himself that he was being an idiot. He had not the slightest desire to investigate Wintringham's death so why was he on his knees looking at deep tyre tracks in the wet grass? The marks were difficult to decipher but it was obvious they had been made by a large vehicle.

'I suppose the police will have seen this?' he asked, getting up with some difficulty and wondering what Fenton would say when he saw the mud on his trousers. 'You are sure these aren't the tyre marks of the ambulance?'

'No, sir, I know the ambulance. It's brand new and has special tyres. Look, do you see?' He pointed to another set of tyre prints.

'You are very observant. By the way, my name's Corinth – could I ask you yours?'

'Fred Rooth, my lord.'

'You know who I am then?' Edward said, rather startled.

'Yes indeed, my lord. The missus reads me your cases from the newspapers.'

'Yes, well . . . this isn't "my case", you know. It's nothing to do with me but . . .'

'Yes, my lord?'

'But, here's my card. If you or any of the staff do stumble across . . .'

'Yes, my lord,' the gardener said with evident satisfaction.

'I was going to say,' Edward corrected him virtuously, 'you must tell the police but certainly telephone me if you wish to. If I am not there, leave a message with Mr Fenton, my valet.'

The gardener touched his hat and grinned. As he watched him walk back to the parterre, Edward kicked himself for being unable to control his apparently insatiable interest in why dead bodies turned up where they ought not to. He reminded himself that he had a more important job in hand – to find out if the Americans had any idea who might want to kill Winston Churchill. He wondered if he could discover Kennedy and Farrell's connection with O'Rourke. That had to be worth investigating. He sighed. Perhaps he should just ask Kennedy and to hell with subtlety.

He walked back via the garages in what had once been a stable block. It so happened that Kennedy's chauffeur was polishing a huge Cadillac. He was a mountain of a man and Edward imagined he must double as the Ambassador's bodyguard.

'What a magnificent machine!' Edward remarked in genuine astonishment. 'May I ask what it is exactly?'

'This beaut's the 16 cylinder 452 D, if you happen to know about cars, sir,' the chauffeur said, straightening up and joining Edward in admiring the vehicle. It was black with whitewall tyres, a spare wheel tucked above the running board.

'You're American?' Edward inquired.

'Yes, sir. Mr Kennedy shipped me over with the automobile six months ago.'

'And do you like it here in England . . . ? I'm sorry, I don't know your name.'

'Washington, my lord,' he grinned.

'Really?'

'Sure. I guess my pa worshipped that man.'

'And England? Do you like what you've seen of it?'

'It's OK but the roads are mighty narrow and twisted. Hard to get above sixty.'

Edward was looking intently at the tyres. Could it have been this car which carried Tom Wintringham's body from wherever he was murdered to the little pavilion?

'What sort of grip does it have? I mean, does it hold the road well? I imagine it's too heavy to travel across grass, for example.' Edward airily gestured across the grounds.

'No, sir. Mr Joseph – that's Mr Kennedy's eldest – was showing it to Lord Astor yesterday and he drove it on the grass by mistake and had no trouble getting it back on the drive.'

'It's certainly a lovely a machine. I drive a Lagonda and you'll forgive me for saying that, in my view, it is the best car in the world – better even than Lord Astor's Rolls.'

'Maybe, sir.' The chauffeur was polite but sceptical.

'May I see what I believe you call the trunk? If the Lagonda has a fault, there's not much room for luggage.'

'There you are,' the chauffeur said, opening the boot. 'It can take several valises and Mr Kennedy's golf clubs, no problem.'

'Very impressive,' Edward murmured. He looked more closely. 'What's that?' he asked mildly, pointing to something that looked like glass on the rubber matting. Washington reached in and took out a broken pair of wire-framed spectacles.

'Mr Kennedy was looking for these,' he said, putting them in his pocket before Edward could examine them properly.

'They're Mr Kennedy's? I haven't seen him wear spectacles.'

'He uses reading glasses. They must have fallen out of his coat. I guess he has another pair.'

Edward hesitated but the moment was gone. He had no authority to take what might be evidence and he knew that no one at Cliveden – not even the Inspector – would thank him for dragging Mr Kennedy into the investigation.

Returning to the house, he came across Lord Lothian who asked him to walk with him on the parterre. Edward accepted a cigarette and the two men admired the dramatic view over the lawns and the woodland beyond. The light was bad but they could just make out the Thames snaking away into the distance.

'Your friend von Trott was here last weekend – did you know?' Lothian remarked.

'Adam? No, I didn't. What's he doing in England?'

'He's playing peacemaker – a last ditch effort to avoid the inevitable.' Lothian sighed heavily. 'We have tried everything but I very much fear . . .'

Edward was hardly listening. He was wondering if Adam would make contact with Verity. He was not in the least concerned that she would be tempted to renew her affair with the good-looking German diplomat. That was over and done with. Adam had let her down, whether from a failure of will or pressure from his superiors. He was not a Nazi – he had consistently refused to join the Party whatever the cost – but, as a patriot, he could not go into exile. He wanted to keep his job in the Foreign Office and that meant making uncomfortable compromises. Verity's love for the young aristocrat might be history but, if he suddenly turned up on her doorstep, her shock and distress would be real. Edward considered telephoning her but in the end decided to let it alone. She would not thank him for nursemaiding her.

CHAPTER 6

Verity had gone straight from the station to the offices of the *Daily Worker* in King Street. She knew that, even though it was a Sunday, there would be people in the office. Her special friend – a blond Irish-Catholic Glaswegian named Jimmy Friel – was the political cartoonist. He always came in on a Sunday afternoon to deliver his biting caricatures of the government and the leaders of the Labour Party, saving undiluted vitriol for the Fascists. He signed his cartoons 'Gabriel' and was, for many readers, the main reason for buying the paper.

He was a fervent Party member and he could not forgive Ernest Bevin and Clem Atlee for trying and more or less succeeding in cutting out the Communist Party from the Trade Union movement. He remembered only too well the desperate deprivation of Glasgow in the early thirties when only he and his sister Cissie were employed out of a family of nine. He always claimed that he had become a cartoonist for one reason and one reason only – money – but Verity knew that he was a man of great integrity and, whenever she was feeling

133

particularly fed up with the Party, she turned to him as her moral conscience to explain why she should stick with it. More to the point, Jimmy had been a close friend of Tom Wintringham.

She found him, as she had hoped, at his desk penning a critique of an art exhibition. Apart from his cartoons, he contributed editorials and other articles on subjects which interested him.

'Jimmy!' Verity said. 'I was hoping to find you here. I'm not interrupting, am I?'

'You are, but that'll no stop you, I'm thinking.' It was odd that Verity, who put up the backs of so many of her journalistic colleagues, had found such an ally in Jimmy. At twenty-six, he was younger than she, from a different class and a different country, but he seemed to recognize in her the same courage and fragility he knew he possessed. Although he had strong views on the class system, he had no personal animus against individuals, judging them as human beings rather than representatives of their social and political background.

'You've heard about Tom Wintringham?'

'I have. In fact, Sheila and Megan are staying with me tonight, just for company.' He was a touch embarrassed.

'How did she hear . . . ?'

'A reporter from the *Express* telephoned to tell her the rumour. Then the polis came and confirmed it. By the sound of it, they were none too gentle. It was a terrible shock for the lassie.'

134

'Oh my God! The thing is, I have an awful feeling that Tom was on his way to see me when he was killed.'

She explained how she had seen Tom with Megan at the Kardomah and how he had visited her at Cranmer Court to warn her about an IRA plot.

'He had a bee in his bonnet about the IRA,' Jimmy said when she had finished. 'But there's no saying O'Rourke isn't behind the London bombings. I ken the kind of shite that bampot is.'

'I wondered if I could do something for Mrs Wintringham and Megan. Are they short of money? Would they accept help from me, do you think? I feel so guilty.'

'I was just about to go and collect them. Why not come with me and talk to them yourself? They'll no eat you. Between ourselves, Tom was not a good husband, though he loved Megan. He was often away for long periods in Spain . . . well, you know about that. And there was talk of other women . . . Sheila had been expecting something bad to happen while he was in Spain but he seemed to bear a charmed life, so this has come just when she hoped he might settle down and take an ordinary job.'

They lived in Camden in a small but pleasant house just off Parkway. Mrs Wintringham opened the door and greeted Jimmy with a kiss. She was puffy about the eyes but, if she had been crying, she was dry-eyed now. A half-eaten pie of some

135

kind sat on the kitchen table. She had been reading to Megan from a book of fairy tales which she still had in her hand.

'Jimmy! I'm not quite ready . . . Oh, you are . . . ?'

'Sheila, this is Verity Browne. She was a friend of Tom's, in Spain.'

'Mrs Wintringham – how are you? I can't tell you how sad I am about Tom,' Verity broke in. 'You see, I was there at Cliveden when . . .' She saw Megan listening and wondered how much she could hear and how much she had been told. 'I think he may have been coming to see me when it happened.'

Mrs Wintringham looked at her in puzzlement and then, collecting herself, said, 'Come in, both of you. It's cold out there. Megan, my dear, will you go upstairs and read your book. I'll be up in a minute or two to finish packing.'

Megan stood up and looked accusingly at Verity. 'I know who you are. You're the lady my pa saw outside the . . .' She hesitated, as though seeking the word.

'Yes, I saw you too. You were wearing a pretty blue coat but I was worried you might be cold. Do you remember how foggy it was that night?'

Megan ignored the question. She had one of her own. 'What did you do to my pa? He's dead, isn't he? Did you do it? He said you wouldn't listen,' she added doubtfully, perhaps not knowing what her father had meant.

'Hush now, Megan,' Jimmy said hurriedly. 'Miss Browne did not hurt your father. She was a friend of his.'

'Were you one of his girls?' Megan said, a note of interest creeping into her voice. 'Mummy says he has girls but, when I asked him, he said I was his only girl. Do you think he was telling the truth?'

Verity knelt down so she was on the same level as the little girl. 'He was telling the truth, I promise you. He told me himself that you were his only girl.' Although not strictly true, she knew it was what Tom would have said. 'I did listen and now I'm listening to you. Your father was a brave man and I'm going to do what I can to find out who . . .'

'Who hurt him?' Megan suggested. 'Where's my *Rupert Annual?*' she asked sharply, turning to her mother.

'Upstairs on your bed. Now, off you go, child. I want to talk to Jimmy and the lady.'

When Megan had left the room, Mrs Wintringham asked them to sit down. 'What do you mean about finding out who killed Tom? What can you do that the police can't?'

'Maybe you have heard of my friend, Edward Corinth – he's a sort of detective.' Why hadn't she said that she was his fiancée? Damn it, she must stop being embarrassed about it.

'Lord Edward Corinth?' Mrs Wintringham asked suspiciously. 'I have heard of him but why would he want to help us?'

'Because . . . because he was there – as I was – when Tom's body was found and because I'm engaged to him so he's got to help, hasn't he?'

At last, Mrs Wintringham smiled. 'I suppose he has.'

'What about a cup of tea, Sheila?' Jimmy said. 'We're frozen. I cannae feel my fingers.'

'I'm sorry, Jimmy. With all this . . .' she waved a hand expressively, 'I've forgotten my manners.'

While they were sipping their tea, Verity said, 'I expect the police have already asked you but is there anything Tom said before he set out for Cliveden . . . anything about why he was going there or what he was going to do when he got there?'

'I knew nothing – except that he was very worried about something. I didn't take him seriously, I'm afraid. I just thought he was going after some girl. It's odd, isn't it? He was hardly Gary Cooper but he never had trouble finding girls. I suppose they liked to mother him.'

'Why do you think he might have been going to Cliveden after a girl?' Jimmy asked. 'It doesn't sound very likely.'

'It was something he said when he came back from the paper one day last week. He said he was going to see a girl but I wasn't to look at him like that because it was only a job.'

'For the *Daily Worker*?' Verity queried.

'Yes,' Jimmy answered. 'We tried to give him work whenever we could. I remember now. He came

138

into the office Wednesday a week ago and had a meeting with the editor and Griffiths-Jones. He had a girl with him called . . . what was her name? Some trollop . . .'

'Was it Lulu?' Verity asked.

'Lulu, that's it. She was putting on all sorts of airs and graces.'

'I wonder what job Mr Rust gave him?' Verity mused. William Rust was the paper's editor.

'I can tell you that,' Jimmy said. 'I suppose it was a secret but Tom wasn't good at keeping secrets. He was going to Cliveden . . .' He hit his head with his hand. 'Of course! What a fool I am. I've only just remembered. He was at Cliveden on a story. Not after a girl at all.' He sounded relieved.

Verity did not challenge his assumption but thought she could see what had happened. He had gone in pursuit of Lulu and someone had wanted him out of the way.

'Did he mention anyone – I mean someone he was worried about or investigating – apart from what Jimmy's just told us, I mean?'

'He had a thing about Danny O'Rourke, but you know that.'

'Anyone else? Did he mention someone called Eamon Farrell or Mr Kennedy, the American Ambassador?'

'The American Ambassador?' Mrs Wintringham opened her eyes wide. 'No. What would he be doing with Mr Kennedy?'

'Nothing, I expect,' Verity said hurriedly. 'It was just an idea. You see, Mr Kennedy was at Cliveden.'

'I see. No, well, he didn't discuss his work with me.'

'Did the police have any theories?'

'They told me nothing at all. They seemed to think that just because he was a Communist he . . .' she gulped back her tears, 'that he got what he deserved.'

'I'm so sorry,' Verity repeated and put her hand out to cover Mrs Wintringham's. She paused and then asked, 'Did the police tell you how he died?'

'They said he'd been stabbed.'

'Did they say anything about the knife?'

'They said it was Italian.'

'Italian!' Verity was taken aback.

'Well, that doesn't mean he was killed by an Italian,' Jimmy put in. 'There must be plenty of Italian knives around – and guns, for that matter.'

Verity thought for a moment. 'I remember now.' She shuddered. 'I didn't take much notice. We were all so shocked but, now I think of it, it reminded me of the type of knife I saw used in Spain. Did Tom have one?' She saw Mrs Wintringham blanch. 'Oh, I'm sorry, I didn't mean to upset you. I just wondered whether Tom might have had difficulty defending himself, taken out a knife and . . . you know, had it taken off him. Didn't he hurt his arm in Spain?'

'I never saw him with a knife like that,'

Mrs Wintringham said quickly. 'He wasn't a violent man. He wasn't strong – physically, I mean. Mentally, he was strong – obstinate even. Once he had decided to do something, no one could persuade him against it.'

Jimmy said, 'He was shot in the arm in the Battle of the Ebro last year. It cut through the tendons in his right arm. He came home because he couldn't fight any more. They wouldn't even let him go on reporting the war. He was very upset – said reporting was all he was capable of doing. He used to send us dispatches from the front so you could really feel what it was like to be there.'

'I know,' Verity recalled. 'He wrote a particularly moving piece about the Basque child refugees. He helped four thousand of them get to England. It was one of the things that inspired me to get the *New Gazette* behind organizing the refugee trains from Germany. They came to Stoneham, didn't they?'

Jimmy added, as Mrs Wintringham looked puzzled, 'Verity – Miss Browne – helped organize trains to bring Jewish refugee children here – *kindertransport*, they call it. They're still coming.'

'But not enough,' Verity added gruffly. 'Tom wasn't Jewish, was he, Mrs Wintringham?'

'His mother was Polish and his father was English – a tailor – but they are both dead now.'

'I remember him telling me that socialism was his religion. I asked him how he had become a Communist and he said he had been at the Battle of Cable Street. I was there too. It seems so long ago. We stopped Mosley and his Fascists marching through the East End and taunting the Jews.'

'Yes,' Jimmy said. 'He joined the Labour Party's League of Youth but, after Cable Street, he joined the Communist Party and then – like so many others – the International Brigade.'

'I didn't really approve,' Mrs Wintringham said sadly. 'I was always Labour. In fact, we met through the Labour Party – at one of their get-togethers. We didn't get married immediately. We were very young – *too* young, my father said. Anyway, we hadn't two pennies to rub together. Also, I knew Tom might not be a perfect husband. And I was right,' she sighed. 'We had just got married and he left me to go to Spain. You can imagine how I felt.' She hugged herself, indignant at the memory.

'But Megan must be . . .'

'She's five,' Mrs Wintringham replied decisively. 'She came a little early, like blessings should.'

'And how old was he when . . . ?'

'He would have been thirty-six in November.'

Before they went, Verity managed to ask if she was all right for money.

'Yes, my father left us this house and a little money. I don't know,' she said vaguely. 'I expect I'll have to try and find a job.'

As she left, Verity managed to have a brief word with Jimmy out of Mrs Wintringham's hearing. 'Is there nothing I can do for them, without her knowing, I mean?'

'The paper has a benevolent fund. If you wanted to give something to me, I could pretend to Sheila that that was where it came from.'

'Thank you, Jimmy. You're a good man,' she said, kissing him on the cheek.'I want to right a wrong if I possibly can. I made a mistake and Tom ended up paying for it. I can't rest easy until I've tried to make amends.'

CHAPTER 7

Before lunch, they all walked over to the cottage where they were welcomed by Dr Channing who was wearing a pullover – with, Edward thought, nothing beneath it – and white ducks with two-tone brogues. He looked as though he were on a yacht in the Mediterranean instead of an English country estate in late February. While Channing was bright-eyed and glabrous, the two girls, Lulu and Angie, appeared very much the worse for wear and complained of headaches. They were dressed in tight-fitting summer frocks and, unsurprisingly, shivered with cold. Edward felt frankly embarrassed but the rest of the party seemed to find nothing odd about the ménage.

They were offered cocktails but Edward joined the Astors in opting for tomato juice. The Kennedy boys persuaded the girls to return to Cliveden to play table tennis – there was a table in the basement. The Ambassador tried to stop Lulu going but she stuck her tongue out at him and called him a naughty boy. Instead of being furious, he appeared to be much amused. Edward was shocked and disgusted.

When they strolled back to the house for lunch, they found Lothian – who had wisely remained behind to read the Sunday papers – in a high state of excitement. Inspector Voss had telephoned to report that his men had found the dead man's missing clothes – a tweed jacket and a trench coat. Someone had attempted to burn them, not very efficiently.

'Did he say where they were found?' Edward asked.

'In the swimming-pool.'

'In the pool!' Nancy – for the first time since the murder – sounded scandalized. 'How horrible! We'll have to have it drained and disinfected.' She shuddered. 'I feel my house is tainted by all this.' She waved her hands theatrically.

Edward was glad that Verity wasn't with them to hear what she would certainly have interpreted as blame for bringing death with her.

'So it looks as though he must have been murdered somewhere on the estate,' Lord Astor opined. 'How beastly. I hope Voss is up to this, my dear, or do you think we should insist on getting someone in from the Yard? I know a very good man there by the name of Pride.'

'Yes,' Edward said drily, 'I know Chief Inspector Pride. However, country police inspectors don't take kindly to someone going over their head.'

'I'll have a word with the Chief Constable,' Lord Astor said. 'He'll see that it's the right thing to do.' He went off to make his telephone call.

Lunch was a sober affair and, when Lee had served coffee in the drawing-room, Edward thought he could decently slip away. Just as he was about to interrupt Nancy, who was in the middle of one of her tirades on the subject of equal pay for women, Kennedy said in his ear, 'What say you and I walk round the golf course? I'm going crazy sitting here listening to our hostess. You noticed that Lothian and our host slid off to the library where I guess we're not welcome.'

'Golf? I'm afraid it's not one of my games, Ambassador.'

'Hey, stop this "Ambassador" stuff. Call me Joe.'

'Well, as I say, I play very badly and I didn't bring any clubs or . . .'

'Just a stroll round the course. I'll lend you what you need. Kick and the boys are going back to town. There's some party tonight they don't want to miss even though I reminded them it's a Sunday. Call me a prude but I don't approve of dancing and drinking on this day of the week.' Edward's gorge rose at the hypocrisy of the man but he managed to keep silent. 'But they don't listen to their pa,' he continued. 'I can't blame them. I never did. Washington, my chauffeur, will caddy for us.'

'I'd like that,' Edward said, realizing what an opportunity had presented itself for having a private word with him. 'My man, Fenton, will give Washington a hand.'

'What's that, Joe?' Lord Astor had returned to

the drawing-room. 'You're not thinking of playing a round at Huntercombe without a caddy? It's not Swinley, of course, but they won't like it, you know. You'll want a course guide, though, even if you don't have a caddy. Why not take Wooster?' Wooster was Lord Astor's black Labrador. 'He knows the course backwards. I always take him. Besides, he needs a leg stretch.'

As Edward had said, he did not play golf on a regular basis and was not a member of any club although, when he did play, his straight eye meant that he never disgraced himself. Many of his friends at Brooks's were keen golfers and he had dined at White's with the Match Club – an exclusive gathering of golf's aristocracy. Huntercombe – a course he had never visited before – was twenty minutes away, and as the Cadillac, with Washington driving and Fenton sitting beside him, purred along the almost empty lanes, he remarked, 'A magnificent automobile, Joe. A bit too large for our roads but . . . well, magnificent. I was talking to Washington about it before lunch and he showed me round it. By the way, we found some spectacles of yours which someone had smashed.'

'Spectacles . . . ? Oh yes, my reading glasses, but I have several pairs.'

They swooped past a man on his horse who cursed them.

'This car is bigger than many people's houses, Joe.'

Kennedy chuckled. 'I guess so. You know,' he said proudly, 'one of the perquisites of being Ambassador in this great country of yours is that I have an honorary membership of most of the top clubs.' Conspiratorially, he added, 'I'm glad we managed to give Casey the slip. I'm not supposed to go on jaunts without him. I feel like a kid playing truant.'

'You mean . . . ?'

'In case someone takes a pot shot at me. I'm not quite as popular as I once was, as I'm sure I don't have to tell you.'

'This is England, Joe,' Edward said, shocked. Then, remembering that this was precisely the threat Winston Churchill faced, he added, 'Actually, that was one of the things I wanted to talk to you about. You know I'm a friend of Mr Churchill's . . . ?'

'Indeed!' Kennedy snorted. 'Why is it that wherever I go people talk to me about Winston? I tell you, he's a warmonger. Without him stirring up hatred of Germany, England might not be facing annihilation.'

'I'm afraid I can't agree with you there, sir,' Edward said firmly, retreating into formality. 'Anyway, I was going to say that Mr Churchill has received a death threat – I suppose in these terrible times other politicians have too, but this is one the security services have had to take seriously. Mr Churchill, also, is not popular with a great many people.'

'What's that to do with me?' Kennedy looked as though he wished he weren't trapped in a car with this English aristocrat.

Edward ploughed on, knowing he was getting nowhere and was merely antagonizing the man whose goodwill he needed.

'Well, sir, there seems to be a connection with the American Embassy.'

'The embassy? Hi! Wait a minute, who are you?' The Ambassador gave Edward a fierce glare. 'You're from Mr Churchill or . . . wait, I've got it! You're a secret service agent. Casey warned me against you. I see it now. He was suspicious about you from the beginning. Don't try and deny it. You and your precious fiancée wormed your way into Cliveden and into the good graces of the Astors to get to me. I'm right, aren't I? I guess I'll stop the car and you can walk back.'

He leant forward to pull open the glass partition but Edward put a hand on his arm. 'Please, Joe, I'm not employed by the secret service or by anybody. I'm just a friend and admirer of Mr Churchill's. Yes, I wanted to meet you and ask for your help, just as your son would do anything he could if he thought your life was in danger.'

Kennedy hesitated but was still angry. 'He sent you to spy on me?'

'No, not at all – it's just that . . .'

'Why didn't he ask me himself? He knows me. I don't bite.'

'He won't take it seriously – the threat, I mean –

but I'm told the security service does.' Edward was being deliberately vague about which service he was in touch with.

'You think an American wants to kill Winston? That's ridiculous.'

'It may not be an American. Our people have reason to believe that someone in the embassy knows about it. That's all.'

'Have you talked to Casey? If there's anything in it, he would know.'

'Casey was as sceptical as you when I raised it with him at dinner the other night. That's why he hasn't mentioned it to you, I suppose.'

'But you believe he's wrong?'

'It's too important for us to take chances. I realize you don't agree, sir, but we feel that, in the event of war with Germany, Mr Churchill is our only hope.'

'So you think it's a Nazi threat?'

'We can't be sure of that. It might be the IRA or the Ghada Party. The Germans might have decided to use some other group to do their dirty work for them. The information we have – and it's very sketchy – emanates from Berlin.'

'What the hell is the Ghada Party?'

'An Indian independence movement, so I'm told.'

'And you think someone at the American Embassy . . . ?'

'Or someone your people know . . .'

'You think we would countenance such a thing?'

'No, of course not, but I thought you might ask Casey to make some inquiries. He won't do anything without your express authority.'

At that moment, the Cadillac drew up in front of the Huntercombe clubhouse and Edward sprang out, almost tripping over Wooster as he did so. It was a relief to be in the fresh air. At least, he thought, he had not been thrown out of the car. But what would happen now? He stretched and looked around him. On a different occasion, he might have found this beautiful place relaxing. Huntercombe, five miles west of Henley, was owned by Lord Nuffield. It had been designed by Willie Park Jr and opened in 1901. It had an exclusive membership and a reputation as one of the finest inland courses in the country.

'Would you like me to return to the house, sir?' he asked Kennedy as Washington held the car door open for his master. He was conscious that both Washington and Fenton were looking at them curiously, sensing that there had been some sort of a quarrel.

'No, I guess not,' Kennedy said grumpily. 'That is, unless you're going to ask me any more damn foolish questions.'

'I promise . . .' Edward grinned and, after a moment's consideration, Kennedy nodded his head.

The Ambassador was obviously expected and Edward guessed that Lee had telephoned ahead to warn the club that he was descending on them.

They were greeted respectfully by Jim Morris, the long-serving Pro, and offered caddies, but to the visible annoyance of the Caddy Master, who saw a handsome tip slip away, Kennedy grunted that they would use his chauffeur and Fenton. Edward added, apologetically, that they were just going to walk the course – not play a proper round.

A few members looked at them with interest but there was something in the Ambassador's face which made them hesitate to greet him. Kennedy was dressed in a gaudy Fair Isle jersey, plus-fours and two-tone shoes with a tartan cap on his head. Edward had removed his jacket and borrowed a jersey from Lord Astor but was otherwise in his normal clothes. As Washington sorted out clubs, Kennedy took out a scorecard and Edward suddenly realized that he intended to take the game seriously.

'Hickory?' Edward inquired, picking up an aluminium-headed putter and weighing it in his hands.

'No,' Kennedy replied with obvious satisfaction, 'it's steel-shafted but coated to look like wood.'

Steel clubs had come in only recently and Edward had never played with one. He swung it thoughtfully. It felt light and almost springy in his hand.

'James Braid designed these specially for me,' Kennedy continued. Braid had won five British Opens and designed numerous golf courses. 'What's your handicap?' he demanded.

'It used to be eighteen.'

'Mine's thirteen,' Kennedy told him complacently.

They walked on to the course and Kennedy teed off with a magnificent stroke which took him almost on to the green. His face, which had promised all kinds of wrath, cleared miraculously. Edward placed his ball on the tee with trepidation.

'It's a Dunlop 65,' Kennedy told him.

'I thought it might be,' Edward replied. 'It's a fraction larger than an ordinary ball, isn't it?'

He had an excellent eye and his first stroke lifted the ball high and true – a hundred and forty yards on to the green, just a yard from the pin. He shrugged his shoulders, rather embarrassed, and muttered something about beginners' luck but he could see that Kennedy was impressed as he marked his scorecard.

As they strolled towards the green, Wooster guiding them rather self-consciously Edward thought, Kennedy said, 'You know, whatever Winston believes, I'm right about Hitler. I'm convinced that he doesn't want to fight. The problem is economic. He simply can't afford it. At present, Germany is on a wartime economy with full production turning out everything Hitler requires, but he can't keep it up for long without a crash.'

'But, if he suddenly moved on to a peacetime economy, his factories would be idle and hundreds

153

of thousands of his people would be thrown out of work. Can he afford that?'

'There's something in what you say but my friend, James Mooney, the head of General Motors in Germany, knows Herr Krupp well and has met Hitler on a number of occasions. He assures me that he won't go to war. For one thing, Hitler despises Slavs and every black man under the sun but he admires the English, another Aryan nation.'

Edward was sceptical. 'What does Joe Jr say? He spent some time in Germany recently, did he not?'

'Indeed, he is my eyes and ears and I trust him absolutely. He also tells me that if England plays her cards right –' like most Americans, he always said England when he meant Britain – 'there will be no war.' He almost shouted the words 'no war' and Edward was once again depressed that this purblind man was the United States Ambassador to the Court of St James. Churchill had told him that Roosevelt had simply wanted him out of his hair and never took him seriously, but it was hard to believe that his views carried no weight in the White House.

'And what about the Jews?' Edward pressed him. 'We can hardly call ourselves civilized and leave them to their fate at the far from tender hands of Herr Himmler.'

'Look, Corinth, I am not anti-Semitic. When I met Dirksen last month' – Herbert von Dirksen was the German Ambassador to Britain – 'he told me why they want to get rid of their Jews and I understood him. They should all be taken to Palestine. It's not the elimination of the Jews that is the problem, it is the fanfare with which Hitler does it. There's a book I commend to you by Brook Adams, brother-in-law to Henry Cabot Lodge. Adams says that there is a moment in history when a particular race reaches a level of achievement where it no longer functions effectively and a more aggressive race takes over. England has been engaged in high living for too long. The new well-educated Germany with its superior armed forces will, if it comes to war, easily knock out England and take over its government. You Brits have two choices – either avoid going to war or submit to being governed by a superior civilization.'

Edward was horrified but recognized that there was no point in arguing. Nothing was going to change Kennedy's mind. Even so, he was tempted to throw down his golf club and stalk off the course – but what was the point? He must make Kennedy promise to pass on any information that might prevent Churchill being assassinated. That was his priority and he couldn't allow personal disgust to destroy his chance of persuading Kennedy to trust him.

'However, Joe,' he risked the familiarity, 'that doesn't mean you would consent to seeing one of our greatest men die by an assassin's bullet, does it?'

'No, of course not. I see you are in earnest, Corinth, and so I will instruct Casey to look into it and report back to both of us, but I can assure you that – if an attack is being planned on Winston – it's nothing to do with us. The United States is not in the business of killing politicians, whatever their views.'

'I know that and thank you,' Edward replied with a sigh. 'I never doubted it. By the way, had you heard of Danny O'Rourke – the IRA man Verity mentioned?'

'O'Rourke?' Edward thought Kennedy was about to deny any knowledge of him but he must have decided that his lie might be found out. 'I was introduced to him once in Boston. He was trying to raise money for the "armed struggle", I guess.'

'And was he successful?' Edward asked lightly.

'I'm afraid he was, Corinth. The English aren't much liked where I come from. Now, let's stop talking politics and play a hole or two.'

After the first hole, Edward's play deteriorated and Kennedy won the next five fairly comfortably. Edward won the seventh and they halved the next three.

'Shall we make this the last?' Kennedy suggested as they prepared to tee off at the eleventh. They were at the farthest point from the clubhouse and it was the longest hole at over five hundred yards, par at five. 'Probably time we were getting back if we are going to be in London before dinner.'

Edward, keen to leave the Kennedys and

Cliveden behind him, agreed while trying not to sound too enthusiastic. 'Indeed, Joe. Best to call it a day. That first hole must have been something of a fluke. I can't seem to hit a barn door.'

On the final hole, for some reason, Kennedy hit hard but wide, his ball falling into the rough. He cursed but seemed gratified when Edward did no better, slicing his ball to the right where it fell not far from his host's. Edward found his ball without much trouble but Kennedy's seemed to have vanished in the undergrowth. They sent Wooster after it – Lord Astor had told them his dog could always find a lost ball – but, instead of returning with the ball in his mouth, he remained in front of a patch of gorse barking noisily. Edward called him but when he refused to move and continued to bark hysterically, Fenton and Washington went over to see what was the matter. As they pushed aside leaves and long grass and Edward was on the point of suggesting they forget about finishing the hole, there was a shout from Washington. The alarm in his voice made them realize immediately that it wasn't a ball Wooster had found. When they reached him, he was holding the dog by his collar and standing over the body of a man.

'Oh Christ!' Kennedy exclaimed. 'What the hell . . . ?'

It was Eamon Farrell. He was lying on his back, his head twisted awkwardly so that they could see the thin silver knife protruding from his neck.

157

CHAPTER 8

Verity was in the shower when she heard the doorbell. She slipped on her dressing-gown and tied a towel round her head. Before opening the door, she called out, 'Who's there?'

'It's me, Adam. Can I come in?'

Hearing that familiar, patrician voice with just a hint of a German accent sent her heart racing. It was a voice she had never expected to hear again. They had been lovers – she and Adam von Trott – in the summer of 1937 and it had been the most intense experience of her life. For a few months she had imagined Adam to be the only man she could ever love. She would have done anything for him. He was so good-looking but that was just the half of it. Her romantic nature – despite thinking herself a hard-bitten, cynical journalist, she was a romantic – had responded to his noble soul, his belief that it was his fate to bring Germany and England together in peace and amity. She admired his courage in deciding to fight Hitler from within Germany. He saw exile as betrayal and he was, above everything, a patriot.

They had gone to Vienna together – she to report on the *Anschluss* and Adam to help her meet the 'right people' who could give her the insight she needed. Before her eyes, he was kidnapped by Himmler's thugs. For months she did not know if he were alive or rotting in some terrible prison camp. Then she had a letter from him. He was safe. He was in the Far East studying philosophy. His tone was cool, casual, matter of fact. She had to face the fact that, for his safety or hers, he had given her up. Their love affair was over.

In time, the pain lessened and she taught herself to think of their love affair as a *coup de foudre* – a summer storm that had passed as suddenly as it had appeared over the horizon, as was the nature of such things. She had turned to Edward who had been standing by, patiently waiting for her. She loved him and was to marry him in just a few weeks so why, at the sound of this voice from the past, was she finding it so difficult to breathe with the blood beating a tom-tom in her temples?

She opened the door and there he was – older, with anxiety etched on his face, but still those cool, clear, steadfast eyes, the high intellectual forehead and determined chin.

'Adam,' she gasped, 'I didn't know you were in England.'

'Yes, I have been staying with Nancy Astor in St James's Square, meeting government people –

even the Prime Minister granted me an interview. Didn't she tell you? Perhaps she thought . . .'

'Have you seen Edward?'

'No. I hear you are to be married. Many congratulations.'

Beneath the banalities another silent colloquy was taking place, the gist of which was 'Do you still love me? Why did you abandon me? Why did you let me down? What do you want from me?'

'Adam, sorry. I don't know why we are standing on the doorstep. Come in. How long are you here for?'

'Just two more days. I have been here a week.'

'Why didn't you come and see me earlier?'

'I've been very busy,' he replied lamely. 'I thought you might not want to see me but, in the end, I had to come.'

He took a step towards her and put his arms round her. He was much taller than she and it had always made her feel safe, protected. 'Let me look at you. Nancy said you had been ill.'

'Yes, but I'm better now.' She hardly knew what she was saying.

'*Meine liebe*,' he muttered and bent to kiss her.

'With a huge effort, she broke away from him. 'No, Adam, it's too late. I'm in love with Edward. You could have had me but you went to the other side of the world.'

'They made me go. It was either the Far East or prison.'

160

'But now I hear you have made your peace with them. You have joined the Nazi Party?'

'No!' He sounded anguished and she was suddenly sorry for him. What a terrible position to be in – to be a patriot and yet to hate your government!

'Have you been to see Diana?' she asked, bitterness once again creeping into her voice. She had learnt after Adam had disappeared that she was not the only Englishwoman he had made love to.

'Please, Verity, don't let's quarrel. We have so little time. My mission has been a failure. I return to Berlin with – how do you say it? – my tail, between my legs. I think this is the last time we shall meet. There will be a war and everything will be destroyed. I shall die – I know that – but not before I have tried to kill the man who has brought down this misery on all of us.'

'Adam, please . . . I *do* still love you – that's why it hurts hurts . . . that's why I feel so bitter.'

'Then let us make love for the last time.' He stretched out his hand to pull off her robe but she stopped him.

'No, I cannot do that. I can't betray Edward. I love you but not in that way any more. I love Edward. Only him . . .'

She kept repeating that she loved Edward as though it was a way of warding off temptation – as though she needed to remind herself with whom her future now lay. For a moment, Adam looked

161

mutinous but then he laughed and relaxed. 'Ah well, it is good that I begin to know what it is to lose what I care for. I think I shall have much practice.'

Verity smiled. 'Now you are trying to make me feel sorry for you.'

'Make me some coffee, will you? I haven't eaten today.' He sounded peremptory but she forgave him. She reckoned it couldn't have been often that a girl said no to him, and it must hurt.

As she boiled the kettle, he said, 'So, Edward, what is he doing now?'

'Jobs . . . I don't know. He's got very friendly with Winston Churchill.'

'Well, tell him that they are after his life.'

'What do you mean? Whose life?' she said, almost spilling the water she was pouring on the coffee.

'Churchill's. Edward's not yet that important. Tell him that Der Adler, the eagle, is in London. Dirksen told me. It is a great secret. Dirksen doesn't approve of political assassinations.'

'But who is Der Adler? How do we recognize him? He can't be allowed to assassinate . . .'

'I didn't ask, Verity. Even if I had, he wouldn't have told me. If it ever gets out that I mentioned Der Adler, then I will hang for sure although, like Dirksen, I don't approve of political assassins.' He laughed. 'What am I saying! If Hitler were killed, I would rejoice.'

'Please, Adam. If there is a war and Churchill is not there to lead us, we will be defeated.'

162

'That is what Mr Kennedy and Lord Lothian believe – that England will be defeated. I have had long talks with them.' There was almost a note of satisfaction in his voice as he said it.

'But Adam, you would not want that. You love England.'

'Do I?' he responded moodily. 'All my English friends blame me . . .'

'For what? Of course we don't blame you. We love and honour you. You make us understand that there are good Germans – patriots who love their country but hate the evil of Hitler and Himmler.'

'You do believe in me?' he asked, sounding momentarily cheered.

'I do. You are a good, brave man who loves women – sometimes too much.'

'Then I shall tell you everything Dirksen told me. If I tell you all our state secrets, will you sleep with me one last time?'

'I cannot!' she cried desperately. 'Please don't ask me again.'

'Very well, then I shan't . . .'

'Adam!' She was exasperated. 'Der Adler. Tell me before I slap you. How will we find him before . . . ?'

'I don't know but I think he may be Italian.'

'Italian?' Verity was incredulous.

'But I may be wrong,' Adam added, maddeningly. 'I am wrong about most things.'

★   ★   ★

As soon as he had gone she had telephoned Edward at Albany but there had been no reply. She then rang Cliveden and discovered that he was staying another night so he could be interviewed by Inspector Voss in the morning about the second murder. When he told her, as succinctly as possible, how they had found Eamon Farrell's body on the golf course, she was horrified but relieved that at least Inspector Voss could not suspect her this time.

She, in turn, told Edward of Adam's visit and then, as opaquely as possible in case anyone was listening in, repeated what he had told her about the would-be assassin's nationality.

Edward had been unimpressed. 'There's nothing to worry about. I'm coming back to town tomorrow and I'll tell you everything then.' After he had put down the receiver, he hesitated before picking up the telephone again and dialling a number. However dubious he was about the value of Adam's information, he thought he had better pass it on to Liddell. He had never had Liddell's telephone number, only a number he could ring and leave a coded message that he needed to speak to him.

Liddell did not return his call until eleven thirty when everyone had gone to bed. Mr Lee had had to summon him from his bedroom, making his disapproval abundantly clear. Edward apologized but the butler had continued to grumble that there had never been so much police activity at Cliveden since he had started working for Lord Astor's father. Edward had the feeling that he thought murder was no reason to disrupt the smooth running of the household.

Liddell stopped Edward the moment he began to tell him of Farrell's death. Telephone operators in the country were the main source of gossip and rumour for the entire neighbourhood. Liddell told him to return to London in the morning after he had seen Inspector Voss and gave him the address of his 'office'.

His interview with the Inspector was brief. Edward restricted himself to describing how he had found Farrell's body and offered no theories about how it might have got there. As soon as he reached town, he went to Liddell's office – not his real office, or certainly not his main office, as Edward knew. He thought Liddell's obsession with security rather absurd but would never have dared say so. Liddell listened to what he had to say about Verity's meeting with von Trott and his own conversation with Kennedy.

'I don't think Churchill is any longer in danger despite what von Trott says.'

'What makes you so sure?' Edward asked.

'Because we've had confirmation from Berlin that Der Adler is dead. He was a German and has been killed by British agents in Buda.'

'Will you tell Churchill?'

'No, at least not yet. I'd rather keep him on his toes. He has our man with him now – Walter Thompson – and I keep him briefed. There's always danger – if not Der Adler, then some other lunatic.'

'And Farrell . . . ?'

'There is something going on at the American Embassy but what it is I don't know. I rely on you to find out. Chief Inspector Pride is now on the case. Between the two of you, you ought to be able to clear up this little mess.'

'You think of murder as mess?' Edward inquired with sarcasm. 'It's a bit more than that, surely?'

'As far as I'm concerned, only if the "mess" gets blown up into a diplomatic row. That we can't afford, so see it doesn't happen, there's a good chap. Now, leave me, will you? I've got a hundred and one things to worry about.'

Dismissed and feeling rather foolish for having taken up the precious time, as Liddell put it, of 'an overworked civil servant', Edward went to Cranmer Court to restore his self-esteem. He found Verity about to go out.

'I want to show my face at the *New Gazette* and remind them that I'm still in the land of the living,' she explained. Edward had some difficulty in persuading her to postpone her outing but she *had* been persuaded. After they had made love for the third time, he said he was hungry after so much exercise and, reluctantly, Verity had risen and put on the kettle. She had looked nervously in the kitchen cupboard and found, rather to her surprise and relief, some stale bread and six eggs

166

she had forgotten buying. A few minutes later, Edward, in a dressing-gown he kept in the flat for just such an occasion, was scrambling the eggs while Verity, with only a towel to cover her 'shame' – as Edward said sententiously – toasted the bread.

'Danny O'Rourke is being held by the police and Der Adler's dead. There's been confirmation from Berlin that a German killed by British agents in Buda was definitely Der Adler,' Edward told her, as he stirred the eggs in a saucepan.

'So there's nothing to fear? I'm confused. Damn! I've burnt the toast.'

'You're not the only one!' Edward, too, was perplexed.

'But Adam said he was Italian and you say Der Adler was German.'

'I don't know why but I can't quite believe in an Italian assassin,' he responded with a laugh.

'So who killed Eamon Farrell?'

'That I can't answer – not yet.'

'Well, Adam certainly seemed to think Churchill is still in danger.'

'Adam, yes. How was he?' Edward's expression changed and his voice was guarded.

'He was well. Look, I know what you want to ask me so let me tell you – I wasn't even tempted,' Verity lied.

He had been surprised – once he had got her into bed – at the enthusiasm she displayed. It crossed his mind that she might be making up to him for some tiny betrayal with Adam although he preferred to think it was love for her future husband. 'I never doubted it,' Edward responded, also lying.

'You were lucky to find me in,' she said after an awkward silence.

'And unengaged . . .' he teased.

'As you keep on reminding me, I am engaged. In fact, I was about to try to get myself re-engaged.' Edward looked at her interrogatively. 'I told you, I was on my way to the *New Gazette* when you . . . when you laid hands on me. Blame yourself if, by forcing me to satisfy your animal lust, my career has gone down the drain.'

'What career?' he risked.

'If I had had a mother, I am sure you are just the sort of man she would have warned me against,' she continued, ignoring his question.

'What career?' he repeated.

'I'm ready to go back to work,' she said firmly. 'You said I was quite recovered.'

'You are but . . . go back to your job? Are you really ready for that? At least wait until after we're married,' Edward pleaded.

'I warn you, I'm perfectly horrid if I'm bored, so don't try to dissuade me. And then I'm lunching with Casey,' she added airily.

Edward sighed. 'You didn't tell me.'

'Didn't I?' she said innocently. 'He's been pestering me so in the end I said I would.' She hurried on, 'So what brought you up to town? You haven't told me yet. Perhaps it's a secret,' she added, her mouth full of egg.

'I saw the chap who is responsible for Churchill's safety,' he said, sticking a finger of toast in his scrambled egg. 'Nanny always called them soldiers,' he mused.

'Soldiers? What soldiers?'

'Fingers of bread or toast. You dip them in the yoke of your egg.'

'I never had a nanny,' Verity replied sharply, although this wasn't strictly true. After her mother's death, her father had employed a succession of young women, all of whom Verity had treated appallingly, so that in the end there had been nothing for it but to send her to boarding school. 'So tell me who you went to see and stop prevaricating. I can see you'll drive me mad if we spend too much time together. Remember that when you try to stop me working as a journalist again.'

'I can't tell you his name – I'm sorry – but I expect you'll meet him some day. I passed on your information and he was very grateful,' he lied. He had to be vague. Although she knew of his connection with Special Branch, he had sworn not to tell anyone about MI5 let alone mention Liddell's name.

'Grateful but dubious . . .'

'No, but he was as puzzled as we are about who killed Farrell. It wasn't our people.'

They considered the possibilities. Then Edward put a hand out and grasped Verity's.

'Hey! Watch out for my coffee.'

'Sorry. I say, V, let's talk about our wedding. I still think we should do the deed on a weekday to avoid unwelcome attention from the press – that is unless you've changed your mind and would like a big show.'

'No, of course not.' She was shocked, not at the idea of getting married – she had become accustomed to that – but at having to discuss the arrangements. Until now, marrying Edward had been something that was going to happen one day and there were always legitimate reasons to put it off.

'Well, I've done some research and – subject to you, of course – I've booked Caxton Hall for . . .' he hesitated, 'March the first. It's a Wednesday.'

The shock hit Verity as though someone had punched her in the stomach. 'But that's only a fortnight away and I haven't got anything to wear.' She knew she sounded absurdly like one of the bourgeois women she so despised. What did it matter what she wore?

'I've spoken to Charlotte and Adrian. They could be our witnesses. Connie and Gerald can make it. You'd have to talk to your father . . .'

'Heavens!' She tried to laugh but it came out as a splutter. 'You have been busy.'

'Well, is there any reason to delay?' Edward sounded belligerent, as though challenging her, as indeed he was. 'You are well now, as you say, and who knows how much time we have before the balloon goes up. I think Hitler will march into Czechoslovakia before the end of March and, as you know, Sunita and Frank are getting married on Saturday the eleventh. We always said we'd get married quietly just before them so no one would notice.' He saw her face. 'Not that I'm remotely worried if there is a fuss. I'm so proud to be marrying you that I want to shout it out from the rooftops but I know you aren't so keen.'

'Edward, I . . .'

'Yes?' he said, expecting her to put forward some reason for postponing.

'You've been so patient. I agree, we should seize the moment.'

'Darling, that's wonderful! You really mean it?'

'I do,' she answered and it was as if a weight had been lifted off her mind. 'Gosh! There's so much to talk about but now I'd better get my skates on. I've got to be at the Hyde Park Hotel in half an hour. What about you?'

'Yes, I'd better be going too. I've got a meeting with Churchill. He telephoned me at Cliveden and asked for a full report.'

Morpeth Mansions was Churchill's London base but it was little more than an anonymous apartment – a place in which to sleep and meet when the House was sitting. For Churchill, home meant Chartwell. They were discussing Chartwell when Churchill disconcerted him by saying,

'There are moments when I'm rather anxious having you in the house, my boy.'

The old man had a twinkle in his eye but Edward was suspicious. 'Why is that, sir?'

'You do seem to attract dead bodies.'

Edward was put out. 'I don't think that is very fair. You and Liddell put me in the way of corpses. My main concern is that you shouldn't be one of them.'

He wondered if he had gone too far but, after a second's hesitation, Churchill burst into laughter. Oddly, this was the first time Edward had seen him laugh but that was probably because for most of the time there wasn't anything very much to laugh about.

'I gather you have fixed a date for your wedding.'

'How on earth did you know that, sir?' Edward was quite put out. 'Apart from Verity and my brother and sister-in-law and our friends the Hassels . . .' he was counting them off on his fingers, 'no one knows. Has Liddell said anything to you? I really think we are becoming a police state.'

'I'm sorry,' Churchill said genuinely penitent. 'I should have resisted the temptation to show off. The truth is I happened to be talking to someone who knew someone at Caxton Hall – just a co-incidence. I promise you, it wasn't Liddell. As far as I know, you are not under surveillance. From what I hear from Liddell, MI5 doesn't have the manpower for one thing.'

'I should hope not,' Edward responded sulkily.

Churchill, sensing his mood, said, 'I'm delighted and I congratulate you. I think Miss Browne is a remarkable woman,' and spoilt it by adding, 'not that I would care to be married to her myself. She's too like Nancy. I prefer women who let me do what I want.' There was another, rather embarrassed, silence and then he announced grandly, 'I would like to give you a wedding present.'

'That's very kind of you, sir, but really . . .'

Churchill carried on regardless. 'It was Brab's idea. You know Brab, don't you?'

'I do, indeed. He was kind enough to show me his cars when I was at Brooklands.'

'A remarkable sportsman and a good man to have by you in a tight situation. He was my PPS for a time, you know.'

Lt.-Col. J.T.C. Moore-Brabazon MC MP was, as Churchill said, an extraordinary sportsman. He was fascinated by engines of all kinds and motor racing was the love of his life. He had been a close friend of Charles Rolls and, as early as 1903, had driven his Mors car at 130 mph and had raced at Brooklands from the day it opened. Like many motor-racing enthusiasts he was also a keen flyer and had the very first Royal Aero Club's pilot's certificate. He had been up in a balloon before the first aeroplane had flown and had won the *Daily Mail*'s £1,000 prize for flying the first circular mile. He was a friend of Wilbur Wright and the Short brothers and had exhibited his 'Bird of Passage' at the first Aero Show at Olympia in 1908. During the war he joined the RFC, despite being in his thirties, and helped develop aerial photography. On the golf course he was something of a legend but, as Edward could testify, he was above all a thoroughly nice man.

'I happened to see Brab yesterday,' Churchill continued, 'and when he heard you were getting married . . .'

'You told him? It's supposed to be a secret but it seems it's common knowledge.'

'. . . he suggested you might like to take a short holiday afterwards.' Churchill was unperturbed by Edward's outburst. 'I hesitate to call it a honeymoon – too sickly sweet for those of us no longer in our first flush of youth, I fancy – but a few days at St Moritz. As you know, Brab is rather a swell there so it might be fun. What do you say?'

'Well, that's very kind of him,' Edward mumbled, still annoyed but trying not to sound ungrateful. 'I'll have to talk to Verity about it but it sounds . . . well, it sounds wonderful,' he said, giving himself a mental shake. 'We'll want to get away for a few days before coming back for my nephew's wedding . . .'

'Good! That's settled then.'

'On the condition that I pay for . . .'

'Now, don't argue, my boy. Three nights at the Kulm Hotel. It's my gift so don't make a fuss. You know how I like to get my own way.'

Edward knew it would offend him if he continued

to protest so, though it went against the grain, he surrendered gracefully. 'Well, that is very kind of you, sir. I am very touched and I know Verity will be too.' In fact, he wasn't at all sure she would be but he would jump that hurdle when he came to it.

'Do you ski?' Churchill asked.

'A little, but Verity doesn't – although I think she might take to it. She likes dangerous sports where she can go very fast.'

'So what does it all mean?' Churchill asked, getting back to business. 'Can I assume that the threat of being assassinated by some madman has disappeared?'

'I'm afraid not,' Edward said firmly. 'Liddell says we must remain vigilant. For one thing, we still have no idea why Farrell was killed. Maybe there's no connection with the attempt on your life, but it's certainly too early for you to lower your guard. There's this warning we had about the Italian . . .'

'So there's no doubt that Wintringham and Farrell were both killed by the same person?'

'They were both killed with the same sort of knife – long and thin and as sharp as a surgeon's scalpel. I've heard it described as a poniard,' Edward told him. 'According to Inspector Voss, they were of Italian make. Both men were killed from behind with the knife protruding from the side of their necks.'

'A knife! At Omdurman I would have used a pistol or a sword but a knife! That's as intimate a piece of killing as using a bayonet. You have to hate to use a knife.' Churchill was thinking of the time he had spent in the trenches in 1916.

'Yes, you're right, sir,' Edward replied grimly. 'A knife is a peculiarly unpleasant way to kill someone – if there is a pleasant way. A knife is savage, elemental and, as you say, intimate. The trouble is, there were no obvious clues where the bodies were found. Wintringham wasn't killed in the Blenheim Pavilion and Farrell wasn't killed on the golf course. Wintringham's jacket and coat were found in the swimming-pool. Someone had made a half-hearted attempt to burn them but had been disturbed or given up. It's surprisingly difficult to burn clothes.'

'I take it most unkindly that the poor man was found in the Blenheim Pavilion. As you know, Blenheim is sacred to me and this tarnishes a name in that splendid roll call of British military victories.'

Edward looked at him quizzically and Churchill appeared momentarily uncomfortable. He had allowed rhetoric to replace sincere revulsion and he knew it.

'And why leave the knife for us to find?' Edward asked, not expecting an answer. 'Verity also noticed that Wintringham's glasses were missing. By chance, I came across Mr Kennedy's car being cleaned by his chauffeur the following morning. I looked in the boot and saw a pair of smashed, wire-rimmed glasses which might have belonged to the dead man. The chauffeur said they were Mr Kennedy's. Perhaps wrongly, I thought it wasn't my place to demand that he hand them over so I could show them to the police. Inspector Voss had made it quite clear that he did not want me involved in the investigation and I had no authority to examine anything. I was also aware that, if I made a fuss about it, I could spark off an embarrassing diplomatic incident. I knew that we couldn't afford to imply that the American Ambassador might be involved in murder.'

Edward spoke with the care he might have used had he been a witness in a court of law. He was rehearsing for himself as much as for Churchill exactly what evidence there was for Kennedy being involved in the two murders. As he listened to himself, he thought it amounted to a prima facie case.

Churchill was silent for a moment and then said, 'I can't see old Joe manhandling dead bodies, let alone murdering anyone himself, although I gather from Liddell that he has close contacts with organized crime in New York and Boston. Being Ambassador means a huge amount to him and he'll do whatever he can to keep his hands clean – at least while he is in England.' Churchill lit a cigar and, after puffing on it and throwing away the match, continued, 'He'll do whatever is needed to keep his reputation, such as it is, intact. Might that not include getting one of his people to dispose of anyone who was trying to blackmail him?'

'It might,' Edward agreed, 'and his most trusted aide is his son, Joe Jr The chauffeur himself told me that the boy had driven the Cadillac – heavy as it is – on the grass without getting it stuck. I think it more than likely that it was he who dumped the body in the pavilion and then "found" it.'

'Of course,' Churchill put in, 'even if that's true, it doesn't mean he killed Wintringham.'

'No, indeed.'

'So what's the next step?' Churchill demanded impatiently.

'Chief Inspector Pride is now on the case. He's a good man – very thorough. I think he'll get results. The local chap, Inspector Voss, was frankly not up to the job.'

'What about Kennedy?'

'I think he's been badly shocked by Farrell's killing,' Edward answered thoughtfully. 'Even if he knew about Wintringham – which, to judge from his reaction when his daughter announced the discovery of the body, I rather doubt – I'm sure he wasn't expecting to find Farrell on the golf course. Why on earth – if for some obscure reason he had wanted Farrell dead – would he have "found" him? He would have made sure he was miles away when the body was discovered.'

'Who was caddying for you?'

'Kennedy's chauffeur and my man, Fenton, were

there when Lord Astor's dog found the body, and Fenton is convinced that Washington was as shocked as we all were.'

'What I don't understand,' Churchill said, 'is how the murderer knew you would slice your ball into the rough at that particular hole. If you hadn't, the body might have lain undiscovered for days, if not weeks.'

'It was Kennedy's slice,' Edward corrected him. 'I agree. On the face of it, it suggests the murderer had no intention of us finding the body. Maybe he was counting on the dog nosing it out.' He shrugged his shoulders. 'It's a mystery.'

'You managed to get close to Kennedy. He even invited you to play golf. What's your relationship with him now?'

'I'm not sure, sir. I don't say he trusts me but I think we have established some sort of relationship. He doesn't like Liddell's chaps and, when it occurred to him that I might be one of them, he almost threw me out of the car. I don't know what Liddell did to him but, whatever it was, it's made him very wary of the security services.'

'I expect he knows MI5 has a file on him as long as my arm,' Churchill said comfortably. 'Of course Joe doesn't trust us. He'd be mad to. He knows we want him gone and he's very bitter about being sidelined by Roosevelt who leaves him out of any important negotiations.'

'Why doesn't the President fire him?' Edward asked.

'He can't until Kennedy does something demonstrably irresponsible. He's got a powerful Irish constituency back in the States and Roosevelt can't afford to alienate them. He needs Kennedy to stay where he is because, if he went back to Washington, he could create a lot of problems. From Roosevelt's point of view, Kennedy's safest here – whatever stupid things he says. His advice can be safely ignored and three thousand miles is about the distance Roosevelt likes him.'

'Well, sir, I will write a report for Chief Inspector Pride and he can then decide how to proceed. It's a ticklish business with the political situation as it is.'

'Quite,' Churchill said drily. 'You've got to go carefully, my boy. Accusing the American Ambassador or his son of murder on the eve of war won't endear us to the people of that great nation.'

'I believe that Casey Bishop, Kennedy's security officer, knows something,' Edward said. 'He certainly ought to if he's doing his job. Verity is lunching with him today. I know him from Cambridge, of course, but he seems to have got a bit of a thing about her. She may come back with something interesting.'

Churchill looked at him and seemed about to say something but obviously thought better of it. If Edward wasn't worried about his fiancée lunching with an attractive American who had a 'thing' about her, who was he to show surprise. 'Feminine wiles, eh?' he risked.

'That sort of thing,' Edward agreed, unperturbed.

CHAPTER 9

Verity had taken some trouble with her appearance – though she would have denied it. She found Casey attractive and she knew he liked the look of her. She wasn't going to lead him on exactly but she wanted to extract all the information she could from him.

As it happened, she had never eaten at the Hyde Park Hotel before but the Grill Room, presided over by Monsieur Favret, was a very pleasant place for luncheon and had the advantage of being within walking distance of the embassy.

Casey was waiting for her. He apologized for rushing her to the table but apparently something had 'blown up', as he put it, and he had to be back at his desk by two thirty.

'I'm real sorry to have to hurry but I hope the next time . . .'

He seemed to know his way around and explained that he used the Grill whenever he wanted to entertain away from the embassy.

'Favret knows what I like. In fact I almost always have the same thing – smoked salmon, *rognons sautés Valenciennes* and cheese. I hate eating too much at lunch but don't let me stop you. I guess you need feeding up.'

'Why does everyone keep on saying I need fattening up? I'm not a chicken or a pig or something.'

'Hey!' He held his hands up in mock surrender. 'I didn't mean anything. I wanted to say how beautiful you looked but I thought I shouldn't since this is only the second time we've met and you're engaged to my friend.'

'Sorry,' Verity said, sipping the champagne the waiter had brought them without being asked. Clearly this was also what Casey normally drank there. 'I know what you're thinking, "Poor Edward getting himself married to such a bad-tempered harridan."'

'Lucky Edward's what I think.' He leant across the table and his perfect teeth gleamed whitely. 'But, if you don't mind, I don't want to discuss Edward throughout the meal. I'd rather discuss you. What you believe in, what you think . . .'

'Well, that will be pleasant,' she teased. 'In my experience, with the exception of Edward, all the men I go out with like to talk about themselves. I suppose they have to preen. In my – admittedly limited – experience the male of the species is much more vain than the female. But I don't suppose you agree.'

'I can't generalize but, if I did, it would be to say that I like British women more than American. The trouble is we put our special woman on a pedestal and worship her until we bore each other to death. You English seem to be more direct, down to earth and . . .'

'Rude?'

'Forthright. You have views and you're not afraid to express them.'

'I hope so but don't judge Englishwomen by me. I'm a reject. Instead of being a good little wife with two children and a string of pearls round my neck waiting meekly for my man to get back from the office and wail about his tough day flirting with his secretary, I go out and make trouble. I've told Edward that, much as I love him, I won't be obedient and I certainly won't stay at home. All his friends will commiserate with him and say, "I told you so."'

Verity leaned over the table and gave Casey the benefit of her powerful personality. He too leant forward and there was a moment when the spark of sexual attraction between them crackled like a firework.

'Cigarette?' he said at last, taking out an elaborate gold case and opening it for her with a practised flick of the finger.

She took one and, as he lit it for her, his hand touched hers. She sat back and dragged on the cigarette, looking at him thoughtfully. Waving the smoke away, she said, 'Edward would be cross with me.'

'Why, because you are lunching with me?'

'Oh no, he trusts me absolutely.'

'Is that wise?' he asked, smiling wolfishly.

'Yes. My days of jumping into bed with attractive men are over. I'm getting married very soon.'

'And you wouldn't contemplate one last adventure before you shut up shop?'

Verity was shocked. Was there a streak of vulgarity in this man? 'That's not why he would be cross.'

'Why then?'

'Because I'm still recovering from TB and I shouldn't be smoking.'

It did the trick and Casey leant back in his chair as though avoiding her germs. Their smoked salmon arrived and they stubbed out their cigarettes.

'Tell me about Eamon Farrell,' she directed him.

'Ah! I wondered if you would ask. A little bird tells me that you and your . . .' he hesitated, 'future husband rather fancy yourselves as sleuths . . . amateur detectives. Is that right?'

Now he was teasing her – even insulting her. 'Don't forget that I'm also a journalist. You had better make me promise not to repeat anything you tell me in the *New Gazette* . . .'

'Or the *Daily Worker*,' he added. 'No need to worry. There's nothing of interest to say about him. He was a nice, clean-living American who did his job well and I'll miss him.'

'Was he an old friend of Mr Kennedy's?' she probed.

'Yes, the old man knew his father and took him on after he had done a stint at the *Boston Globe*.

185

I'm told that, if he had stayed, he would have made a first-rate journalist.'

'So why did he give it up to take on Mr Kennedy's publicity?'

'He admired him and there was a brief period when we thought the old man might have become President but that isn't going to happen. Eamon soon understood that. The Ambassador has – what shall I say? – a few too many skeletons in the cupboard. Now there I go! You must promise not to quote me on this!'

'Also, he was in love with Kick.' It was a wild guess but she had hit the mark.

'How on earth did you know that?'

'It was the way he looked at her when we had dinner with the family. He obviously adored her. I'm not surprised. She's a lovely girl but it is common knowledge that she's in love with . . . someone else.'

'That's right and Eamon knew it. He loved her but not in that way. In any case, the old man would never have let him marry his daughter. He was aiming much higher.'

The waiter cleared away their plates and, while he did so, they were silent. When he had gone, Verity said, 'It must be quite a battle running security at the embassy.'

'Why do you say that?' Casey asked shortly. 'Well, you're right in the sense that Mr Kennedy doesn't take kindly to being told what he can and can't do.'

'Meaning . . . ?' She felt rather uneasy and wondered if she had gone too far but she couldn't draw back now. 'That girl Dr Channing brought – Lulu – Mr Kennedy seemed to like her?'

Damn! she thought. Why had she said that? She was pretty certain that David Griffiths-Jones was using Lulu to trap Kennedy so he could be black-mailed and, if he ever found out she had warned Casey about her, he would be very angry. However, she didn't approve of blackmail even if it was done with good reason – for the sake of the Party. Well, what did it matter anyway? Soon she wouldn't be a Party member. The thought almost panicked her, as if she was being expelled from school, as she so often had been.

'You think it's a set-up?' Casey asked with interest. 'I thought so myself, but who would she be working for?'

'Don't ask me!' Verity replied airily, feeling that she had already said enough.

'Thanks for the tip, anyway. Now, is there anything you want to ask me?'

'Yes, there is. Do you think there's any connection between Tom Wintringham's death and Eamon's?'

'You obviously think so.'

'Murder isn't yet so common in England that one can believe two bodies "discovered" more or less by the American Ambassador within a few miles of each other is pure coincidence. And the way they were killed by a knife in the neck. They must be connected, mustn't they?'

187

'You don't think Mr Kennedy killed either of them, I hope?' Casey's snort of derision spurred Verity on.

'No, of course not. If he had, he'd hardly be anywhere close when their bodies were found.'

'Mind you,' Casey said in a low voice, 'and this is off the record, I'm sure he could – maybe even has – killed an enemy if it was absolutely necessary. Not over here though – not in a job which means so much to him.'

'Someone close to him, then?'

'You don't give up easily, do you? I assume you mean me?'

'As you said about Mr Kennedy, I think you could if you had to.'

He laughed. 'You let me take you out to lunch and then call me a murderer? Not cricket, eh?' he added in an exaggerated English accent.

'No, I don't think you would stoop to murdering anyone. You're too clever for that. However, I imagine you have "heavies" to do the job for you.'

'You think I'm too clever?' Casey looked pleased. 'Nah! You've been reading too much Dashiell Hammett. That's not the way it works in real life.'

You're vain, Verity said to herself. I thought so. You think you're smart but I wonder . . . She put on her most admiring voice, hoping to appeal to his sense of self-importance. 'Would you know if there was someone in the embassy . . . or a friend of the family perhaps . . . who was . . . I don't know . . . doing something he or she shouldn't?

188

I mean, you must suspect that whoever killed Eamon may kill again. For the head of security, that must be a worrying thought.'

Casey grinned as the waiter served the kidneys. 'Are you happy to keep to champagne or would you like . . .'

'I've drunk enough. Otherwise I'll sleep all afternoon.'

'But not with me,' he said as the waiter retreated.

'Not with you. Don't try and make me feel sorry for you. I'm sure there's no shortage of women in your life.'

'None like you,' he responded quickly. When she did not reply, he went on, 'You've given me something to think about. Let me talk to a few people and, if I find anything, I'll get back to you. I don't know why I should but there's something about you, Verity, which makes me want to invent excuses for seeing you again.'

After lunch he put her in a cab and walked back to Grosvenor Square. Were things getting out of control? He rather thought they might be and decided he must take firm action to avoid a precipitate termination of Mr Kennedy's tenure as United States Ambassador to the Court of St James.

'We've had some bad news,' Liddell said, pacing the room. 'Our German source says it'll happen soon.'

'The attack on Churchill?'

'What else? Or did you think Herr Hitler has announced he's sorry he's caused so much trouble and wants to resign?' Liddell snarled.

'The invasion of Czechoslovakia – that's what I thought you were going to say,' Edward replied mildly. He knew that Liddell was under a fearful strain. Would he ever be forgiven if he let the only person who might save Britain be murdered right under his nose?

They were in Edward's rooms in Albany. Edward thought Liddell's visit must be because he could not stay in his office without going mad with frustration and anxiety.

'So Der Adler isn't dead?'

'We killed Der Adler and they have resurrected him or, more likely, found someone else to take his place.'

'Von Trott could have been telling the truth. What are you doing to keep Churchill safe?'

'The whole works. I've tightened security around him. Walter Thompson's armed but Churchill's a nightmare to guard. He simply refuses to lie low and wait till we've caught the bastard. Says he hasn't got the time.' Liddell laughed but there was no humour in it. 'I'd admire his sheer recklessness if it wasn't so damned irresponsible. His food is tasted before he eats it. We even examine his cigars.'

'Nothing else? No clues as to who Der Adler is?'

'Nothing! We have put in an official request for help to the Americans but they continue to say they know nothing. Blast and damn! What are we *not* doing?'

'Has Pride had a chance of examining the files on the two murders?'

'He's started. He's very thorough but if Der Adler committed the murders – and it's a big "if" – have we the time for an exhaustive investigation? By the way, he says he's going to talk to you tomorrow.'

Edward nodded. 'What about the Italian connection – those knives?'

'It turns out they can be bought in Seven Dials without difficulty.'

'Maybe, but presumably we have people in Rome?'

'We have spies in Mussolini's court. That's no problem. You know the Italians,' Liddell added contemptuously, 'they can't keep a secret.'

'Well, it's just a hunch but put out the word and see if anything comes back. You never know.'

'What about you? You trip over corpses in your usual way but that's not what we want. We want information. We'll have corpses enough in six months and Churchill must not be one of them.'

'"So shalt thou feed on Death, that feeds on men, and Death once dead, there's no more dying then."'

'What the hell does that mean,' Liddell asked irritably.

'Sorry, nothing – just that death is the last enemy. What about the IRA?'

'We rounded up two of the three men Wintringham told Miss Browne he had seen talking in that pub. The trouble is that talking in a pub isn't illegal so we had to let Danny O'Rourke go. We'll have to let MacDade go tomorrow. I'm sorry to say that we haven't found the one they call "Bomber" Kelly because he's the most dangerous of them. He'll be picked up soon no doubt.'

'Have you got a photograph of him? If you have, I'd like to see it in case . . .'

'Good idea. We circulated it to ports and airports. I'll get it sent over to you. It was taken about three years ago when he was in custody in Northern Ireland. They thought he'd planted a bomb which killed a police officer but they were never able to prove anything against him.'

As he saw Liddell out, Fenton informed Edward that a Mr Rooth had rung from a public telephone box.

'Did he leave a message?' he asked sharply.

'Yes, sir.' Fenton passed him a sheet of paper which Edward scanned impatiently.

'Ah! I would never have guessed it,' he said. 'It sheds a new light on things, that's for sure.'

From the bed where they had just made what passed for love, Lulu watched Joe Kennedy dress. He was covered up to his neck in a thick pelt of hair which she found both attractive and, at the same time, repellent. He did not resemble any

192

man she had ever slept with and she had slept with more than most women of her age. He had a heavy Boston accent – at least he had told her it was Boston – which she had some difficulty understanding. She thought he looked working-class, almost uncouth, not at all like an ambassador – not that she had ever met one before. She was surprised how easy it had been to ensnare him and she almost pitied his simplicity. He put on his spectacles and continued to tell her about his success in Hollywood but not the stories she wanted hear about Errol Flynn whom she had seen in *Captain Blood* and very recently in *Robin Hood*. She had longed to be Olivia de Havilland and be clasped in his strong, manly arms. Instead of which she had to sleep with this old man.

She pulled the sheet over her breasts and tried to concentrate. Why did old men always talk about money?

'When I got to Hollywood, nobody knew how to depreciate, amortize, capitalize – the very thing that makes for success or failure in any business.'

He did not tell her about the women – how he had raped Gloria Swanson, destroyed her marriage and her film career. At the same time as he was bedding all the women he could buy, he was married to Rose who swore she would make him pay for his infidelities. She made him hand over clothes, jewels – anything she wanted – but it didn't make for a happy marriage and the children suffered.

Given the sins he so cheerfully admitted to, Lulu wondered if David Griffiths-Jones' attempt to blackmail the Ambassador would succeed. David seemed to believe that times had changed and, although a Boston hoodlum could get away with murder – literally – in the United States, in England the United States Ambassador could not afford even to be caught in adultery let alone anything worse.

She was rather frightened of Mr Kennedy and would be glad when it was all over. If he ever found out that she was bait for blackmail, she thought he might kill her. They had met in the flat in Curzon Street – conveniently near the embassy – which David had provided and she had ensured that the photographs, which had been taken through a two-way mirror, were quite explicit. Lulu prayed fervently that neither Kennedy nor David discovered that she had also slept with the Ambassador's twenty-two-year-old son, Jack. She knew all hell would break loose if that ever came out. Jack did not love her, she knew. She was just an 'easy lay' – he had told her so with icy contempt – but, despite the way he treated her, she adored him. He was so handsome, but that wasn't it. He had an attraction that grew – paradoxically – from his coldness. He never seemed to question his charm. He knew he could have her – would have her – from the moment he had set eyes on her at that dinner at Cliveden. It wasn't important to him but it was convenient.

Lulu was one of those girls who found that sort of arrogance irresistible.

As Joe Kennedy slipped out of the flat into a waiting car – not the Cadillac, he wasn't that stupid – and told Washington to take him back to the embassy, he did not know that he would never see Lulu again. Her duty done, she would disappear. What had David said when he had ordered her to seduce the old man and she had demurred? 'Lie back and think of England.' She had guessed it was some sort of joke and had tried to laugh.

Chief Inspector Pride looked at Edward gloomily. They were in his cramped, spartan office at the Yard discussing whether there was a connection between the murders and the possible attack on Churchill. 'Between ourselves, Lord Edward, Voss would have done well to have invited me to take over the case right at the start. These country coppers can never resist the temptation to show off, as though investigating a murder case was not very different to arresting a "drunk and disorderly". He's gathered very little evidence and his interviews with the staff and guests at Cliveden were inadequate.'

'I doubt he could have done more without causing the most frightful fuss, Chief Inspector. As it is, the papers have had a field day. Mr Kennedy cannot understand why they have turned on him so savagely since the Munich Agreement. And then my presence didn't help.

Was I investigating something murky, they want to know? Or was I part of the so-called Cliveden Set? Well, no doubt you read the beastly rags. A combination of the Astors and the Kennedys topped with Cliveden conspiracy theories – I think we were lucky to get away without being lynched. If Voss had impounded Kennedy's Cadillac because he suspected it had been used to transfer Wintringham's body from wherever he was murdered to the pavilion, the press would have slavered at the mouth. I imagine the Foreign Office would have had a few things to say about damaging our relations with the United States.'

'You're right,' Pride said, sounding even more gloomy. 'It always doubles the difficulty when I have to investigate a crime where public figures are involved and the United States Ambassador is one of the biggest fishes I've ever had to interview.'

'Did you ask him about the spectacles in the boot of the Cadillac? He told me they were one of his pairs of reading glasses, but then he would.'

'I didn't. He would hardly have confessed that they belonged to Wintringham. It would just have increased his suspicion that we were trying to pin something on him.'

'And it would have put me in a difficult position because he would have known that I was the source of any evidence against him. He suspected I worked for Liddell's mob and I had to do a good deal of spadework to convince him I didn't. I don't want him now to think I'm just a "copper's nark". I think that's the phrase, isn't it?'

'That's the phrase. I certainly don't want to queer your pitch. At the moment, you are our best chance of getting information out of him. You say you found his chauffeur cleaning the Cadillac?'

'Very thoroughly,' Edward agreed.

'And the chauffeur found Farrell's body?'

'Strictly speaking, Wooster, Lord Astor's Labrador, found it. Washington and Fenton were caddying for us so Washington was the first person to see the body, but would he have "found" it if he had actually murdered the man?'

'He might have if he wanted to throw suspicion on Mr Kennedy.'

'The logistics don't work unless he had a partner in crime. He was with us in the car and then was never out of my sight. He couldn't have been ferrying a corpse around at the same time.'

'Who knew that you and Kennedy were going to Huntercombe to play golf?'

'Anyone at Cliveden. Lord Astor – or rather his butler – rang the club secretary so there would be no trouble about us playing a round even though neither of us is a member. I say, Chief Inspector, are you sure Farrell wasn't murdered where he was found? Did Voss establish when he was last seen alive?'

Pride looked through Voss's notes. 'He was last

197

seen about an hour before you went off to play golf. Where he was in that hour we have yet to discover. As for the time of death, the doctor says it is very difficult to estimate how long Farrell had been dead. It was a cold day, as you remember, and you noticed that his body was cold yet there was no rigor mortis. The doctor says Farrell was probably killed about an hour before he was found but it's little more than a guess. It's not an exact science.

'The body was taken to the golf course in a car or van,' he continued, reading from Voss's notes. 'Before you ask, no one saw a van or car and the tyre prints weren't clear. Photographs and casts were taken but won't be conclusive.'

'The gardener thinks Dr Channing's car was used to transport Wintringham's body to the Blenheim Pavilion. He rang me to say he thought the tyre marks outside the pavilion were from his car.'

The Chief Inspector raised his hands in a gesture of despair. 'I don't know – even the gardener turns out to have been a better detect-ive than Voss. I've had the forensic boys go over the car but they found nothing conclusive – nothing that would stand up in court. As far as Farrell's body is concerned, it could have been transported in Mr Kennedy's Cadillac. It could have been taken in Channing's Ford. It might have been taken in a completely different car. Unfortunately the ground was dry and we couldn't follow the tracks very far. However, there's a quiet lane leading from the eleventh hole to the village but we've found no one in the village who has admitted to seeing a car or anything unusual last Sunday.'

'Thank you, Chief Inspector, for sharing all this with me. Voss wouldn't tell me anything.'

'It is irregular but we have – what shall I say? – cooperated on several occasions in the past and I think, with your entrée to the Astors and the Kennedys, you should be able to help us.'

Edward nodded. 'So both the victims were transported from where they were murdered to where their bodies were found. No clue . . . nothing has been found near either body which could tell us anything about their murderers?'

'Nothing, Lord Edward, and I rather doubt we are going to get lucky and find something. The murderer has had ample time to clean up and destroy anything incriminating.'

'The golf course has been searched?'

'With a fine-tooth comb.'

'What have you learnt about Farrell, Chief Inspector?'

'I suppose it's not surprising but I can't help noticing that the Kennedys aren't interested in Wintringham's murder but they are cut up about Farrell's. He was almost one of the family. Kennedy relied on him to get him a good press and he would have been particularly useful now. Kennedy was a friend of his father's and had to telephone him to break the news. It can't have been an easy call to make. One thing though – for what it's worth, Farrell was homosexual.'

'I didn't know that.' Edward was surprised. 'I thought he was in love with Kick Kennedy.'

Pride shrugged. 'Maybe he worshipped her without any . . . you know, sexual feelings.'

It was the nearest Edward had ever seen him to showing embarrassment.

'That's possible, I suppose. Have you found out about any . . .' he hesitated and settled for, 'friends of his?'

'As far as we can tell, he lived a celibate life over here but in Boston it was well known that he had "leanings" in that direction. Mr Kennedy made no secret of it. He said Farrell's father had sent him as a young man to doctors and psychiatrists but none of them had been able to cure him.'

'Kennedy told you that?'

'Yes.'

Edward meditated. 'I don't think it can be "cured". It can be suppressed, of course, but that can lead to all sorts of psychological problems.'

'It's against the law,' Pride reminded him.

'Yes, and I'm inclined to think the law is an ass. Be that as it may, could Farrell have been murdered in some sort of mix-up with either a lover or someone who was going to get it into the press?'

'But why would they do that?'

'To embarrass Kennedy? The more I think about it, the more I'm convinced that all this is aimed at harming Kennedy.'

'And you could be right at that,' Pride agreed.

CHAPTER 10

As the cab cut through Belgrave Square, Verity mused on the two very different Londons which existed in the same city, each totally ignorant of the other. It was not yet nine o'clock and the square was still empty. A few bowler-hatted, overcoated gentlemen, briefcase in hand, strode purposefully towards Sloane Square to catch a bus or the Tube, although in this area most were collected by chauffeur-driven cars rather later in the morning. Doorsteps had already been scrubbed and there was no life to be seen or heard behind the heavy doors and windows – some still shuttered – which, blind and hostile, seemed determined to ignore the world outside.

She had no difficulty imagining the ladies of the household still abed – not even breakfasted – and certainly not ready to begin the laborious daily endeavour of hiding the advancing years behind elaborate but discreetly applied make-up. If there were small children, they would be breakfasting in the nursery before Nanny took them out, the babies in perambulators large and heavy enough to intimidate anyone in their way. The grandest baby carriages bore the family coat of arms and the nannies wore starched uniforms. Slightly older children, smartly dressed in coats and hats never to be muddied in boisterous play, would walk beside the pram, perhaps trying not to walk on the cracks between the paving stones in case the bears got them. The older children would be dropped off at exclusive nursery schools in the New King's Road.

Less than a mile away, in Victoria and Pimlico, children of an altogether different class would be shivering in cellars and vermin-infested rooms, perhaps several siblings to a bed, with little prospect of breakfast or schooling, condemned to a life of poverty and deprivation. On the other hand, if they survived infancy, they enjoyed a freedom undreamed of by the children of Belgravia. They could play in the street from morning to night the age-old games of the poor – hopscotch and tag – skipping to rhymes so ancient as to be unintelligible even to the children who chanted them.

Verity believed in social mobility and equal opportunity but was well aware that the class system was rigid and power was concentrated in the hands of the few. These might be civilized and benignant like Edward – people hard to dislike – but she firmly believed this was wrong and that it was necessary to bring about a revolution in society whatever the cost. So what was she doing marrying into the class she so despised? It was a conundrum to which she had no answer and she was dreading another meeting with David Griffiths-Jones.

He was steel to her soft lead. He would not hesitate to accuse her of apostasy but neither would he hesitate to use her position in society for the sake of the Party, which he equated with the historical imperative. It did not worry him that the Communist Party had lost most of the popular support it had gained during the General Strike. To its leaders, popularity was at best irrelevant or at worst a distraction. A Communist government in Britain would never be won at the ballot box and Labour had now established itself as the visible champion of the working class. David had agreed with Verity when she said that the working class was innately conservative and suspicious of change. The proletariat had to be 'mobilized' – a favourite word of his – and made to see where its future lay. He would point to the way in which the Bolsheviks – a tiny splinter party – had instigated and led a revolution in Russia. He sincerely if, in Verity's view, mistakenly believed that a 'coup' of this kind was possible in England.

He had summoned her to a meeting to discuss Wintringham's murder and find out if she had made herself, as he had instructed, one of Kennedy's trusted intimates. He said he had a message he wanted her to give him – a message he could hardly give her over the telephone. As Party headquarters were under continuous surveillance by Special Branch, they were meeting at Ransom Street.

When the cab stopped outside George Castle's lodging, it was immediately surrounded by small children – street Arabs – unused to seeing respectable folk alighting from cars or even taxis in their neighbourhood. Just a few streets away outside Heal's in the Tottenham Court Road cabs stood in ranks, and in Fitzroy Square the houses were substantial and their owners prosperous middle class, but the world of these children encompassed little more than three or four streets from which they seldom if ever strayed.

'Why a cab?' David asked crossly as he took her coat. 'If anyone were watching, they would have noticed you arriving.'

'So what?' Verity answered defiantly. 'I'm not ashamed of being seen here. Hello, George,' she said, wondering if she dared kiss him but deciding that it was better just to shake his hand. 'Where's Mary?'

'She's at work and that's where I'm going once the kettle has boiled and I've made you a nice cup of tea. You look perished.'

'It is cold,' she agreed, 'and since . . . since I've been ill I do seem to feel the cold.'

If David recognized this as a plea for sympathy, he ignored it. 'You should have come by Tube. It's perfectly warm. I despair of you sometimes, Verity. Well, come in and sit down.'

George brought her tea in a mug, which she

held in both hands to warm herself. There would be no fires in Ransom Street until the evening and then only a few coals smouldering in the tiny grate. When George had left for work, slamming the door behind him, David made Verity recount in detail exactly what had happened since they had last met.

'So you think Wintringham came to Cliveden to see you?'

'Don't you?' She looked at him speculatively. He was still very good-looking but he appeared noticeably older than when they had been lovers. There were creases in his face and his hair was thinning. She wondered if the constant travel – he was never in one place for more than a few days at a time – and the absence of any sort of home life were beginning to take its toll. So far as she knew, he had no woman in his life and the knowledge that, at least in this country, his movements were monitored by the security services must be a terrible strain.

How could it be otherwise? He protected himself by developing a carapace beneath which no one was allowed to probe. His eyes were steel blue and his gaze was steady but she detected a tiny tremor in one hand when he lifted his mug of tea. He wasn't the same man she had met five years ago and there was a moment when she wanted to soothe him. The impulse faded as quickly as it had come. She had always been rather frightened of him. It had been part of his attraction but now she was frankly scared. What would he do if she told him she had decided to leave the Party? To what would he not resort to protect himself? Would he kill? She was sure he had it in him to kill. Would he betray his friends? Of course he would, because he had no friends. His life was the Party and yet he must know that the Party had no gratitude. Once his usefulness was deemed to be at an end, he would be jettisoned and probably destroyed as he had jettisoned and destroyed others. After all, he knew too much to be allowed to sink into obscure retirement. Would he think the same about her? She shivered.

'Are you ill?' For a moment she thought she detected real concern in his voice.

'No, not ill. Exhausted. Those people at Cliveden – it was all I could do to be polite.'

He looked at her so fiercely that she had to lower her eyes. 'That is good. They are the enemy. This is the war – the real war – and don't you forget it.'

She told him everything without glossing over the smallest detail. Long ago she had resolved never to lie to him except once or twice by omission – because she recognized that he would immediately know it.

'Wintringham didn't come to see you,' he said when she had finished.

'No? Then why was he at Cliveden?'

'He fancied he was in love with Lucinda.'

'With Lulu?' she asked, surprised. 'I didn't know they knew one another.'

'Well, they did.' David sounded irritated. He hated giving information. 'He met her with me.'

'With you?' She was puzzled until she remembered Tom had told her that he had been following David. He had called him a bad man but she hadn't wanted to listen. She had said she was busy. She realized – now that it was too late – that she ought to have asked him what he meant. She decided to change the subject. 'What about Dr Channing?'

'What about him?'

'Who is he? Does he work for you?'

'He's not really a doctor. He's a . . . what do you call it? An osteopath, but he also practises what he calls natural medicine – herbs, massages with natural oils – that sort of thing.'

'I thought he was a charlatan the moment I saw him,' Verity cut in. 'Is he a member of the Party?'

'No, but he has been useful. I suppose you'd call him a pimp.'

'And he's pimping Lulu to Kennedy?'

'She's useful too,' David admitted.

'We're all either useful or not useful – is that it?'

'Don't be impertinent, Verity. It doesn't suit you. If the Party . . .'

She interrupted him again. 'So you're planning to blackmail Kennedy?'

Her face must have shown her disgust because he replied, almost defensively, 'Not for money but because we need to influence him. In fact, that's what we want you to do. Go to him and tell him that he has been photographed in delicto flagrante with Lulu and, if he doesn't want the pictures to be sent to every newspaper in Fleet Street, he has to co-operate with us.'

'But he hasn't been photographed in bed with Lulu, has he?'

David nodded.

'He has! That's awful. No! I can't possibly do that,' she said without hesitation.

'Why on earth not?' He seemed genuinely surprised.

'Because I'm not a blackmailer – because black-mail's a crime and because I won't do it. Is that enough?'

David was pensive. 'I take it you want to marry that man of yours?'

'Edward? You know I do.' It was as though someone had made her swallow a cold sponge.

'Well then, you won't want me to show him the photographs we have of you and Leonard Bladon, will you?' Bladon was the good-looking young doctor who ran the clinic where Verity had con-valesced from TB the previous summer.

'What photographs?' she demanded in a low voice. 'There are no photographs.'

'There could be. We have skills in that dir-ection . . .' David replied.

Lulu looked down at Jack Kennedy and smiled. 'Was that good?' she inquired. She compared him mentally to his father. She didn't mind old men in general. She had made love to many of them. For the most part, what they lacked in physical prowess and bodily beauty they made up for by being gentle and imaginative. Joe Kennedy had not been gentle and she had hated having to service him – she could not call it 'love-making'. He was ugly – but that was not his fault – and he smelt bad but it was the way he liked smacking her about which frightened and disgusted her. His son had that same cold look in his eyes but he was so charming. His smile was irresistible even if it was as superficial as the skin on a peach. Why had she thought of peaches? Was it the faint blur of hair on his skin or the taste of his flesh? She licked her lips in anticipation but there was to be no second bout. Jack raised himself, pushing her off him none too gently. Perhaps, when he was an old man, he too would be cruel, she thought. His father had provided him with the worst possible example. How could his son ever believe in a lasting relationship with a woman based on mutual respect?

'Why do you have to go?' she whined, picking herself up from the floor where she had fallen among the tangled bedclothes.

'Why is it so fucking cold in this godforsaken country?' Jack complained, wrapping a bathrobe round him.

'Don't cover yourself up,' she said, sinking back on the bed. 'I like looking at you naked. When you're cold, the fur on your stomach stands up and your skin is covered in goose bumps.'

'Damn it, I don't want to go but I have to make an appearance at some dance this evening. I hate them – those dumb English girls with their cold eyes and small breasts. And their gowns . . . Isn't there a decent dressmaker in the whole of London?'

'But that won't stop you fucking one of them,' Lulu said viciously.

'Gently, gently,' he chided her. 'Why, my little cat, I do believe you're jealous. Can a whore be jealous?'

'You treat me like shit, just like your father . . .'

She stopped, realizing that she had gone too far. 'I only meant . . .'

He turned and looked at her with such loathing that she was suddenly frightened.

'You little bitch!' he shouted, his voice taut with anger. 'Get out of here, will you, before I throw you out. Here . . .' He threw some money on the bed.

'Please, Jack, I'm sorry. I don't want . . . I didn't mean . . .'

'I expect to find the room empty when I get out of the shower. Go out the back way. I don't want anyone to think I need women like you.'

He went into the bathroom and she heard the water beat against the shower curtain. Hurriedly, she threw on her clothes and glanced in the mirror. Tears had streaked her face with mascara. She wiped away the worst of the mess and then – leaving the money on the bed but taking something from the bedside table – she slipped out of the room. She crept down the back stairs and into Prince's Gate believing that no one had seen her, but she was wrong.

CHAPTER 11

'This is one hell of a mess. The press are baying for my blood and I've had the devil of a time trying to keep the Kennedy connection out of the papers.'

'How are the Astors taking it, Chief Inspector?' Edward asked.

'None too well, as you can imagine.'

'Have you arrested Dr Channing?'

'On what grounds? The girl's body was found in his house but she wasn't murdered there and he didn't put it there.'

'Can you be sure – absolutely sure?'

'The post-mortem shows she had been dead several hours when she was found and there was no blood on the carpet. The girl was a whore and Channing had been told to put her in Kennedy's way.'

'Told by whom?'

'He's not saying. I think he fears for his life and I can't say I blame him.'

'Kennedy took the bait?'

'The police constable on guard outside the residence says he saw her enter the building last night but didn't see her leave. She must have left through the back – if she did leave alive.'

'You think Kennedy may have killed her in the residence? Surely not! He could hardly keep that a secret.'

'I haven't told you the worst of it. The Ambassador wasn't at home last night. He was at a public dinner until late.'

'So if Joe wasn't entertaining Lulu, who was?'

'Jack Kennedy. She had his watch in her bag. It was found underneath the body.'

'How do you know it's his watch?'

'It's a very expensive watch and there's an inscription engraved on the back – "From J.P.K. to J.F.K. with love May 29 1938".'

'That's Jack's birthday?'

'Yes, his twenty-first.'

'Have you questioned him?'

'Not yet. It's a damnable business. The embassy and the residence are both United States territory. We can't search them without an invitation – so far we've had none – and the Foreign Office has told us to back off.'

'May I see the photographs again?' Pride threw them across the desk. 'Channing refuses to say who told him to introduce Lulu to the Ambassador?' Edward mused as he examined them.

'He does. Why? Have you any ideas on that score?'

'Verity told me that she was introduced to Lulu at a local Party meeting.'

'Introduced to her by whom?' The Chief Inspector sat up in his chair.

'David Griffiths-Jones. We have both known him for a long time off and on. He was in Spain when Verity was there. He's a top Communist Party official. A nasty piece of work – Liddell has quite a file on him.'

'Of course! You and he quarrelled over . . .' He saw Edward's face and realized he was on sensitive ground. Hastily, he changed the subject. 'So what might Griffiths-Jones want with Kennedy?'

'You'll have to ask him that but both Verity and I thought he might be – you know . . .'

'Trying to trap him – photograph him with the girl and then blackmail him?'

'Something like that,' Edward agreed drily.

'That is a lead. Thank you, Lord Edward. I knew I was right to involve you despite what Voss said.'

Edward grunted. 'The Inspector doesn't like me and I can understand why. Who needs some amateur sleuth muddling up a perfectly good investigation?'

'Only it isn't a perfectly good investigation. Where are we now?' Pride leant back in his chair and closed his eyes. 'Let me see. We have three murders involving the Kennedy family. Is one of them a murderer? Or is it someone who wants to discredit them at a crucial moment in Britain's relations with the US? The Communist Party, for instance.'

'And the other significant point is that all three

victims were moved somewhere else after they were murdered.'

'Yes, Wintringham and Farrell were left where one of the Kennedy family would find the body. On the other hand, the girl was moved away from the Kennedy residence where she was last seen and possibly murdered and taken to somewhere she had been staying – the Astor estate.'

'Yes,' Edward agreed, 'she was one victim who wasn't dumped in a place a Kennedy would find her but was actually moved so it didn't implicate the family.'

'True, but the murderer didn't bother to remove Jack's watch – assuming he didn't plant it on her. And Kennedy senior was always likely to be implicated. Quite a few people may have known or guessed what was going on. I think we need to concentrate on Cliveden. Only a handful of people saw Lulu being introduced to Kennedy by Channing.'

'Where did she live, by the way?' Edward asked.

'She had a small flat in Clapham. Apparently she liked to pretend that she lived in Kensington but that was just fantasy.'

'That was what Verity thought. She had this double-barrelled name but her vowels didn't support her pretensions. And Channing – what have you found out about him, Chief Inspector?'

'He's not a doctor but he is an osteopath who has developed a practice – if you can call it that – dispensing homeopathic medicines to the

216

desperate or deluded – mostly, but by no means exclusively, women.'

'Why women in particular?'

'He also offers beauty treatments and dispenses slimming pills.'

'And that's not illegal?'

'Apparently not – at least not until someone complains of being defrauded or poisoned. I think he has performed an abortion or two but I don't have the evidence yet. By the way – it's probably not relevant – but he's homosexual.'

'I wonder if he knew Farrell?'

'That occurred to me but so far we haven't turned up any evidence that he did,' Pride said.

'It's lucky for him that the murderer favoured knives not poison.' Edward was looking at the photographs of the murdered girl. 'She was stabbed in the side of the neck like the others . . .'

'But in her case the murder weapon was removed. There was no knife.'

'But didn't the post-mortem show she had been stabbed with a similar weapon to the one used on Wintringham and Farrell?'

'It did,' Pride confirmed. 'Before I interview Griffiths-Jones – you don't know where he lives, do you . . . ?' Edward shook his head. 'I must speak to Miss Browne. Presumably you know where she is.'

'She's waiting outside,' he said coolly.

Verity had been kicking her heels for a full thirty minutes before Pride came through from his office pretending – she thought – to be unaware that she had been left waiting for his summons. He was apologetic and Edward looked guilty which assuaged her anger.

'We've been talking about Lulu,' Edward said. 'Here, have a look at these.' He passed her the photographs.

As she examined them Verity felt her eyes mist over. She hated sentiment and she hadn't liked Lulu but to see this young girl – so alive at Cliveden, flaunting her sex appeal – reduced to dead matter by some arrogant, brutal man made her angry and scared. No one had said it but this could have been her. There was too much death in her life. It made her sick to the stomach.

'Only a man could have been so callous,' she said at last.

'I'm inclined to agree,' Pride nodded. 'Do you know anything about her background?'

'No, you'll have to ask David Griffiths-Jones. He knew her and probably employed her.'

'Employed her . . . ?'

'Yes, Chief Inspector.' She found that, in her mood of despair and disgust, she had no feelings of loyalty to David. He used people and did not care very much what happened to them. 'I believe they may have been lovers though I suppose you could say that she spread her favours widely.'

'But at his direction?'

'Possibly. She called herself Lucinda Arbuthnot-Grey but I'm sure that wasn't her real name.

She just liked sounding posh but her vowels gave her away.'

'We think her real name was Mary Potts.'

'No wonder she wanted to change it,' Edward put in.

'I don't know why you say that,' Verity snapped. 'I would describe her as an East End girl trying to make her way in the world using her only asset – her body.'

'She was a whore,' Pride said, scandalized.

'She was a woman in a nasty, cruel man's world, Chief Inspector. She was a victim long before she was murdered.'

Pride looked at Edward and he lowered his gaze. Verity could still shock him but there was something in what she said. It was the men who pimped her – Channing and maybe David Griffiths-Jones – who were to blame for her ending up dead.

'She wanted to ingratiate herself with people like the Astors,' Verity continued unnecessarily, feeling that, in some small way, Edward had failed her.

'You notice that once again there is no blood, V? She was murdered elsewhere and her body taken back to Cliveden.'

'What does Channing say?'

'He knows nothing about it, or says he doesn't,' Pride answered her, 'and I'm inclined to believe him – at least as far as the murder is concerned.'

'I think he might make an intelligent guess, though, at who the murderer could be,' Edward added. 'After all, he put her in the way of Joe Kennedy and her death must be related to that in some way. If I were him, I'd be worried.'

'Well, I shall be questioning the gentleman again in due course,' Pride said grimly. 'If he knows anything, we'll sweat it out of him.' He hesitated. 'Could you tell me who else was at the meeting you went to, Miss Browne, in addition to Mr Griffiths-Jones and Miss Arbuthnot-Grey?' He asked the question blandly enough but it was intended as a test and Verity knew it.

She chewed her lower lip, wondering whether she would be betraying her comrades if she volunteered their names. On the one hand, the police were generally considered to be the enemy – the instrument of government. On the other, this was a murder case and there was nothing secret or illegal about a meeting of Party members.

'I don't know that it is particularly relevant, but there is no reason why I shouldn't tell you provided you give me your word that it won't result in anyone being harassed for political reasons.'

'I give you my word,' Pride said without hesitation.

'Well, there were about fifteen of us. I can't remember everyone but no doubt I could get a list if you persuaded me that it was absolutely necessary.'

'Was there a special reason why you went to the meeting?'

'It was a normal local gathering of Party members and I've missed so many of them as a result of being away so much. But yes, there was a reason why I went to that particular meeting. I wanted to hear a friend of mine speak. He was fighting in Spain when I was there – an Italian – Fernando Ruffino.'

'I thought the Italians support General Franco,' Pride said, puzzled.

'Mussolini and the Fascists do, of course, but there were about five thousand Italian anti-Fascists in Spain fighting for the Republic.'

'I didn't know that,' Edward said.

'To be honest, they weren't very effective because they quarrelled among themselves so much.' Feeling disloyal, she added, 'But Fernando was as brave as a lion. He was wounded and I never saw him again until the other night. He spoke very well about the fight against Fascism in Italy.'

'Who else was at the meeting?' Pride pressed her.

'The District Secretary, George Castle, and his wife, Mary. Harold Knight – the local Party treasurer. Danny O'Rourke – I hear you've arrested him . . . ?'

'The IRA man – yes, he was being held on suspicion of being involved in the bombings but we've had to let him go. You don't approve of the IRA killing innocent civilians, I presume?' Pride said grimly.

221

'Of course I don't, nor would any self-respecting Party member. We're not terrorists, you know, Chief Inspector,' Verity said wearily. 'We believe in social justice. Isn't that what you believe in?'

Pride did not answer but looked sceptical. 'Anyone else you remember?'

'There were some young people, some students. A girl called Alice Paling and a spotty youth – I think his name was Leonard Baskin. I think Alice was a friend of Danny's but,' she added hastily, 'I'm quite sure she wouldn't have known about Danny's links with the IRA – assuming he had any – let alone been involved. She's English for one thing.' She caught Edward and the Chief Inspector exchanging a sceptical glance and it made her angry. 'Apart perhaps from Danny, they are all good, honest, patriotic citizens and I insist you don't assume that being a Communist makes you a criminal.'

Pride snorted as though he wasn't convinced but said politely, 'That's very helpful, Miss Browne. I must admit I can't see anyone other than Mr Griffiths-Jones having any links with Miss Arbuthnot-Grey's murder but we'll poke about and see if we turn up anything.'

Verity looked embarrassed. 'Chief Inspector – although, as I say, none of us at the meeting have anything to hide I'd be grateful if – when you talk to David, Mr Griffiths-Jones – you'll keep my name out of it. I think he might misunder-stand . . .'

'Don't worry,' Pride said soothingly. 'He'll not hear your name from me, I promise you.'

On the way back to Cranmer Court in a taxi – her mind still running on her decision to leave the Party – Verity said suddenly, almost as though she were arguing with herself, 'I think I have known for some time but couldn't admit it that I'm not what David would call a Communist. I don't believe in the dictatorship of the proletariat, which appears to mean unquestioning obedience to Comrade Stalin. It seems one can't take an independent line any more. I mean, if you disagree with anything the Party tells you, then you are a "deviationist" and can be "liquidated". I hate all the jargon that prevents one understanding what the real truth is. I don't believe in – I don't even understand – all the "isms" David spouts – "formalism", "sectarianism", "reformism", "social chauvinism", "socialist realism", "social demo-cratism" . . . I just believe that children should not be allowed to starve in a wealthy country like ours, that workers should have rights and that capital-ism is heartless.'

The taxi was a neutral, transitory place in which to deny her faith – a secular confessional but with no priest to offer absolution. Edward said nothing. There was either nothing to say or too much.

At last, in a voice as free of emotion as he could manage, he volunteered, 'Was there any particular moment when you finally decided . . . ?'

'David asked me to blackmail Joe Kennedy. Apparently, he had photographs taken of him in bed with Lulu. I couldn't do that and, before you ask, I couldn't tell Pride about it either.'

'Yes, I quite see. You are the last person in the world who could ever blackmail someone.'

'And . . . and . . .' She hesitated. It was a test. Would he pass it? 'He said he had photographs of me with Leonard Bladon that he would show you if I didn't do what he asked.'

'The blackguard!' Edward could barely restrain himself. 'I hope you told him to go to hell.'

'More or less,' she said, turning to him and smiling for the first time since they had left Pride's office. 'Is there anything you want to ask me?'

Edward looked puzzled. 'No, why should there be? I always knew he was . . . if you'll forgive me using the word, a shit, so it doesn't come as much of a surprise.'

She nodded. He had passed the test. He had not felt it necessary to ask whether the photographs of her with Bladon actually existed. Had he done so, she doubted whether she could have married him.

When he was back in Albany, Edward thought he would take the bull by the proverbial horns and see if Casey Bishop would talk to him. He had been disappointed that Verity had been unable to get as much out of him over dinner as he had hoped. But then Casey was not a fellow who could

224

be pumped for information without being aware of it and giving away precisely nothing. Casey obviously liked the look of Verity and, though Edward would not have admitted it, he had hoped that, if she flirted with him, he would become careless or try to impress her by letting her into some secret. He didn't for one minute believe that she had had an affair with Leonard Bladon. He didn't even think she would have renewed her affair with Adam von Trott. That was over. Verity did not forgive men who had let her down. But Casey . . . ? No, he was quite sure . . . but, then again, he was damned attractive and had stolen women from him before.

He telephoned the embassy. Casey was on the point of going home but he agreed – rather reluctantly, Edward thought – to meet him the following evening.

'I can't do anything before then, I'm afraid. I'm going to have a hell of a day but, if you don't mind a late dinner, we could meet at a little place I know in Greek Street called the Golden Gate.' Edward hadn't heard of it but was always ready to extend his knowledge of London nightlife. When he asked what sort of place it was, Casey said it was 'a kind of nightclub where people like him could relax'.

When Edward dropped her at Cranmer Court, Verity suddenly found herself fagged out. She wanted to throw herself on her bed and sleep.

It didn't please her, therefore, to find Alice Paling waiting for her outside the flat. She was sitting on the top stair holding her knees to her chest in a foetal position. She had obviously been there some time. When she looked up as the lift doors opened, Verity saw that her eyes were red and her ineffective attempts at make-up had dissolved and then crusted. She wore a cheap hat, which had been sat upon quite recently, and her thin coat was missing a button.

'Alice!' Verity said breezily. 'Whatever are you doing here? You look a mess. What's the matter?' She knew she sounded unsympathetic but the last thing she felt like was mothering Alice, whom she had always rather despised. Verity had always thought that women's propensity to cry was a weakness which should be resisted if at all possible. It only bolstered men's stereotypical ideas of the 'weaker sex'.

'It can't be that bad,' she continued, fumbling for her key. She almost added, 'Buck up, old thing,' which she remembered a hockey mistress telling her when she had been concussed for a few moments after being whacked on the forehead by an opponent's stick.

'But it's not all right,' Alice wailed. 'He's left me and he promised to marry me.'

'Who promised to marry you?'

'Fernando, of course. He said he wasn't in love with you any longer. He told me so.'

'In love with me? How ridiculous! Of course he

was never in love with me. He just enjoys flirting, like all Italians.'

'He said you'd been lovers in Spain. He said you were ever so brave.'

'I'm afraid he was telling fibs, Alice. We were never lovers and I was never especially brave.'

It was obvious that Fernando had said whatever it took to get the wretched girl into bed and had then grown bored with her – as was inevitable – and dumped her.

'Alice, he led you up the garden path. He was trying to impress you just to get you to . . . you know.'

'To sleep with him? Oh no, he truly loved me. He often said so.'

Verity promised herself that, if she ever saw Fernando again, she would give him a piece of her mind. To bamboozle this simple-minded girl was below him.

'You know he's married?'

'He said he was lonely. He said his wife didn't . . .'

'. . . understand him?' Verity groaned. Surely Fernando could have come up with something a little more original. Perhaps Alice was just too easy a conquest and he simply couldn't be bothered.

'Come in.' She unlocked the front door and shoved the girl – now weeping again – in front of her. She went into her tiny kitchen and put on the kettle. It was nearly five and she felt like a cup of tea, though if Alice stayed around much longer

227

she would need something stronger. 'So he's left you? Did he say why – where he was going?'

'He said he had an important job to do and wouldn't be coming back.'

'An important job . . . ? I wonder what that could be? Was he speaking somewhere?'

'No, he'd finished his lecture tour. He had raised quite a lot of money for the fight against Fascism. He's so brave . . . the stories he told about dodging the police and Mussolini's thugs. I admire him immensely,' Alice added unnecessarily, cheering up for a moment.

'But now he's gone,' Verity said flatly, wanting to bring the silly girl to her senses. 'He seduced you and left you – a typical man! Presumably you . . . I mean he protected you when you were making love.' It was ridiculous to be coy about condoms but there was enough bourgeois reticence left in her to make her feel embarrassed at having to spell it out.

'Oh, no. He said, as a Catholic, he didn't believe in birth control.'

'How very irresponsible of him.' Verity was exasperated and anxious. She felt she had to impress on Alice the potential seriousness of her situation. The girl's next words confirmed her worst fears.

'That's what I wanted to talk to you about. You're the only person I can talk to. I know you've had a lot of lovers. You see, I think I'm pregnant.'

'Alice, are you sure? Have you seen a doctor?'

'No, I haven't got one.'

'Your parents must have a doctor.'

'But he tells them everything. When I was a child, I cut my finger breaking into my piggy bank. I made Dr Evans swear not to tell my father but he did. My father was furious with me.'

Verity could see it all – the tyrannical father and the put-upon mother. If he had been furious with Alice for trying to break into her piggy bank, what would his reaction be to the news that she was pregnant? The imagination boggled. 'How pregnant are you? I mean, how long has it been . . . ?'

'About a month . . . I'm not sure.'

'That's not long. Perhaps you are mistaken.'

'No, I'm quite certain,' the girl said, almost triumphantly. 'I feel sick at the sight of food and I've missed my period.'

Verity was annoyed with herself for being surprised – even slightly shocked – to hear Alice refer to her menses so casually even though she had long advocated open discussion of 'women's problems', as such matters were coyly described. It was clear to her that much misery could be avoided if a little light could be shone on the dark ignorance of most young women about how their bodies worked.

'At the meeting in George Castle's house – you were sleeping with him then?'

'Oh yes.'

Verity thought savagely of the easy way he had

tried to seduce her with quotations from Dante, with Alice – his lover – in the same room. She remembered him telling her quite brazenly that his little boy was the apple of his wife's eye – or words to that effect. Her opinion of Fernando dropped to zero.

'I thought you would be able to arrange an abortion for me,' Alice continued naively. 'I asked a friend and she said that if I went to some struck-off doctor, I might be hacked open and die of blood poisoning.'

The friend had obviously been determined to prevent Alice having an abortion by frightening her with horror stories. Verity, too, had heard stories of bungled abortions carried out by drunk or incompetent doctors and was not going to contradict her.

She sighed. 'Oh, Alice, you are a little fool. Have you tried gin and a boiling hot bath?'

'Yes, and I've jumped off a chair.'

Verity remembered guiltily that for the past month or two she and Edward had not bothered about using the Durex she kept in her bedside table. She realized that she did not have a leg to stand on when it came to criticizing Alice. True, she was engaged to be married and Edward would never desert her but even so . . .

'I want to talk to Fernando. Where did he say this "important job" was?'

'He said he was going down to Kent – a place called Westerham. Do you know it?'

'Yes, I know it but why would he be going there? It's not a big town . . .'

'I know it wasn't to give a lecture. I think he said he was going to . . . what was it? It was a quotation, I think. Fernando's so clever. I remember – "Kill Claudio". I asked him who Claudio was – another Italian, I suppose – but he just laughed.'

CHAPTER 12

'Your hunch was right,' Liddell said grimly. 'Our man in Rome has heard about a plot to kill Mr Churchill. At first he dismissed it as one of those wild rumours which abound in Mussolini's court. The Italians are so indiscreet it's almost impossible to keep a secret, however important, for more than a few hours. Il Duce is always looking for ways to please Hitler and apparently he thinks this plan he's cooked up with the Abwehr will do the trick.'

'And do we have a name yet?' Edward asked.

'Not yet but our man's working on it. I feel a little easier in my mind now we have something to go on. I've had a list drawn up of every Italian in Britain with a criminal connection and known Fascist sympathies. It's a long list, I'm afraid, and it'll take some time to go through. The damnable thing is that we don't know how much time we've got,' he added grimly.

'Mr Churchill has invited me to stay at Chartwell for a few days but I've told him I have to be back in London by the end of the month.'

'For your wedding?' Liddell said with a grin. 'Yes, you mustn't be late for that.'

'After that Mr Churchill, or rather Colonel Moore-Brabazon, has very kindly arranged for us to spend two or three days in St Moritz. A sort of honeymoon,' Edward smiled shyly. 'I know it's absurd to talk of honeymoons at my time of life but, God knows, if we don't have a few days together then, I don't think we ever shall. Verity has convinced herself that she's well enough to go back to work and she's angling for a posting to Czechoslovakia, but Lord Weaver has refused to promise her anything for the moment, thank goodness.'

'She'll be lucky to get back to Prague,' Liddell replied grimly. 'I have it on the best authority that Hitler is about to march across the border.'

'Surely not?' Edward said in surprise. 'I thought the Prime Minister had made it clear that, if he did, we would go to war.'

Liddell shrugged. 'The politicians are fooling themselves and everyone else if they think Hitler will stop now. He's like a runaway steamroller. He can't stop even if he wanted to.'

With an anxious heart, Edward walked out into Trafalgar Square. He glanced up at Nelson on his column and hoped he saw more clearly with his one eye than Mr Chamberlain did with two. It was a cold day but the sun was out so he decided to stroll round to his club for a bite of lunch. When he reached St James's Street he found that, after all, he wasn't hungry and on a whim hailed a cab and asked to be taken to Prince's Gate. He thought he might have a look at the cars parked near the Kennedys' residence. He realized it was hardly worthwhile but he was possessed by a restlessness that made him want to do *something*, however futile. He grinned. How different he was from an American 'private eye', he thought. Why couldn't he knock down some door with a 'gat' in his hand and rescue some 'dame'? No, that wasn't his style but he'd give a lot to force his way into the residence and look for clues as to how poor Lulu had died. But that wasn't going to happen.

He paid off the cab and strolled across the street. There were no large American cars in view. Disconsolately, he walked into the mews behind the building where he knew Casey lived. He had told him that he had a flat over the garage where some of the embassy cars were parked. Edward noted that security was lax. Not a single policeman was on duty and, if the Americans had their own people patrolling the building, none was in evidence. The doors to several of the garages in the mews were open and chauffeurs in shirt-sleeves and mechanics in boiler suits were tending their machines. Edward's latent interest in cars was sparked by the American ones which stood out among the Rolls-Royces which were also on view. A huge, streamlined Lincoln Continental caught his fancy and the chauffeur who was polishing it allowed him to look it over and answered questions about its speed and reliability.

The chauffeur admitted that the Ambassador had imported a total of four cars. Apart from the Lincoln, there was a Duesneberg – a sporting model that Joe Jr had bought in California at the urging of Gloria Swanson, his father's mistress – and two Cadillacs. He was unable to hide his enthusiasm for these beauties and, when Edward asked if he could see either of them, he looked shifty and said he had been told not to let anyone into the garage. However, when Edward produced a banknote, the chauffeur told him that he could have a quick look as no one was around.

He led him into the back of the garage and, switching on a light, revealed a magnificent Cadillac Sixty Special. It had been designed by William L. Mitchell, a protégé of the great General Motors designer, Harley Earl. Elegant but compact despite its size, it sported chrome-edged windows and squareback fenders. Edward's mouth fell open and he experienced a moment of disloyalty to his beloved Lagonda.

When he asked to see the other Cadillac, the one Washington had driven to Cliveden, he was told that it was being used to take the Ambassador to an event and was not expected back for at least a couple of hours. With expressions of mutual esteem, Edward and the chauffeur parted company. As he turned to go, Edward asked if his friend Mr Bishop lived above the garage.

'When I lunched with him the other day,' Edward said, trying to sound casual, 'he asked me to drop in on him but, to tell the truth, I can't remember the number.'

The chauffeur, who had obviously never been told that anyone using the phrase 'to tell the truth' was almost certainly lying, pointed to a door a little further along the mews but said he thought Mr Bishop had accompanied the Ambassador on his outing.

Edward thanked him again and went over to the door. There was no bell so he rapped on it with his knuckles and, to his surprise, the door swung open. He glanced right and left but for the moment there was no one in view so, taking a deep breath, he slipped inside and closed the door behind him. There was something about the place that made him sure no one was at home but he called out anyway. When there was no reply, he decided he might as well explore. He knew that technically he was house-breaking but, if Casey did return unexpectedly, he could say he was just looking for him.

There was a tiny entrance hall and then a steep flight of narrow stairs to the flat. As he stepped into the living-room, he saw that it was small but had been expensively modernized. The room, which stretched the whole depth of the garage below, was divided by a counter around which stood two or three stools. On one side of the counter there was a tiny kitchen and, on the side on which Edward was standing, a table at which six people could sit. At the far end, he saw a seating area with an uncomfortable-looking white leather sofa, a couple of armchairs, a glass-topped table and a radiogram.

He looked round, searching for something personal – photographs perhaps – which might give him a clue to Casey's interests and character. He saw nothing, which was in itself revealing. Here was a man who concealed his personality even from his friends.

Seeing a door which he presumed led into the bedroom, he went through it and was startled to find a large double bed with white silk sheets and a huge abstract painting on the wall behind it. He wondered whom Casey entertained between such luxurious – not to say decadent – sheets on that grand bed. He decided he was in the room of a practised seducer and it made his stomach churn. He pushed open the bathroom door and looked in. It was scrupulously clean with just shaving kit and a toothbrush in evidence. There was a cupboard with a mirror attached to the wall behind the basin. Feeling he had gone so far that he might as well go further, he opened it and saw a row of bottles, some containing pills and others fluids. He looked at the labels on two of the bottles and was shocked.

Returning to the bedroom, he noticed two framed photographs on the bedside table. One was of an elderly couple who, he guessed, must be Casey's parents and the other of Casey in his graduation robes. It seemed rather odd to Edward to have a photograph of yourself in your bedroom when you could look in a mirror if you wanted to be reminded what you looked like. It must, he supposed, have some special significance for him – perhaps a moment of success or optimism. The bedside table had drawers. He opened the top drawer and was momentarily startled to find it contained a gun – a Mauser pocket pistol – and some ammunition but, given that Casey was head of security at the embassy, he supposed they were official.

Edward decided that he had pushed his luck about as far as it would go and he had better make himself scarce before the owner returned. He had suspected Casey was not quite the clean-living defender of democracy he pretended. Tonight, when they met for dinner, he would do what he could to make him reveal his true self. How far was he prepared to go to protect his boss? Edward was inclined to think he would commit murder.

As he slipped out of the flat into the mews he thought he had escaped unobserved. He was wrong. The chauffeur who had told him where Casey lived had thought it strange to be asked so many questions and had hung around to see if the Englishman with the absurd accent was up to no good. He had seen him go into the flat and now he watched him leave.

*　　*　　*

238

Verity was in a fever of indecision. Fernando! How could she suspect this friend of hers from such dangerous days, her companion in arms, this principled fighter against tyranny? And yet he was Italian and the word was that Churchill's would-be assassin was Italian. He was going to Westerham. No doubt hundreds of innocent men and women went to Westerham every day. But why should *he* be going there? What possible motive had he for going to this sleepy Kent town if not to see Churchill? Perhaps he just wanted to talk to him . . . perhaps he had even been invited to visit Chartwell to report on the situation in Italy . . .

But what had he meant when he said to Alice Paling that he had an important job to do? And what . . . yes, most of all, what had he meant by the words 'Kill Claudio'? Verity had not read much Shakespeare but one could not be around Edward for any length of time without picking up famous quotations and she happened to know that this was Beatrice's shocking command to Benedick. It was that bizarre moment when *Much Ado About Nothing* lurches from light comedy to chilling revenge tragedy. As though you were in an aeroplane which suddenly plunges several thousand feet in a few seconds, those two words, 'Kill Claudio', signal a descent into hell and leave the audience with their collective stomach in their mouth.

She telephoned Edward's rooms in Albany but

Fenton said he was out and he had no idea when he would return. She left an urgent message for him to call her. She looked in on Alice who was now asleep on her bed. By confessing all to Verity, she had unburdened herself and could now sleep the deep, innocent sleep of the shriven. What to do about Alice? Because something needed to be done – of that she was certain. She could not be left to the untender mercy of some back-street abortionist. On the other hand, to have the child might ruin her life. She might be confined in some home for girls who had let down their sex and her baby taken and given to an orphanage. Verity had read about such things and was determined that silly, ingenuous Alice would not be one of those girls.

She would have telephoned Edward's friend at Special Branch about Fernando – what was his name? Colonel something – but he had never told her how to get in touch with him. It had never occurred to her that one day she might actually *want* to speak to him. Up to now, in her mind, he had simply been the man who persecuted the Communist Party instead of the real danger to society, the British Union of Fascists. What sort of traitor was she to turn over a comrade to the police? She could never do that. There was Pride, of course. She had at last managed to trust him, at least to some degree. But . . . it was stupid even to think of it. She knew she could never bring herself to telephone Scotland Yard and inform on a friend. And yet if something were to happen to Churchill . . . something bad . . . something she could have prevented, Edward would never forgive her. She would never forgive herself.

In the end, she dialled the operator and asked for the number for Chartwell. She thought she might try light-heartedly . . . apologetically, to warn the man himself. The butler answered and to her relief knew who she was. Mr Churchill was in the garden building a wall – could he give him a message? She wondered what message to leave – 'I think one of my friends in the Party is on his way to kill you'? She just couldn't say it. The butler seemed to understand her hesitation and asked if she would prefer to speak to Mr Thompson. For a second she did not know to whom he was refer-ring but then she remembered Edward saying something about Special Branch insisting that Churchill had a personal detective with him at all times, much against his wishes.

'Yes, I'll speak to him. Thank you.'

There was a wait of some minutes during which Verity was tempted to replace the receiver. Just as she was about to do so, Thompson came on the line and apologized for the delay.

'I was in the garden, miss. I try always to have Mr Churchill in sight but not to crowd him, if you see what I mean.'

His level voice soothed and reassured her. 'You know who I am, Mr Thompson?'

'Indeed, miss. You are Lord Edward Corinth's

fiancée. Mr Churchill introduced me to the gentleman when he was last here.'

'Very well then . . .'

'Yes, miss? Was there something you wished me to pass on to Mr Churchill . . . a message?'

'Well, I'm not quite sure . . . it may be nothing but . . .'

'But what, miss?'

'There's a man called Fernando Ruffino – a friend of mine,' she added stoutly, 'an Italian Communist. I heard he is coming to Westerham and I am worried . . . I have no evidence, you understand . . . that he might be . . . he might try to kill Mr Churchill.'

She had said it. Her horrible, unjustified suspicion was out. Had she betrayed an innocent man? He would be caught and deported or put in prison and it was all her fault.

Thompson was speaking and his voice was suddenly urgent. 'Miss Browne, why do you think he might be coming here?'

'He told his girlfriend that he had an important job to do and that he should be coming to Westerham and he said . . .'

'He said what, miss?' There was an insistence in his voice that she could not resist.

'He quoted Shakespeare – "Kill Claudio". It may be nothing. I can't think what possible motive he might have for wanting to kill Mr Churchill but I thought . . . I haven't been able to speak to Lord Edward . . . I thought I should tell someone.'

'You did right, Miss Browne,' Thompson said soothingly. 'Better safe than sorry. Don't worry about it. We'll deal with it but I'm afraid someone from Special Branch may want to speak to you. Will you be at your flat for the rest of the day?'

'I . . . probably . . . I'm not sure.'

'Thank you, miss. I must go now and see to it that, if the gentleman you mentioned comes here, we are ready for him.'

When Verity put down the receiver she still felt uneasy and anxious but thought she had, on balance, done the right thing.

CHAPTER 13

'So how did your night of dissipation with Casey go? What sort of nightclub was it? Was it very seedy? Do tell.'

'Sorry to disappoint you, V, but Casey cancelled at the last moment.'

'Why?'

'I'm not really sure. He said something about a crisis blowing up and he couldn't get away. To be fair he had warned me he was expecting to have a bad day.'

'But . . . ?'

'But he was so abrupt I wondered if by any chance he had heard I had been mooching around. Anyway, enough about that. V, I heard what you did.' He took her hand. 'I know it can't have been easy but you did what you had to do. I don't agree with Morgan Forster. There are times when you have to choose country over friendship.'

'You think I was right?' she asked, her eyes lighting up.

'Dearest V, of course it was. It was brave and it was difficult – like most right things are. I'm so proud of you.'

Verity tried to hide the tears that came into her eyes. 'So you don't want to postpone the wedding?' she said, her voice unsteady.

'Over my dead body.'

'Don't joke, Edward. I have a horrible feeling that we're not at the end of all this yet. What was that thing you quoted at me? "So shalt thou feed on death, that feeds on men . . ."'

'"And death once dead, there's no more dying then,"' he finished.

She shuddered. 'No more dying! If only . . .'

Several days had passed and still Chief Inspector Pride had nothing to report.

'You are convinced Casey Bishop is the murderer?' Edward asked.

'Aren't you?'

'Yes. I think Casey, or maybe Washington on his orders, killed Tom Wintringham and Lulu but I'm pretty sure Washington didn't kill Eamon Farrell. Fenton was there when Wooster found the body on the course. Washington seemed as shocked as the rest of us. What do you say, Fenton? Did you think Washington's shock was genuine?'

'I did, my lord. I am convinced his surprise at finding the body was unfeigned. However, might I suggest that perhaps he had killed Mr Farrell elsewhere and had not expected to stumble across his corpse at the eleventh?'

'Good point,' Pride said. 'The question then is who moved the body?'

Edward sighed. He suddenly felt very tired. 'Washington would not kill anyone without orders,' he repeated. 'Casey or Mr Kennedy must be behind all this.'

'You really think Kennedy would involve himself in murder? This isn't Boston, don't forget.'

'I'm not forgetting. I don't think Kennedy would *want* to be involved in murder but he might have been forced into it. Or – if not Joe Kennedy himself – then Casey may have taken it upon himself to protect the Kennedy family. Damn and blast! It's going round and round in my brain but I always come back to that.'

'A funny way to do it – protect the Kennedys by letting the old man trip over dead bodies all over the place.'

'I know. Maybe I've got it all wrong. I thought at the time that Kennedy's surprise at finding Farrell's body was as real as mine but now I'm not so sure. He was so keen for us to play that round of golf and, when we came to the eleventh, he said it was to be our last hole.'

Pride shook his head. 'But you can't explain why Kennedy would want to be anywhere nearby when the body of one of his closest associates was found. Furthermore, as you said yourself, Farrell was almost like a son to him. Would he have had him killed? I doubt it.'

'True', Edward conceded.

'And my hands are tied,' Pride said. 'I can't carry out a proper investigation. I was called in by my chief this morning and told that I must on no account harass Mr Kennedy. The political situation with regard to the United States is so sensitive that any hint that we were treating the Ambassador as a murder suspect would put American popular opinion against us just when we need President Roosevelt's support. To put it bluntly, if Joe Kennedy is behind these killings, I haven't a hope in hell of bringing him to justice.'

'What about Casey? Surely you can interrogate him?'

'I could if I were able to find him,' Pride agreed gloomily. 'I spoke to the embassy yesterday and they said – cool as anything – that he has taken leave of absence – a holiday on the Continent. They don't know exactly where. Can you beat it?'

'Damn! I've just remembered. I haven't told you. I found a bottle of Salvarsan in Casey's bathroom cupboard.'

'What the hell is Salvarsan?'

'It's an arsenic-based drug used in the treatment of syphilis. I noticed that it had been prescribed in Switzerland. Perhaps he has gone to consult his doctor.'

'Syphilis! You think Casey has syphilis?'

'I do. In his bedside cupboard I found a Mauser and a book by William Hinton on the treatment of the disease.'

'Syphilis sends you mad, doesn't it?'

'Eventually, Chief Inspector, if it isn't treated early enough.'

Edward ceased his pacing and stood staring out of the window. He had a vision of Casey's bedroom and it sent a shiver down his spine. How many women had he infected between those silk sheets? He took another step and then stood still again. Verity had had lunch with Casey. He was absolutely certain that it had just been lunch. He trusted her but what if . . . ? Without explaining himself, he went into the hall and telephoned Cranmer Court. He drummed his fingers on the wall as the phone continued to ring and Verity did not answer.

They both stood stock-still staring at each other as the persistent ringing of the telephone echoed round the flat. It went on for so long that Verity was certain it was Edward and longed to answer it but Fernando's black semiautomatic Beretta was pointing at her breast.

When the ringing at last ceased, she said, 'I had to do it. Mr Churchill is the one politician who has the guts to stand up to Hitler. If you had killed him, we might lose the war. You have spent a lifetime fighting Fascism, surely you understand?'

She spoke as calmly as she could but she could see that Fernando was possessed by a powerful cocktail of rage, fear and frustration. He had been on the run for two days and nights, sleeping rough, not daring to trust anyone. Finally, he had made his way to Alice's flat and accused her of betraying him. She had been badly scared but stood up for herself, pointing out that he had not confided in her what was the 'important job' he had to do.

'But I told you where I was going – *idiota!*' he had yelled and slapped Alice's face.

'I wasn't to know it was a secret!' she had wailed. 'Anyway, I didn't tell anyone . . . wait a minute, I did tell Verity Browne but she wouldn't . . . would she?'

Now he was determined on revenge. He needed to vent his feelings on someone whom he could blame for his failure but, underneath the rage, Verity thought she could detect relief. She was convinced that, whatever else he was, Fernando wasn't a murderer. She hoped she wasn't fooling herself.

'You meddling bitch! *Mio bambino, mia moglie!* They are in prison . . . my baby in prison! I cannot think about it without weeping. I have been tried by the *Tribunale Speciale* and sentenced to death. I have one chance – if I carry out this *assassinio* I will be pardoned and my family restored to me. They say that in the *Casellario Politico Centrale* my file is the longest.' He sounded almost proud. 'Now you understand why I have to do it. Why you betray me?'

'Oh my God! I knew there must be some reason . . . I'm so sorry but, truly, I did not betray you, Fernando. You never entrusted me with your secret. If you had, I would have told you straight away that I would have to go to the police. You are a patriot. I, too, am a patriot.'

249

It was not the language she would normally have used but she needed to make him understand and to do so she had to use high-flown words like patriotism – a word she normally distrusted.

'Shoot me if you like but you're not a murderer. I know you could never have killed Churchill. We must find some other way to get your family out of Italy. Tell me what happened. You went to Westerham but you were not arrested . . . ?'

'No, I saw all the police – they were checking every passenger – and I knew I had been betrayed. I thought it was Alice but she said she had told you I was going to Westerham. I knew then it was you.'

'You didn't hurt Alice? You know she is pregnant with your child?'

'I do not believe it! I was very careful . . .'

'Well, she thinks she is. She is seeing a doctor this afternoon unless you prevent her.'

Fernando suddenly threw down his gun, sank into an armchair and put his head in his hands. It was theatrical but she did not doubt that he was sincere.

'You are right. I could not have done it. I am not an *assassino*.'

Greatly relieved, Verity knelt down beside him and took his hands in hers. 'How did you plan to do it? Mr Churchill is well guarded.'

'I was going to knock on the door, explain who I was and ask to see him. Then I suppose I would have shot him.'

'But, even if you had done such a thing, how did you expect to get away with it?'

'They said there would be a submarine waiting for me off the coast but I have been thinking about it and I believe they would have let me be captured. I am a well-known Communist. The Party would be blamed for what I had done, whatever I said.'

Verity thought it was all too likely. 'Tell me, Fernando, did you have a code name?'

He almost giggled, as one can do when the situation is so serious that it is beyond normal reactions. 'Would you believe it – they called me Der Adler, L'Aquila, The Eagle. But I always knew I was more like Il Passero – the sparrow.'

She smiled weakly and stroked his hand as she would a child's. What should she do now? Telephone the police? No, she had done enough. There was no longer a threat to Churchill. Why should she persecute a poor, tortured man who had been forced to choose between his family and killing a politician? She knew Churchill well enough to be certain that it was the last thing he would want. Fernando had done nothing wrong. No, she would get in touch with David. It was his job to preserve the reputation of the Party. He must get Fernando out of the country. And Fernando's wife and child – what about them? She told him what she intended to do but he was apathetic. He had surrendered to fate. His resolve had vanished at the sight of those policemen at

Westerham. It was a blessed excuse for calling it off. As he said, he wasn't a killer and the Abwehr was foolish to think he might be, but how would he be able to live knowing that he had sentenced his wife and child to death?

A thought occurred to her. What if Fernando was being watched by a German agent? It was possible. What if – when they realized he was not going to do what he had promised – they decided to dispose of him? They could hardly risk him blurting out everything he knew to the British. What if they sent a replacement? One eagle had failed. Could they not send another? Well, one thing at a time. She must find David. She did not even know if he was still in the country. She decided to telephone George Castle. The Party had paid to have a telephone installed in his house and it was used by any Party member who needed help urgently. Mary answered the phone and listened in silence to what Verity had to say before telling her to stay where she was. She would find David Griffiths-Jones and ask him for instructions.

Verity looked across at Fernando and saw that he was almost asleep in his chair. The constant worry about the killing he had agreed to carry out, on top of several months of constant travel, the lectures he had given in so many towns, the knowledge that he was probably being watched by Special Branch and, perhaps, agents of OVRA and the Abwehr had taken their toll. He was exhausted. She managed to rouse him and half carry him into the bedroom where he slumped on the bed. She took off his shoes and jacket and immediately he fell into a deep sleep.

She felt her nervous energy evaporate and sat down in the armchair Fernando had vacated, staring without seeing through the window. She thought she would telephone Edward even though the effort of getting up and going over to the hall table was almost too much for her.

'V, is that you? I've been so worried. I've been trying to ring you but you didn't answer. Is everything all right?' Edward's anxiety made his voice high-pitched, almost strangulated.

'Not really. Could you come over here? I've got Fernando. He arrived with a gun.'

'A gun? Where is he now? Are you safe?'

'Oh yes, I'm all right. He broke down and cried. Now he's asleep on my bed.'

'But what . . . ?'

'He admitted he's Der Adler. He says I betrayed him.'

'Did he say why he wanted to kill Churchill? I thought he was on our side.'

'He was but they took his wife and child hostage.'

'Who have?'

'The Abwehr, OVRA – Mussolini's thugs . . . I don't know. Look, I can't tell you any more on the telephone. Just come over here, will you?'

'Stay where you are. I'll be there in fifteen minutes.'

It was more like thirty minutes before there was

a knock on the door. Verity woke with a start from a shallow doze.

'Darling V, are you all right?' Edward asked, clasping her in his arms.

'I'm all right, though it takes it out of a girl having a friend hold a gun to her bosom and threaten to pull the trigger.' She tried to speak lightly but Edward could see that she was suffering from delayed shock.

'He didn't do anything, that's the main thing.'

'No, but he's desperately worried. The Italian secret police are holding his wife and baby hostage. What can we do? We can't just hand him over to the police and forget about him.'

'No, of course not. Where is he?'

'In the bedroom, sleeping the sleep of the dead. We must help him, Edward. We can't let him be carted off to prison.'

'I know, but it might be safer for him if the Abwehr *think* he's in prison after being caught trying to carry out the assassination. We may have to resort to a little blackmail ourselves.' Edward thought for a moment. 'If our people at the Rome embassy explain that, unless wife and baby are restored to their loving father, he will stand up in an English court and tell the world exactly what he was asked to do and by whom – naming names . . .'

'You think that would work?' Verity was doubtful. 'They'll just say it's lies and point out that he's a Communist.'

254

'Mussolini hasn't decided yet whether to go in with Hitler as a junior partner in a war which might end in disaster for Italy or stay out. He won't want it to become common knowledge that the OVRA is just a cat's-paw for the Germans.'

'Well, it's worth a try, I suppose. And what happens to Fernando in the meantime?'

At that moment there was another knock on the door.

'Who could that be?' Edward asked sharply.

'David Griffiths-Jones, I expect. I telephoned the Castles and left a message for him. All this concerns the Party and Fernando is a member of the Party. I thought David might be able to smuggle him out of the country or something.'

There was another knock on the door and Verity went to open it.

'David, I . . .'

'Where is he?' Griffiths-Jones strode into the flat as if he owned it. 'Corinth – what are you doing here?'

The two men looked at each other with the intensity of schoolboys trying to outstare each other. Edward blinked first. 'We were trying to decide what to do with Ruffino. Apparently – if we are to believe him – he was told that if he did not assassinate Churchill, his wife and baby would suffer. I thought the best thing might be to broadcast the news that he had tried but failed and was now behind bars.'

'But he hasn't done anything,' Verity protested.

'Apart from planning to assassinate a leading politician, no. But surely you agree, David, it must be better for Ruffino if OVRA think he tried and failed to kill Churchill rather than discover that he didn't try at all.'

'But there would have to be a trial and he might say stupid things about . . . the Party,' David objected.

'Not necessarily . . . I mean, for security reasons the trial could be held in camera so no one – not the Party, not the British intelligence service, not even Mussolini – would be embarrassed. The Foreign Office still believe Italy might remain neutral if Mussolini is not provoked.'

David barked his dissent. 'No, the jackal will dog the heels of the wolf to get a share of the spoils. Your plan is all too complicated. I can get him out of the country tonight. That is unless you alert Mr Liddell and we're stopped at Dover.'

'Liddell? Who's he?' Verity asked.

She had been watching fascinated as the two men measured up to one another like boxers in the ring. Both were tall, good-looking and determined. She had slept with both of them but loved only Edward. She could not help feeling that they were tussling over her as much as Fernando and, if she were honest, though it made her uneasy, it also excited her.

'Ask your precious fiancé to tell you who Liddell

is,' David told her roughly. 'Though I don't suppose he will. He's been ordered to keep it secret, especially from you.'

'Guy Liddell is the head of one section of the intelligence service and, for obvious reasons, it is important that as few people as possible know,' Edward replied levelly, looking at David.

'Well, I think Fernando should decide how he wants to play this,' Verity said, putting to one side Edward's admission that he kept secrets from her.

'But before we talk to him,' Edward said, 'I'd like to ask David a few things about Tom Wintringham's murder. Was that your doing, David? Did you kill him and dump his body in the Blenheim Pavilion?'

'You're barking up the wrong tree there, Sherlock,' David sneered. 'I wasn't at Cliveden and, if I had been, why would I want to kill Wintringham? I hardly knew him.'

'You tell me why. Perhaps it was part of your plan to smear Joe Kennedy. After all, it was you who set up Lulu to blackmail him. You won't deny that, I presume?'

'I don't deny it. For good reasons, "for the sake of the country",' he replied with exaggerated emphasis, 'Kennedy has to go. He's doing everything possible to keep Roosevelt out of the war. Now, that's something you'll agree with, Corinth.'

'Yes, I do agree but there's no cause to stoop to blackmail. Roosevelt is no fool. He doesn't take much stock of Kennedy. He has other sources of information about our determination to stand up to Hitler.'

'So who did kill Tom and Lulu?' Verity demanded.

'Your friend Casey Bishop, of course. Why do you think he's skipped the country?' David answered her.

'But why?'

'I'm sorry, Verity, but I haven't time to play Holmes and Watson. Work it out for yourself. I have to get going. By the way, I should warn you that you will be disciplined by the Party – as I told you you would – for insubordination. You can't seem to understand that wiser heads than yours decide Party policy. It's not for you to question Party directives. I shall decide what you should or should not do. You are too much under the influence of this absurd aristocrat you say you intend to marry. Marriage and family are bourgeois institutions, outworn and outmoded. I urge you to think again.'

For a moment or two Verity was unable to speak. She had always known that one day she would have to face up to her position. She had to choose and she could no longer postpone that moment. She saw that both men were looking at her expectantly.

'I'm glad you raised the question of my marriage, David. I agree with you. I cannot be married to Edward and remain a member of the Party. In any case, I don't want to. Here . . .' She went to her handbag and took out her Party card. 'The Party I joined has been destroyed by people like you and the men in Moscow whose every word you believe and whose every order you obey without question. I joined a party of like-minded fighters for freedom and social justice. Maybe we were naive. I'm sure we were. We thought we could build utopia but instead we helped build a prison camp. It took me years – much too long – to understand what had happened. How we had been duped. How good men like George Castle and Harold Knight are being fooled or, worse still, used. When I first knew you, David, I admired you and I thought your ruthlessness was necessary if we were ever to defeat Fascism, but you have turned into a monster and it makes me unbearably sad.'

David, to Edward's surprise, did not try to interrupt her tirade. He listened as one might listen to a child stamp his foot and scream. He appeared not to have heard a word Verity said. Edward wondered if he would strike her but he remained icily calm, only saying in response, 'We'll talk about all this some other time. You are ill and don't know what you are saying.'

He strode over to the bedroom door and shouted, 'Ruffino, wake up! It's time we got you out of here.'

Fernando emerged from the bedroom dishevelled, badly in need of a shave, with that hangdog look of the school-boy caught in a prank which had just gone spectacularly wrong. As soon as Edward saw him gaze at David as though he were his father or dominating schoolmaster, he knew which option Fernando would choose. He would trust David to save him. He hardly listened to Edward as he suggested he might like to surrender to the police and spend a few weeks behind bars. When David said they could be in France in twenty-four hours, Fernando nodded happily. Verity sent him off to shower and shave with instructions to use the razor Edward kept in her bathroom.

When, after twenty minutes, he re-emerged looking much more his old self, Fernando embraced her warmly.

'Forgive me, *cara*, for being such a fool. I shall always think of England with love and gratitude, and I think of you as England. Please look after Alice for me. I should have left her alone but I can never resist a woman. It is my weakness.' He sounded almost proud to confess it. 'And Lord Edward . . . you are an English gentleman and I shall never forget how you have treated me. You could have given me to your police and I would have suffered . . . maybe died in their hands. *Grazie mille!*'

To Edward's embarrassment, Fernando proceeded to kiss him on both cheeks.

When at last David and Fernando had left, Verity turned to Edward. 'You keep secrets from me, do you? You know I can't marry you if you won't tell me who you work for. I have sacrificed – as you see – my Party, my life you could say. I expect to be repaid in the same coin.'

'I understand. You have my word. No more secrets. Come to bed and I'll tell you all about Liddell even if I go to prison for it but first I must make a telephone call.'

'A telephone call? Who are you going to telephone?'

'Liddell, of course. I can't allow David to spirit Ruffino out of the country. He has a few questions to answer before he goes anywhere,' he added grimly.

Verity looked at him with dismay. 'I . . . Is it necessary . . . ?'

'It's necessary,' Edward said and there was something in his face that stifled her protests before she could utter them.

CHAPTER 14

Verity had insisted on the most low key wedding that could possibly be devised. She had a horror of a press photographer capturing the moment when, against every principle she had ever espoused, she married her aristocratic lover. That day had come and although she had reluctantly agreed to a small luncheon party in a private room above Gennaro's in New Compton Street, where she and Edward had first dined *à deux*, she had insisted there should be only five witnesses at the actual wedding. They had finally agreed on her father – assuming he returned from Rome in time – their old friend, Tommie Fox, now a North London vicar, Edward's sister-in-law, the Duchess of Mersham, and Adrian and Charlotte Hassel. Edward knew that his brother, Gerald, was hurt that he was not being allowed to sign the marriage certificate but Verity had been adamant.

'He's never pretended to like me. He certainly doesn't approve of you marrying me and I'm simply not having him standing in a corner glowering at me. I am going to be nervous enough as it is.'

Edward had sighed but submitted. If he had to choose between offending Verity or his brother, there could be no question which of them had to take a back seat. Tommie, too, had been hurt because Verity had made him swear that he would not say a prayer or bless them or do anything that might imply she accepted a religious element to her commitment.

'You'll just have to draw on your reserve of Christian charity, Tommie,' she had said. 'I don't mind sitting in a church or cathedral and seeing Frank marry Sunita. I shall probably cry in the approved manner, but I've had such a rocky journey to find a justification for marrying at all that I just daren't make any other compromises without feeling the most awful hypocrite. You do understand, don't you, dear?'

'But I don't, Verity.' Tommie made one final protest. 'If you can't believe there is a God, then why does it bother you if I give you His blessing? I think Edward would like it.'

'No, Tommie, that's very underhand. "Get thee behind me, Satan." Not even for Edward will I ask a non-existent God to bless our union. If He wants to do something useful, why doesn't He do away with Hitler or Franco? If He does exist, He has so much to do that I don't want him wasting time on me. In that respect at least, I'm a lost cause.'

'Like so many of the battles you choose to fight,' Tommie had replied meanly. Seeing her face, he realized he had gone too far. 'I'm sorry, Verity. I shouldn't have said that. The fight for truth and honesty is never a lost cause even in our corrupt world. I beg your pardon.'

Even though she had accepted his apology, he could see that he had damaged their relationship and kicked himself for not respecting the sincerity of her views, however much he disapproved of them.

The next problem was what to wear. It was easy for Edward. He just wore a smart pinstripe suit, tie – a dull red not associated with any school, university or similar organization – and a red carnation in his buttonhole.

Charlotte and Connie had taken Verity off to Chanel. When she heard how much a custom-made outfit would cost, Charlotte had almost physically to keep her from bolting out of the door. Connie had to use all her powers of persuasion. She announced that she and Gerald would like to give her a wedding outfit since, as she said, 'You and Edward are quite impossible to give presents to but we all know that, if you have a weakness, it's for clothes and we want you to look your best on this rather important day. I know you want to stop everything spiralling out of control but you must give your friends and relations some pleasure. Don't deny us that just to satisfy some abstract principle.'

'And you want Edward to be proud of you,' Charlotte added deviously. 'I gather you aren't even allowing him to put a wedding ring on your finger.'

Verity blushed. 'Did he tell you that?'

'He mentioned it in passing,' Connie said.

'Well, I know you think I'm an idiot but for me it's a symbol not of commitment but of servitude and I really can't do it.'

In the end she was measured for a pink wool suit trimmed in shiny black leather and with gold buttons. The tight-fitting skirt emphasized her slim figure. Pink shoes and a pert little hat crowned with a pink feather completed the creation.

'Won't I look like an exotic bird or something?' she demanded, on the verge of tears. But when she went to try it on she could not but take pleasure in the way it fitted so perfectly and, examining herself in the mirror, she had to agree that she looked very much herself but different. It was, as Charlotte said, 'an outfit difficult to be sad in'.

To her surprise and delight her father appeared the day before the wedding and presented her with an interesting black box from Cartier. She gasped as she examined the three rows of perfect pearls within. Then she laughed.

'Daddy, they're gorgeous but I always said I despised girls in pearls waiting for their husbands to come home from the office.'

'Don't be ridiculous, child,' he said crossly. 'No one could ever imagine that you would stay at home for anything or anybody. You're my daughter, aren't you? I only hope Edward understands what he's taking on,' he added grimly.

'He does. He surely does,' she said, kissing him. 'Thank you, these are wonderful. Too good for me but, for this particular day, they are just what I need.'

However, Verity was given what she was pleased to call her best present on the morning of her wedding. Basil, her curly-coated retriever, had been brought up from Mersham for the big day. When he dropped a big juicy bone at her feet, wagging his tail frantically, she was hard put not to cry. She knelt while he nuzzled her affectionately, as if wanting her to know that he was her dog, however rarely she was able to be with him. Connie had tied a ribbon round his collar and Verity felt Basil understood that, for his mistress, this was a special day.

She had asked Edward not to give her a present. 'When we get our home sorted out, then you can give me something if you aren't already fed up with me,' she had said. 'I know I'm mad but, if you gave me a wedding present, it would somehow rub it in.'

'Rub what in?' he had inquired mildly.

'I can't really say . . . that you made me change my mind – that you won. Oh, I'm sorry! I didn't mean that,' she said, seeing a hurt look wipe the smile off his face. 'I love you, I trust you and, if I can live with any man, it's you, but still . . .'

'You feel you are surrendering something?' he

asked gently. 'Don't we always have to surrender something to gain something?'

'I suppose so but the only things I really possess are my principles and now I seem to be losing those. I'm determined to leave the Party and in marrying you . . . well, if I were a politician I would say, "How typical! She's said one thing and done another." Tell me you understand.'

'"Unhappy that I am, I cannot heave my heart into my mouth", as Cordelia says. I don't really understand but I do love you. All I can say is that a less complicated woman might bore me quite quickly. You sometimes madden me but you never bore me.'

The wedding itself passed so quickly that she could remember little about it except the registrar's evident disapproval that there was no ring and his insisting that Edward signed the marriage certificate with the pen provided which was filled with a special ink that did not fade. And she remembered the kiss he gave her when they were declared man and wife. It was the first time Edward had kissed her on the lips in public and she was momentarily embarrassed and then thrilled, kissing him back with enthusiasm.

After they had been congratulated by the witnesses, they stood with Basil on the steps of Caxton Hall and allowed themselves to be photographed by the press who had somehow discovered their secret. It wasn't quite as bad as Verity had feared. She could imagine the disparaging and faintly sarcastic stories that would appear alongside no doubt unflattering images of the two of them, expatiating on her hypocrisy at marrying an aristocrat. However, to her surprise, she found that she didn't care what people might say or write. She jutted out her chin pugnaciously but fortunately, perhaps, no one noticed. She looked at Edward, who she knew guarded his privacy fiercely, but he seemed unmoved by the intrusion of the press on this most private celebration. He nudged her and pointed to one of the photographers.

'Bandi!' she squealed, waving frantically. 'How . . . ?'

'I asked him to be here. I hope you don't mind.'

André Kavan, the celebrated war photographer, did not usually cover weddings but Edward had discovered that, fortuitously, he was in London and asked whether, as a special favour and as a surprise for Verity, he would take some photographs as they came out of Caxton Hall and join them afterwards at Gennaro's. Verity had not met him for two years and seeing him now brought back memories of the terrible days in 1937 when Guernica was razed to the ground by the Luftwaffe. Tears came into her eyes but she dared not cry and smudge her discreetly applied mascara.

'How wonderful!' she said, turning to her husband with a beaming smile. 'I couldn't have asked for anything better. I love you so much for thinking of asking him.'

Edward looked smug. 'I thought you'd be pleased. Now smile. Whether we like it or not, we're going to be plastered over the picture papers tomorrow.'

Strictly against the rules, Charlotte and Connie threw handfuls of confetti over them as they walked down the steps to the waiting Lagonda in which Fenton was to drive them to the wedding lunch. He had decorated the car with white ribbons and Frank and Sunita had insisted on attaching the traditional tin cans and old boots. For a 'quiet' wedding, Edward thought, it had been quite noisy and, somewhat to his surprise, he had not minded at all.

At Gennaro's, Freddy, the head waiter, pink with excitement, greeted them with much bowing and smiling. 'Lady Edward,' he said, ushering her into the private room. For a second or two, Verity could not think whom he meant before it dawned on her. The waiters lined the way resplendent in penguin suits complete with white gloves, and Edward suppressed a notion that they might all burst into song, like the chorus of peers in *Iolanthe*. Freddy's daughter, bursting with pride, presented Verity with a bouquet of white jasmine.

Gerald had suggested Claridge's or the Savoy but Verity and Edward had been absolute in their decision to celebrate their union in the place where it could be said to have begun almost four years earlier. She confessed to Edward in a whisper that

269

she had never been happier in her life. To be with the only man she had ever really loved and surrounded by thirty of their closest friends was her idea of a perfect wedding. She wished Frank and Sunita well of their grand celebration in Winchester Cathedral with hundreds of friends and acquaintances, many of whom they hardly knew, and tables groaning with expensive, and for the most part useless, presents but she knew she would have hated it.

She said to Adrian who was sitting across the table from her, 'This is just perfect. If I had to get married, this is exactly how it should be. I suppose I can't smoke a cigarette?'

'No, you can't,' he replied firmly.

'Well, I can't eat a thing,' she retorted, before finding that she was, in fact, starving.

Most of the guests, when they had admired her outfit and Edward's profile, directed their attention on Verity's father. Donald Browne was a highly successful barrister who could have made a fortune had he not chosen to appear in a succession of politically charged cases on behalf of trades unions, left-wing politicians and agitators including, on two occasions, the Communist Party of Great Britain. Although not himself a member of the Party he supported it both in the courts and financially. He bank-rolled the *Daily Worker*, the organ of the Communist Party, to his great cost but still managed to run a Rolls-Royce of which he was inordinately proud. He was frequently lampooned

by the *Daily Mail* and the *Telegraph* as a 'champagne socialist' and a Communist stooge who
undermined the 'values' that made Britain great,
but he took no notice. He was often abroad
advising on political cases and he had three times
the work he could deal with comfortably. Verity
had long ago accepted that, much as he loved her,
she would always take second place to his work
and had no illusions that, if some important case
had come up, he would, regretfully, not have been
there for her wedding.

But here he was, by some miracle, sitting beside
her and his presence made this day perfect.

'Are you very busy, daddy?' she asked.

'Of course. I was in Berlin last week trying to
get a friend of mine out of Dachau.'

'That's the camp near Munich?'

'Yes, it's a terrible place. Starvation, disease, even
torture . . . It chilled my blood.'

'Were you successful?'

'I was. I happen to be a friend of Winifred
Wagner. You know she's English?'

'The composer's daughter? No, I don't know
anything about her.'

'She's Wagner's daughter-in-law. She was
brought up in an orphanage – East Grinstead, I
believe.'

'How did she end up married to Wagner's son?'

'He was a homosexual – dead now. It was an
arranged marriage but it worked. She saved
Bayreuth.'

271

'Bayreuth? I've never heard of it.'

'It's a theatre Wagner built specially for his operas in the town of Bayreuth. Winnie runs it.'

'And is she a Communist?'

Her father laughed. 'Far from it. She's a personal friend of Hitler's and can ask him favours no one else can.'

'And she would help a Communist?'

'I don't know about that but she helped get my Jewish friend out of Dachau. She's convinced herself that "Wolf", as she calls Hitler, has no idea what is being done in his name.'

'And she's a friend of yours?' Verity was doubtful.

'I like her. She's a silly woman but her heart's in the right place.'

'But how can you like a Nazi?' she protested.

'There are a lot of people on our side who are no better,' he replied grimly.

'I don't believe it,' she said, knowing that she did.

'Take your friend David Griffiths-Jones.'

'David . . . ?' She felt her blood chill. 'What about him?'

'He's a ruthless man responsible to my certain knowledge for the death of many good men – all done in the name of the Party. I have been meaning to warn you about him. I heard the other day that he was involved in the death of that journalist fellow – Tom Wintringham. Did you know him?'

'Yes, he was a friend of mine. But, are you saying David killed him?'

Her father saw that she was upset. 'We shouldn't be having this conversation on your wedding day.'

'Just tell me how you know . . .' Verity was angry.

'I don't *know*. I don't suppose he did actually kill Wintringham. It's just a rumour but he was involved in some way. I shouldn't have repeated it.'

Before Verity could say anything more, Edward leant over and suggested this might be the time to propose a toast. There were to be no speeches at Verity's insistence but her father had been asked to propose the toast to the bride and groom.

'Don't be soppy, daddy,' she implored him as he rose to his feet but, of course, he was and by the time Edward had responded the tears were running down her cheeks.

CHAPTER 15

'Isn't this heaven?' Verity said, snuggling up to Edward in the huge bed.

They had wakened at the same time. It was either very late or very early because moonlight still shone through the gap in the curtains. They lay beneath a vast feather duvet – neither she nor Edward had ever slept under one before – which settled on them like a blanket of snow. They were tired after their journey but had slept lightly. The Rhätische Bahn, an extraordinary feat of engineering, chugs ever higher, over the mountains, through countless tunnels and a hundred or more bridges and stone viaducts, across freezing rivers and dramatic gorges. They had felt very alone and intimate in their first-class compartment as they embarked on this magical journey, their first as a married couple, but they had been glad to get to St Moritz at last. They had reached the hotel just in time for dinner but had not felt much like eating so they had had a bottle of wine and sandwiches sent up to their room. This night in a fairy-tale bed was the fitting culmination of a momentous few days.

Suddenly, feeling suffocated under the heavy duvet, Edward put her gently to one side, slid out of bed and went over to the window. He drew the curtains and looked out. He picked up his watch from the bedside table and was able to read it by the silver stream of light reflecting off the snow. It was four o'clock. He could see snowflakes falling across the window in soft, silent streams. His feelings, too, seemed to swirl about him. He knew they would settle, like the snow, but at this moment before dawn there was trepidation along with joy, doubt along with certainty, and pain along with pleasure. He was married to the woman he had wanted for so long but from whom he would soon be parted. He loved her but feared, deep in his heart, that she would tire of him. The gods had given him what he had asked of them but would his happiness turn to dust between his fingers? He told himself that it was madness to think this way. He was tempting fate. He knew that if he didn't snap out of it he risked losing all. And yet, he wondered, how many men had stood, as he was standing now, on the first morning of their honeymoon, tormented by demons?

He shivered. It was odd to be standing here quite naked yet warm looking out on such coldness. He could see a barn roof, its eaves seeming to bend under the weight of whiteness. The world was strange to him – made anew for him alone – and he must meet it with courage. He had made solemn promises to Verity and these must now be honoured. He would never have been happy without her. Now he must bear the pain of knowing that, in the coming war, he stood to lose her. Bitterness filled his heart and he pressed his forehead against the cold glass and closed his eyes until the pain eased.

Verity must have felt something of his turmoil because she flung back the duvet and came to him. She did not speak and he did not turn as she put her arms around him and laid her head against his back. He was so much taller that she could only cling to him like a child asking for comfort and giving it. At last – it was only a few seconds but it seemed an eternity – he gently prised her hands away and turned to look at her. He knew her so well but at this moment not at all. He stroked her face, between her breasts, down her stomach and she felt his hand explore between her thighs. Then he pressed himself to her and she felt his hardness. He lifted her in one graceful movement and carried her back to the bed.

As he made love to her, he felt the doubts and the pain flow from him. He did not close his eyes. She always said it was one of the things she most liked – that he looked at her while he made love to her. She said it showed he was sensitive to her needs and was not wholly absorbed in his own pleasure. Together, they came to a climax. Verity stroked him feverishly – scratching his back and leaving weals for which, in due course, she would have to apologize – feeling his hard muscular body as it bowed and bent over hers. At last, she let go a cry, half a sigh of regret that it was over and half an acknowledgement that she had been satisfied. He loved her.

It was after nine when the sun reflecting off the snow woke them. Edward was immediately alert, happy and energetic, the travails of the night forgotten. He splashed his face in cold water and then came back to turf Verity out of bed. She was less eager to meet the new day and hid her face in the pillows.

'Don't be such a bully,' she complained. 'This is supposed to be our honeymoon, isn't it? I know what happens on honeymoons. All my girlfriends have told me about it. You get brought breakfast in bed and you are left to . . . No, damn you, Edward . . .' He was sprinkling her with cold water. 'You beast!' She grabbed him round the neck and they wrestled together until the inevitable happened and he was drawn protesting back to bed where, under her tuition, he made long, languorous love to her.

'Enough of this, my girl,' he said at last. 'I don't intend to miss my breakfast and then you've got a skiing lesson.'

'Must I really? I'd much rather watch you,' she grumbled, burrowing back under the bedclothes.

'No, I'm sorry, V. We've only got four days. We can't stay in bed when the world is this beautiful.' He carried her to the window and showed her a

277

panorama of glistening white and she was enchanted.

'It's a fairy tale!' she exclaimed unoriginally. 'What's that droning noise?'

'I'm singing. I always sing when I'm first married.' He stropped his razor and covered his face with shaving cream. 'Boo! I'm Father Christmas,' he said, kissing her.

'Get off me!' she complained. 'You've made me all wet.'

It was unexpected, she thought, to find such pleasure in being naked together. Like children, they had no embarrassment about baring all to one another. Of course, they knew each other well so there was none of the shyness she supposed some young marrieds must feel about revealing their imperfections to each other. But still, it was something more. She thought it might be an expression of the honesty they had promised themselves. It was also, perhaps, the feeling that they had broken so many taboos, acknowledged and unacknowledged, that to be shy now would be absurd. Verity had not always liked her lovers to see her naked but Edward was different. She loved him unreservedly. She took pleasure in every part of his body and his few small imperfections amused and reassured her. He had hurt his leg, not so many months ago, in a fight to the death with one of the Nazis' most ruthless agents and the encounter had left him with an almost imperceptible limp. And there was a scar on his chest from a bullet wound that made her shiver whenever she touched it. She, too, had scars – the one on her forehead he sometimes touched, as if for luck – and other more intimate physical defects but, as Edward said, how boring perfection would be.

They were staying – courtesy of Colonel Moore-Brabazon – at the Kulm Hotel overlooking the St Moritzsee. Edward had read in his Baedeker that the large lake was too cold for swimming even in summer and in winter freezes solid – so solid in fact that horses race across it and the English play cricket on it. St Moritz is dominated by the Palace Hotel with its spectacular green-capped tower and the more solid, yellow, Kulm just above it. Behind soar the mountains, the most dramatic of all, Piz Corviglia, is ten thousand feet high. The most famous and fashionable winter sports resort in the world, St Moritz sits six thousand feet above sea level in the Engadine River Valley. Edward had been impressed to read that, at peak season, the town's population of four thousand is doubled by the influx of tourists – mostly English, American and German – who come to enjoy the settled weather.

Baedeker points out that the sun shines on average two hundred days in the year and heavy snowfalls – which cause avalanches in Austria and France – are unusual. It's no surprise that the English, who first 'discovered' St Moritz, were enraptured. It was the English – and Colonel

Moore-Brabazon in particular – who developed the sporting facilities and were instrumental in creating the Cresta Run. The Kulm was dedicated to the Cresta and, standing in the Sunny Bar waiting for Verity, surrounded by memorabilia of Cresta heroes, Edward decided he must investigate it, although the mere thought of hurling himself head first down a sheet of solid ice on a flimsy toboggan made him feel sick.

One of his friends, when he had heard where Edward was going, had told him that that minute on the Cresta Run was the most exciting of his life – 'better', he had added in a half whisper, 'than sex.' The Run was only a five-minute walk from the hotel and from what he could see, examining the photographs on the walls and reading the comments beneath them, it was the ultimate speed experience. Lying on your stomach on a wooden toboggan – known to enthusiasts as the wagon – with your chin just an inch or two above the unforgiving ice, it was possible to travel the run at over fifty miles an hour, which was faster than most cars.

When at last Verity appeared and they sat down to breakfast, the first people they saw were Moore-Brabazon himself and Joe Kennedy Jr Brab greeted them warmly and Edward haltingly expressed their thanks for arranging the holiday.

'Not at all, young man,' Brab said, beaming. 'Winston speaks very warmly of you and any friend of his I count a friend of mine. You know

Kennedy, don't you? He's one of our most promising riders.' They shook hands and Joe Jr said how delighted he was that they were in St Moritz at the same time while promising not to dog their heels.

'I know you'll want to be left alone but perhaps we could meet this evening for a drink and, if you felt like it, we could dine together?' Brab suggested.

After Kennedy and Brab had left and they were settling into their hot chocolate and croissants, Verity voiced Edward's thoughts. 'Is it just a coincidence Joe Jr being here, do you think?'

'I don't see why it shouldn't be,' he said carefully. 'We know he's a great sportsman and, if Moore-Brabazon is with him, it must all be above board.'

Rather to Edward's annoyance – he had hoped to be the patient teacher – Verity immediately hit it off with her instructor, Karl – one of those brown-faced, superbly fit athletes who looked good in goggles. Perhaps because she was small and had no fear of falling, she took to skiing with all the confidence and enthusiasm of a novice who had never seen a nasty accident on the slopes.

She would have skied all day if Edward had not insisted they stop for lunch. He had laid on a sleigh to take them to the charming little Stazer See beyond the town. The horses, decorated with bells and feathers, tossed their heads as the sleigh slid over the crisp snow which had hardly melted in the midday sun. Cuddled beneath the heavy blanket the driver had thrown over their laps, Verity relaxed and surrendered herself to the happiness of being looked after by someone she loved and trusted. When they reached the lake, they left the horses stamping, their breath steaming in the cold air, and entered a small hut built of pine and furnished with tables and benches hewn from logs. There they ate long, smoky sausages smothered in the light mustard of the area and drank the local beer. On the return journey Verity slept in Edward's arms and he felt as happy as he could ever remember.

When they arrived at the Kulm, she begged to go skiing again but it was almost four and getting cold so Edward was firm in his refusal. Instead, they walked about the town and indulged in creamy coffee and the most delicious chocolate cake Verity had ever tasted. Then they went to bed and made love and slept and loved again. She had thought that after so much food she would never be hungry but whether it was the air or the love, when the time came to dress for dinner, she decided that she might after all manage an omelette.

'Do you mind eating with Joe Jr and Brab if we run into them?' Edward asked.

'No, it might be interesting. After all, we don't want to use up all our conversation in the first few days of marriage, do we?'

She devoured vegetable soup and a veal chop – rather leathery to be sure but even shoe leather would have tasted delicious in the mood she was in now – while Brab told them about the Cresta Run.

'It's three-quarters of a mile long and has a drop of over five hundred feet, roughly the height of a fifty storey building. The track's about six feet wide and has an average gradient of one in seven with some bits as steep as one in two. It's solid ice all the way down or, as we say, from Top to Finish and it's watered every night so as to be virgin ice in the morning. I can never believe at this time of year that in summer it completely disappears and turns into grass. It has to be reconstructed every year by men with shovels. The important thing is that the Cresta Run is for amateurs,' he went on. 'There are races and cups – the Morgan Cup, for instance, and the Heaton Gold Cup and the Bott Cup which was first presented in 1905 and is the oldest of all, but there are no money prizes. It's all for the honour and glory. Guests are welcome, Corinth, so I do hope you'll have a go.'

'Can women do it?' Verity asked, predictably.

'Miss Wheble won the Bott Cup in 1908 but soon after that women were banned. It's just too dangerous.'

'Is it *very* dangerous?' she pressed.

'Very,' Brab replied breezily, 'It's easy to be knocked about – bruises, damaged fingers, that

283

sort of thing. Serious injuries are rare but not unknown. We can't use the Run the day after tomorrow because we're marking the death of poor old Capadrutt who was killed on the Bob Run, not the Cresta, thank God. So, if you want to have a shot at it, Corinth, you should go tomorrow. As it happens, it's a very good time to be here because last year the course was opened from Top.'

'How do you mean?' Edward asked.

'Well, for some years the Run started at Junction – look, I'll show you.' Brab pulled out his pocket map of the Run. 'Many races still do start there, particularly early in the season, but now we can start much higher, weather permitting.'

Edward examined the map. 'It looks frightening.'

'It is, but exhilarating. You see . . .' he pointed on the map with a stubby finger, 'you begin very steep, flatten out a little, then at Church Leap – the steepest part of the entire run – you can run right out of control as you slide up three steep banks. It's like jumping off a cliff and you have to rake hard if you don't want to break your neck. But if you survive to reach Shuttlecock, that's where the fun really starts. There's a sharp right-hander called Battledore which throws you into the low, left-hand turn of Shuttlecock. If you don't get into it high and early, centrifugal force will carry you up and over the edge. You have to ride well. There are no short cuts which don't lead to hospital. Unless you are pretty good, you can literally fly off the track at Shuttlecock or at Scylla

284

and Charybdis. I've often seen it happen, even with experienced men like Joe here. You have to remember that the Cresta is not a "slide" but a "run" that wants riding.'

'Gosh! Have you ever injured yourself?' Verity couldn't help asking him, thinking of Edward.

'Not badly. Despite what I said, if he's properly kitted out with helmet and gloves and so on, he'll be all right,' Brab replied reassuringly. 'You wear goggles, of course, and leather pads to protect your knees and elbows.'

'How do you steer the toboggan?' she asked faintly. It was a question Edward wanted to ask and he was glad Verity had asked it for him. He did not want to sound feeble.

'Well, you have heavy metal spikes on your boots which you use to slow yourself up – we call it raking – and you shift your body to steer. The further forward you are on the toboggan, the faster you go. It's huge fun, isn't it, Joe?'

'The greatest!' the young man said. 'You must have a go, Edward.'

After drinking several bottles of indifferent Italian wine and then brandy with their cigars, Verity and Edward said good night to Joe and Brab and went up to bed too sleepy to do much but lie in each other's arms.

'I have bad feelings about the Cresta Run,' Verity said, her voice muffled by Edward's shoulder on which she was lying. 'I forbid you to try it. You're too old.'

But Edward was already asleep.

In contrast to their first night, he slept deeply without dreaming, purring rather than snoring. Verity, on the other hand, lay awake for an hour thinking over what had been a perfect day. They had not discussed the murders. They had never mentioned the possibility of war and separation. She owed Colonel Moore-Brabazon for that. They had been content to listen as he recollected past triumphs and lectured them on the history of the Cresta Run. She thought about skiing and how she could get to love it – that moment of flying downhill hardly able to see or think but feeling utterly alive. And she luxuriated in the knowledge that she had done what she had resisted for so long. She had made the commitment to the man whose bed she shared and their lives were now totally entwined.

She nuzzled against him, tasting his flesh, and he stirred but did not wake. She recalled something he had quoted at her – it was an infuriating habit of which she had yet to cure him – 'For present joys are more to flesh and blood than a dull prospect of a distant good.' She couldn't remember who had said it but it was certainly what she now felt. And yet there was unresolved business. Perhaps there always would be. Only in fairy tales were the ends neatly tied up, the monster killed and the beautiful princess rescued by the prince to live happily ever after.

Just when she was drifting into sleep, she thought

286

of Casey and was instantly wide awake again. As David had suggested, he must have killed Lulu and Tom and probably Mr Kennedy's friend Eamon Farrell as well. But why? Edward had come up with motives and she had been convinced but now, in the loneliness of a sleepless night, they rang hollow. Casey had run off, disappeared, seeming to admit his guilt. But she couldn't get it out of her head that there was something wrong – that she and Edward had got something badly wrong.

Early the following morning they walked on to the bridge over the Cresta Run just beyond the hotel. For half an hour they watched as unidentifiable men hurtled beneath them on fragile-looking toboggans until Verity complained that her feet were getting cold and they went back to the Kulm for hot coffee.

'I absolutely forbid you to try it,' she said seriously. 'You'll only hurt yourself trying to show that you are as game as Joe Jr. You don't have to prove anything, at least not to me, and you're too old.'

Edward did not disagree. He had already, reluctantly, decided against attempting the Cresta Run. He didn't want to injure himself on their honeymoon but he worried that Brab and Joe Jr might think him a coward. 'Brab's older than me,' he said weakly.

'I don't care. He's an extraordinary man. You know he was telling me that he had the first pilot's licence?'

287

'So I'm ordinary?'

'Don't be silly,' she said impatiently. 'You know what I mean.'

'"You are old, sir. Let it satisfy you, you are too old"', he quoted, and, when she made no comment, couldn't resist adding, '*All's Well That Ends Well*.'

'Look, Edward,' she sounded exasperated, 'I'm only going to say this once – stop quoting at me. It just makes me feel under educated and inadequate, which I know I am.'

'Sorry,' he said humbly, suppressing an apposite quotation.

When they had warmed themselves they made their way to the nursery slopes and, under Karl's watchful eye, Verity skiied with an ease and grace which surprised even her. At last, she began to feel tired.

'You know, whether it's the mountain air or skiing or being married to you but for the first time in ages I really feel well.'

'I'm so pleased,' he responded, taking her arm and squeezing it. 'I've noticed it too. Your colour is better and you are breathing more easily. And you have given up smoking. I believe that's made a difference.'

'I wish you hadn't said that. I immediately felt a pang of regret. It was bad enough having to watch you smoke a cigar. If you offered me a cigarette now, I'd . . .'

'Well, I'm not going to,' he said hurriedly. 'Instead, I'm going to take you skating.'

'Skating! How wonderful!' They had passed the ice rink – the *Eis-Stadion* – the previous afternoon and Verity had asked if they could try it sometime.

For a few minutes, drinking hot spiced wine, they stood watching from the side of the rink and then – impatient as ever – she dragged Edward off to the hire skates.

'Skiing's easy compared to this!' she said, sitting down on the ice with a bump for the third time.

'Just hold on to me, V. Hey, don't pull me . . .'

They collapsed on the ice in a tangle of limbs. Verity in fits of laughter. In her present mood, everything was fun and nothing could hurt her. She was in a state of blessed forgetfulness.

When she thought she had got the hang of it she set off gingerly on her own, keeping as close to the barrier as possible. Edward let her go, feeling proud that this beautiful, spirited woman was 'his' – as far as she could ever be anyone's. He lost sight of her behind a group of skaters and was momentarily overwhelmed with fear, as though he were a parent who had lost a child in a crowd. It was quite absurd, he knew, so for a minute or two he practised turns and stops but, when she still hadn't appeared, he skated across the ice to check that she hadn't fallen and hurt herself. He reached the barrier on the far side but still could not see her. Panic rose like bile in his mouth and his heart thumped. It was not possible. Was this a repeat of the unforgettable, haunting incident the previous summer when she had been taken hostage and almost drowned? No, he would not even think about it.

Suddenly, to his huge relief, he saw her. She was with a man and they were talking earnestly. As he skated towards them, the man looked up and, seeing Edward, disappeared into the crowd. He thought he saw him press something into Verity's hand as he skated off. It was Casey. There could be no doubt of it. What was he doing in St Moritz and what had he got to say to Verity? A nightmare vision passed like a curtain over his mind. Casey was her lover. He had come to claim her, to steal her from him. They had been talking with the self-absorption of lovers. He had run off when he had seen him. It all added up.

No, he was being ridiculous, he chided himself. Hadn't she proved how much she loved him in bed that morning? But he was still racked with irrational, unforgiving jealousy. He tried to regain control of his emotions, like the reins of a runaway horse. It was much more likely, he told himself, and much more to be feared that Casey was trying to persuade her that he was not a murderer. Verity had always doubted the evidence which was, it had to be admitted, circumstantial. Edward, on the other hand, was convinced that he had fled London from guilt and for no other reason.

With a heart as cold as the ice below him, he slid up to Verity and halted with a spray of ice. She raised her head and seemed surprised and not altogether pleased to see him. 'Edward!' she exclaimed. 'Where did you get to?'

Instead of saying 'Wasn't that Casey I saw you talking to?' he held his tongue like some over-proud Othello – he had a vivid memory of Laurence Olivier as Iago at the Old Vic. Why should he question her? She would explain everything without him having to ask. But she did not.

At dinner that evening they ate alone, hardly exchanging a word, and that night they did not make love. Neither of them remarked on the fact that this was the first since their wedding that they had not done so but both felt it. Neither slept well and, in the early hours before dawn, he did take her – roughly and without joy. She did not resist him but he knew she felt nothing but discomfort as he entered her.

After breakfast, during which she made a great effort to throw off her air of preoccupation, Verity reminded him that Karl was giving her a private lesson on the nursery slopes while he went off with a guide to attempt a tricky 'black' run. His first thought was to cancel and spend the morning spying on Verity. He immediately checked the impulse. He was ashamed of himself. If not now, when would he ever trust her? The idea that she might betray him was ridiculous and to try to protect her when she had not asked for protection might end in disaster. She must have a plan and, if he disrupted it without knowing what it was, he might put her in more danger. Even if he did try to find out what she was up to – if she had arranged another meeting with Casey, for instance – was it practicable? She would see him. Casey would see him. There was nowhere to hide on the nursery slopes and she would want to know what he was doing. When he confessed, as he knew he would, her fury would be corrosive. Their marriage was based on trust and, whatever he did, he must not undermine it.

So, reluctantly, he departed with his guide to a distant north-facing slope leaving Verity with Karl. When she kissed him goodbye, he thought she might, after all, ask him to stay with her but she did not.

The skiing was difficult and even dangerous for someone of his age who had not skied for several years and he was aware of his guide's concern that he was clearly struggling. Just after midday, he was grateful when the guide suggested they had done enough. Although Edward had managed to stay upright and was feeling more confident, his legs and thighs hurt from the strain he was putting on under-used muscles. However, one good thing had come out of it. There had been no time to brood on what Verity was up to.

They went to a small log cabin serving sausage in a bun which hungry skiers washed down with beer or *glühwein*. There his guide left him. Edward parked his skis, removed his woollen hat and gloves and stepped into the dark interior. He was almost blind after the brightness outside but a pleasant girl in a dirndl took his order. He took his sausage and beer outside and sat on a bench in the sun. It would have been a moment of pure happiness had Verity been sitting beside him. As it was, though his body was warm, he still felt cold. Restless, he got up from the bench and took his beer to the rail. A dread of something to come spoilt his enjoyment and disturbed his equanimity. The view was breathtaking. The snow, stretching like a linen tablecloth down the mountain, was speckled with the figures of skiers carving lines of grace and beauty on the pristine white. Looking upwards towards the mountain tops he saw grandeur and purity. The peaks appeared unsullied and unapproachable, and the rocks stood out black against the all-encompassing white. The air was so cold and pure that it almost made him giddy.

Reluctantly, he took his empty tankard back into the cabin. He contemplated ordering a second beer but decided that, coupled with the champagne air, it would make him drowsy. As his eyes got used to the gloom, he saw a couple in the corner, heads bowed towards one another. He thought at first that they must be lovers. Then, with a start of recognition, he realized that it was Verity and Casey. As he watched, she leant forward and took his hand.

Edward stumbled back out on to the wooden balcony feeling quite faint. His worst nightmare had come true. He had witnessed a secret assignation.

293

They must be lovers. In his bitterness, he vowed he would have revenge. He would have justice. Recovering a little, he decided that, whatever Verity might say, he must challenge her. Anything was better than not knowing. Then, if she admitted that Casey Bishop was her lover, he would seek him out and . . . He wiped his forehead with his hand as he always did when he had worked himself up into a fever. He re-entered the cabin but there was no sign of them. Had he been hallucinating? Had he seen what he imagined he'd seen? Yes, he had. He went and retrieved his skis. He would search them out. They could not have gone far. He would find them.

CHAPTER 16

Verity knew she ought to have been more surprised than she had been when Casey appeared beside her on the ice rink like a genie out of a bottle. The fact was she *thought* she had seen him the day before in a bunch of skiers, mostly novices like herself. He had been so muffled in a woollen scarf and hat, goggles covering his eyes, that she could not be sure and he had quickly dived out of sight when he caught her looking at him. She had not said anything to Edward because, for some reason, she did not feel threatened by Casey's presence here of all places. She knew he must have followed them to St Moritz and she also knew that he would make himself known to her when he was ready. The more she thought about the murders, the more she felt uneasy about pinning them on Casey. True, he was the obvious suspect. He had opportunity, and his association with the Kennedys might have provided him with motive, but even so . . .

Then, on the ice rink, there had been very little time but he had said to her that she had to believe he was innocent and that the letter he pressed into her hand would explain everything. He asked her to meet him at lunchtime the next day and told her where they could talk without being observed. He had disappeared as quickly as he had arrived. Edward had skated over to her immediately after Casey had left her but she was fairly sure that he had seen nothing. Even though he had seemed unusually silent that evening, she put it down to his sensing her own unease. No doubt he had recognized that something was amiss but he was sensitive enough not to mention it, for which she was grateful.

The letter, which she had read in a cubicle in the ladies' lavatory attached to the ice rink, was short but long enough to confirm what she already suspected. According to Casey, it had been David Griffiths-Jones who had killed Tom Wintringham, Eamon Farrell and the wretched Lulu. He asked her to meet him, without telling Edward, in the log cabin restaurant at the top of the second chair-lift at twelve o'clock the next day when he would prove it to her. He said that David was also in St Moritz and would 'seek her out' as he put it. She must be watchful. She knew as soon as she had read Casey's note that she would meet him as he had asked even though she was aware it could be a trap.

If, on the other hand, David really was the murderer, she alone must make him pay the reckoning. David had been her political mentor and she was his creature. If he wanted to kill her, it would not be too difficult to engineer a fatal accident, or he might not even bother trying to disguise her death. The murderer had not tried to pretend that the other deaths were accidental. She would feel a sudden, stabbing pain and there would be a knife in her neck. Whatever happened to her, she must not involve Edward. This was her battle, not his. Too long she had known that David was ruthless and cruel with no belief in the principles which had brought her into the Party and which he himself might once have held. Too long she had made excuses for him. Too long she had procrastinated.

It had been easier than she had imagined to persuade Edward to leave her with Karl on the nursery slopes while he went off to try a black run. She had explained to Karl that she had to meet a man without her husband knowing and had blushed when she saw him add two and two together to make five. He had seemed rather surprised, not so much that this attractive girl had a lover – many married women he taught to ski had a lover and he was often persuaded to be that lover if the girl was pretty or rich – but because he had really thought Verity and Edward were genuinely in love and was disappointed to be proved wrong. Verity, reading his mind without difficulty, decided not to try and explain. It was all too complicated.

After the lesson, Karl escorted her to the chair-lift and left her with a look of regret. He thought it a shame that, if she were really silly enough not to be satisfied with her aristocratic-looking husband, she would not settle for him.

She entered the cabin uncertain of what she would find and began to wish that she had not been so determined to follow up this particular 'investigation' without Edward. When her eyes had adapted to the dark, she saw Casey in a corner reading the *New York Herald Tribune*. He rose courteously when she went over to him but she saw that he wasn't quite the cocky, self-satisfied embassy official he had been when they had lunched in London. His hair was not as well brushed, his eyes were red-rimmed and his hand shook a little as he lit a cigarette for her – she just had to have one if she was going to do what she had decided was necessary.

'Why are you here?' she demanded.

'Why am I here in Switzerland or here in St Moritz?'

'Both.'

'I had to come to Geneva to see a doctor. I've got . . . well, it doesn't matter what I've got . . . but I needed some sort of cure. Then I saw Griffiths-Jones.'

'You saw David in Geneva?'

'Yes, I was expecting him. I had left a trail for him to follow because I *wanted* him to come after me. I figured it was much easier for us to slug it out in Switzerland than back in England under the bright lights. We both knew that the police and the rest of them were watching our every move. He was waiting for me at the railway station in Geneva and I let him follow me to St Moritz. I knew he planned to kill both of us, you and me.'

'Me! What do you mean? We're both members of the Party. He's not my enemy. Perhaps you mean Edward?' Verity said disingenuously.

'No doubt he would like to kill Edward but it's you he's after. That's why I had to get hold of you – to warn you.'

'How did you know Edward and I would be here?'

'It was in the newspapers that you were honey-mooning in St Moritz.'

Verity recalled Edward's annoyance on the train when he had opened his paper to find it reported that the 'happy couple' were to spend a few days at St Moritz on honeymoon. He had made rude remarks about *The Times* turning into a gossip paper.

'By that stage, I don't know who was following who. I bought a ticket for St Moritz and he followed in my footsteps. He knew I would want to warn you of the danger you were in. And now I have.'

Crepi il lupo – kill the wolf. Fernando's phrase echoed in her mind. 'But David . . . ?'

'He's your murderer, not me. Do you want me to explain?'

'Of course I want you to explain.'

'Well, here goes then.'

She said very little as he told her how he had been set up by the man who hated capitalism, America, Americans and the Kennedys in particular. David had made sure that the three dead bodies had all turned up in close proximity to Joe Kennedy and his family. He had succeeded in making it obvious – almost too obvious – that Kennedy was connected to his victims.

'Griffiths-Jones wanted Joe out for what you might call patriotic reasons but beyond that, he had come to believe that the US of A was the epitome of everything he, as a Communist, hated. America is capitalism incarnate and I don't disagree with him. Where I do take issue with him is in believing that the Soviet system is any better.'

'How do you know all this?'

'I've had my suspicions for months, even before Wintringham was murdered. All my informants had led me to believe that the Communist Party – and especially Griffiths-Jones – were determined to bring down Mr Kennedy. Now I don't pretend the old man's a saint but it was my job to keep him safe. I may have let things slide a bit too long but when first Wintringham was killed at Cliveden and then Lulu, who we were pretty sure was out to blackmail Joe, I knew I had to make my move.

'Anyway, after Wintringham was murdered, I worked out a plan of action with Eamon Farrell but Griffiths-Jones got to him before I could get to Griffiths-Jones. Eamon was one of the good guys but he made the fatal mistake of underestimating the enemy. He arranged a meeting – I'm not sure where – without telling me and confronted him. Griffiths-Jones never hesitated. He killed him. His death hit us hard, Joe and me, and I swore to him that I would avenge it. I decided on a face-to-face meeting on neutral ground. So, as I say, I lured him here. Yesterday we met up near the ice rink. He seemed almost – what shall I say? – drunk with power. He had got away with three murders and he seemed to think he was some kind of sword of justice. He didn't deny anything. In fact, he seemed almost uninterested when I accused him of murder. I got the feeling he thought murder was a triviality.'

'A triviality!' Verity shivered. 'But why did Tom have to die? To be honest, I don't mind about the others – not so much, anyway – but Tom was a good man.'

'He was also a good journalist. He had known Griffiths-Jones in Spain and became convinced that the Soviet-financed Communist Party had done more to destroy the Popular Front than the Fascists. He saw many of his friends "liquidated" for opposing the Party and identified Griffiths-Jones as the author of what he regarded as the great betrayal. I don't suppose this was entirely fair. No doubt Griffiths-Jones was only obeying orders from above but Wintringham made it his personal crusade to expose what was happening to the party he had loved. Unsurprisingly, he couldn't get anyone to print the story and that was why the *Daily Worker* was reluctant to employ him.'

'So it wasn't because of his wound?'

'That was just a convenient excuse. Anyway, rightly or wrongly, he blamed Griffiths-Jones for getting him fired as a foreign correspondent and determined to pursue him until he had incontrovertible proof that he was a murderer.'

'David knew about this?'

'He did and he warned Wintringham to desist. When he refused, his fate was sealed. Wintringham discovered that Griffiths-Jones was determined to smear Mr Kennedy – he met Lulu and wormed it out of her what she was supposed to do – so he went to Cliveden to warn him. You being there was a bonus because he thought that, if he couldn't get to Kennedy, he could tell you and you would relay his message.'

'You make it sound as though you talked to him.'

'I did. He tried to get to Joe but got me instead. He told me everything and I'm afraid I didn't take him seriously enough. I said no one would believe Griffiths-Jones if he alleged that the Ambassador used prostitutes and even if they did believe him, no newspaper would print the story. You can imagine how I blamed myself when we found him murdered. I was sure then that I knew who the killer was.'

'Oh God. I only wish you had confided in Edward. We might have prevented the other deaths.'

302

'I didn't trust him and he doesn't like me, and I don't blame him. I'd stolen his girl once before and he must have thought I was trying to steal you.'

'But that's ridiculous!'

'Thank you, Verity. It makes me glad to hear you say that,' Casey responded with a wry smile.

'No, but I mean, I like you . . . and in other circumstances . . .'

'Don't worry. I knew I could never get you into bed and, quite frankly, I didn't try that hard. You see, I'm not . . . I'm not very well. You had TB but I've got something worse.'

'I'm so sorry. I didn't realize.'

'Hardly anyone does, though I think Edward found out when he burgled my apartment. That's one of the reasons I wanted to keep clear of him. I just pray he never sees us together and suspects . . .'

'So Tom was killed because David feared that he would interfere with his blackmail attempt?'

'He just knew too much and Griffiths-Jones must have felt he had no choice but to get rid of him. He feared Wintringham had already told you what he suspected or worse, told Edward.'

'But he hadn't!'

'No, but he had told me and I had told Eamon. The afternoon you arrived at Cliveden, Griffiths-Jones followed Wintringham and killed him as he approached the house. He used the thin-bladed poniard he had learnt to kill with in Spain. It was quick, silent and much less easy to trace than a gun. It was also rather dramatic. Don't forget, he wanted the press to tell the story the way he wanted it told with Joe Kennedy as the villain. For the same reason, he decided – almost literally – to muddy the waters by setting fire to some of Wintringham's clothes and dropping them in the swimming-pool. He then dumped the body in the boot of his car – or rather Channing's – he had been hiding in Channing's cottage so he could keep a close eye on Lulu. He drove the car down the drive – it was dark by then and no one was about – and left the body in the Blenheim Pavilion. What he didn't know was that we were exploring the grounds but that worked to his advantage. Kick and Joe Jr found the body almost immediately.'

'But why did he move it – the body, I mean?'

'As I say, he wanted to add drama to the story, which he knew the newspapers would appreciate. He wanted reporters to get interested in the Kennedy connection with the murder, and the fact that Joe was staying with the Astors at Cliveden was great. The Cliveden Set is already regarded as the enemy so a conspiracy theory was there for the making by any imaginative journalist.'

'Edward jumped to the conclusion that the murderer had used the Ambassador's car to transport the body but he was wrong. The broken spectacles really were the Ambassador's as Washington said,' Verity mused. 'But why did Lulu have to die? Surely she had done everything that had been asked of her? She had seduced Joe . . .'

'Yes, but Griffiths-Jones discovered to his fury that she had "fallen in love" – or what she thought was love – with Jack Kennedy. In any case, he had the compromising photographs of Lulu with the old man. If she was then found murdered – what a story that would be for the press. The government would hardly be able to suppress it, however inconvenient and embarrassing.'

'He used her and tossed her away like a dirty handkerchief,' Verity said bitterly. 'But why did he take her body to Cliveden? Wouldn't it have been better to have left it near the residence if he wanted to embarrass Mr Kennedy?'

'He did. I found Lulu's body – almost tripped over it as a matter of fact. Jack tells me everything and, when he found she had vamoosed, he telephoned and asked me to go after her to see she came to no harm. I was too late. If only I had been a few minutes earlier, I might have saved her.'

'You found her dead? You swear to me that you didn't kill her?'

'I do so swear. Griffiths-Jones killed her.'

'But why did you take her body to Cliveden?'

Casey looked a bit sheepish. 'I felt I couldn't just dump her in the river – I might have been seen for one thing but . . .'

'But?'

'But I guess I felt sorry for the poor kid. The Kennedy family hadn't treated her well and maybe she wouldn't have died if Jack hadn't thrown her out. You knew she was sleeping with both the old man and his son?'

'How could I not? You left Jack's watch on her when you dumped the body.'

'Sure, that was careless but I thought it right that poor Lulu should be found somewhere she might be treated with respect. I thought the Astors would make sure she was looked after. I guess it was foolish but . . .'

'No, I think you were right.' Verity looked at him with a new respect. He did have feelings after all. 'So David killed her because she had disobeyed his orders and let Jack Kennedy seduce her?'

'Yes, and because he had no more use for her. He was waiting for her outside the residence. I guess he couldn't let her run around in the state she was in. God knows to whom she would have blurted out the truth.'

'So he killed her?'

'He must have hoped it would look as though I had done so in order to protect the old man.'

'It was plausible enough,' Verity admitted.

'I know. I don't blame Edward for being fooled. I guess I might have been. Then I made a big mistake.'

'What was that?'

'I felt I needed some advice on how to handle the situation, which I could see was rapidly running out of control.'

'That was when you told Eamon Farrell?'

'Yes. He was very close to me but his loyalty, first and last, was to the old man. I asked him if he thought I should tell the British police what I knew. He advised me not to. Without telling me, he decided he would confront Griffiths-Jones. He was too angry to think clearly. Don't forget, Eamon owed Joe Kennedy everything and he loved Kick although "love" doesn't go far enough. She was his star and he worshipped her. That he was homosexual and knew that she would never be his wife did not affect his love for her. This, he believed, was the moment when his loyalty to the family would be tested. But Eamon was no match for a practised killer, and Griffiths-Jones stabbed him. Leaving his body on the golf course was just another attempt to implicate Mr Kennedy in something the newspapers would love. A third death, he must have thought, would surely destroy Joe's reputation and he would have to resign. That's when I knew I had to disappear and draw him after me. I had to meet him on my terms. I dropped some hints that I was going to Switzerland to see my doctor.'

'Oh my God! I knew David was ruthless but I had no idea he had gone mad.'

'Is he mad? I don't know if he's mad or just a typical product of the Soviet system. Friendship, family . . . it means nothing to those people. They only care about the Party and the Great Leader. Well, there you have it – my story. It's hardly believable, is it?'

'I believe it,' Verity said firmly, taking his hand. 'You may have saved our lives but, you know, I've got to have it out with him. I can't go on with my life until I do. I can't walk around always expecting David to jump out at me.'

'I thought you'd say that,' Casey said excitedly, 'so I've made a plan. Will you trust me?'

Why should she trust him? Casey thought, trying to put himself in her shoes. Ought she not to fear him rather than Griffiths-Jones? He could declare himself to be innocent until he was blue in the face, blame everything on Griffiths-Jones, but he could not prove it. He knew he would not believe his story if he were Verity. He must somehow get them face to face so she could hear it from Griffiths-Jones' own lips, but, of course, that would be very dangerous. He scanned her face anxiously.

'What do you want me to do?' she said at last.

'So you do trust me?' he said, the relief in his voice almost palpable.

'I do, Casey. I know David has always hated Edward and only tolerated my relationship with him because he thought I could spy on his friends. When he found out we were getting married, I think he realized for the first time that I had gone over to the enemy.'

'And have you?'

'I don't think so. I'm still a Communist at heart but I've come to believe that the Party itself is no longer the one I joined. People like David have betrayed the ideals we had.' Verity spoke sadly but she had never been a sentimentalist. She would not hang on to dreams for comfort. She would rather face reality, however ugly. 'So you are convinced David intends to try and kill me?'

'I'm afraid I am, yes,' Casey said bleakly. 'He no longer trusts you. He thinks you betrayed O'Rourke to the police for one thing, but the main point is you know more about him than almost anyone. He simply can't afford to let you live.'

'I see.' She suddenly felt very cold.

'And . . .'

'And what? Tell me, Casey.'

'He would never acknowledge it but he thinks he loves you. He's certainly deadly jealous of Edward.'

Verity did not want to think about it. It sounded absurd . . . mad . . . She took a deep breath and turned back to Casey. 'So what must we do?'

'He knows where you are staying. He'll be watching the hotel and waiting for you to return. He'll want to catch you on your own – without Edward. I suggest you go along with it. Maybe, if he doesn't approach you, look out for him and act surprised. Take him somewhere quiet and let him tell you why he's in St Moritz.'

'Isn't that rather dangerous?' She could just imagine what Edward would think of the plan.

'Come outside. I've got something for you but I can't hand it over in public.'

Behind the log cabin, he looked round to make

sure that no one was watching. 'Take this.' He took out of his pocket a small, sleek, black pistol and handed it to her. 'You won't need it because I'll be close by and when, or if, he tries any rough stuff I'll jump in and . . . you know, stop him.'

'I'm not sure. It all sounds rather vague.' Verity looked at the gun and then at Casey. 'I'm not very good with guns. How does this one work?'

'Take the safety catch off . . . see . . .' he showed her, 'and then aim and pull the trigger.'

'Is it loaded?'

'Of course, but you won't need to use it.'

'I'm still not sure . . .'

'Well, you could always run away,' Casey said calmly, 'but I thought you said you wanted to have it out with him.'

'I did. I do. You don't think it would be better to wait for Edward?'

'No, I don't. He won't come near you if he sees Edward.'

'He'll be most awfully cross if I don't tell him about this. He is my husband, after all,' she added for no good reason.

'You don't need to worry. I'll be there and you said you trusted me.' Casey sounded reproachful. 'Take Griffiths-Jones up to the top of the Cresta Run. There's a pavilion at the start where no one will see you. I'll hide behind a pillar.'

'Won't there be lots of people around?'

'Not today. There's no racing today as a mark of respect for some fellow who died recently.'

310

'Yes, I remember. Brab mentioned it. You're right,' she said, suddenly coming to a decision. 'This is my battle. I don't want to put Edward in danger.'

'Don't forget that he thinks I'm a murderer.'

Verity's eyes widened. 'But you're not, are you?' she said, shrinking back. Before he could answer she answered for him, 'No, you aren't. I believe you are a true friend.' She shook her head as if to clear away the confusion she felt. 'Let's get this over with.'

'Good girl! Then you can go back to London with Edward and live happily ever after. You deserve a little happiness.'

She stopped in her tracks. 'But what's the point of getting David to incriminate himself if there's only me and you to hear it? I mean, what's my word against his?'

'I've thought of that.' Casey sounded excited. 'I've managed to get hold of a clever new machine our technical people have come up with.'

'What machine?' she asked flatly.

'It's a wire recorder. A very small one but it works just as well as one of those big machines you had to hide under a bed or something. You wear the wire round your neck and switch it on by pressing a button on a wire in your pocket. He'll talk and you'll record. Simple.'

'And what if he suspects?'

'He won't.'

Verity was silent for a moment and then sighed

heavily. She had a horrible feeling in her stomach that something would go wrong but what was the alternative? 'All right. I can't leave here with nothing resolved, as you say. I'll do what you suggest but just be nearby, will you? To tell the truth, I'm afraid.'

'No need to be, I promise you. I have *my* revolver,' he said, patting his pocket, 'and I'm a trained shooter.'

'I wanted to talk to David anyway. I want to make sure he's understood that I no longer consider myself a member of the Party. I tore up my Party card in front of him but I'm not certain he noticed,' she added with a grim little laugh.

CHAPTER 17

It all went according to plan – but whose plan, Verity wasn't sure. They skied back to the village and stopped off at Casey's hotel, hardly more than a bed-and-breakfast. He smuggled her up to his room and fitted her with the tape recorder. It was a clumsy machine despite what he had said and made odd bulges under her clothes.

'I can't wear this,' she said at last, tearing the wires off. 'I'm sorry, Casey, but it's bad enough having a gun in my pocket. All these wires . . .'

'All right then,' he said, seeing she had made up her mind. 'I'll wear it and hope I can get near enough to record whatever you can get him to confess. When we leave here, you go first and I'll trail you. For all we know, we may already be being watched.'

When she arrived at the Kulm, she could not see David so she parked her skis and went to have a drink on the terrace. She had been there ten minutes and was beginning to think he would not show. The adrenalin stopped pumping and her eyes closed. The sun was still on the terrace and she had an almost overwhelming desire to sleep. She hadn't slept much the night before and all the unaccustomed exercise and fresh air was soporific. Her anxiety had left her. It was her fate to meet her enemy today, at this place, and she would not avoid him.

She suddenly realized the shadow David had cast over her for so many years. She didn't see him for months and then he would turn up and require her to do something she found . . . distasteful was a feeble word but that was often all it was. He never asked her to commit a crime but there was always something underhand and mean about what he proposed, and it was always 'for the good of the Party'. She knew now that she could no longer believe in the Party. Friends, whose probity she could not question, had returned from Moscow with terrible stories of persecution, torture and plain murder. And the victims were not just political enemies but totally innocent, loyal members of the Party who had been – what was the word? – 'denounced' by neighbours or so-called friends. There was no trust left and the utopia she had once imagined the Soviet Union to be had never existed. The Revolution had been just another false start on the road to the egalitarian society she yearned for. Communism had become yet another tyranny, as vicious and ruthless as that in Germany. It hurt her to admit it but she was no coward and she had to face up to it. Her 'truth' had become a lie.

She felt, rather than saw, David sit down beside her on a wicker chair. The sun was behind him and she had to shade her eyes to make out his features. He was so handsome and, as he looked at her with an expression she could not read, she felt a moment of regret. How easy it would be to surrender herself to him and worship at the altar he had set up. He was wearing dark glasses so she could not see his eyes. As if he could read her mind, he took them off and looked at her without saying anything.

'I thought I saw you. Did you come specially to see me?' she inquired calmly, though her heart was pounding.

'How like you, Verity, to think that the world revolves around you. No, of course I didn't come to Switzerland especially to see you. I had business in Geneva.'

'Party business?'

'What other business would I have? You think I might turn into one of those fat businessmen . . .' He gestured to a party of skiers who had just come on to the terrace with their women and were shouting at the waiter to bring them drinks. 'Come for a walk with me. I have something to say to you.'

'Can't you say it here?'

'No, I can't. I can't hear myself above this noise.' And it was true that the loud, braying voices of the men and the screams of the women were ugly and intrusive. 'Let's walk up beside the Run. There's no one about today.'

'Yes, let's. As it happens, I wanted to speak to you, David, so I'm glad you found me.'

They walked in silence for the ten minutes it took them to get to Top Hut – an octagonal wooden pagoda with a single entrance a yard or two from the start of the Run. About twelve feet wide with benches along the walls, it had a small stove in the centre to warm riders waiting their turn but today this was unlit. Apart from a dart-board on one wall, there was no other furniture. A few toboggans lay scattered around.

'It's strange to be here, David, because this is so like the pavilion at Cliveden where you dumped Tom Wintringham's body after you had killed him.'

He looked at her properly for the first time. 'So Casey's been telling you a tale, has he?'

'You deny you killed Tom, then?' Verity spoke almost wearily, as though she could hardly be bothered to listen to his lies and excuses. 'It was for the good of the Party, was it?'

'You always were a little idiot, Verity, but I tolerated you for – yes – the sake of the Party. You were useful despite your love of the bourgeois life which ought to have disgusted you.'

'There was a moment when I thought you loved me,' she could not resist saying, almost wistfully.

'How pathetic!' he sneered. 'A week or two of not very good sex and you think it's love. I never loved you and I never pretended to. How could I love someone as selfish, snobbish and thoroughly rotten as you?'

She was stirred to anger. 'Don't call me rotten. I joined the Party to fight Fascism in Spain and at home and you used me, as you used so many of us, to build a new tyranny. It is you and the Party that have gone rotten. I never thought I would be ashamed to call myself a Communist.'

Now it was David who was angry and there was something snake-like in the way he hissed at her: 'Your infatuation with your pet aristocrat has led you to this. Do you know what we do with comrades who have betrayed the Party?'

'I have betrayed only myself,' she replied, jutting out her chin. 'Yes, I do know what you do with your enemies. You torture them, imprison them and persecute their family and friends.'

'And then we kill them,' David said, drawing a knife from the pocket of his jacket.

'There it is! Did you use it in Spain? The assassin's poniard, the coward's weapon, the stab in the dark. How many have you got? Did you buy a quiverful because you must need them often? That's how you killed Tom, isn't it? And poor, stupid little Lulu, and Eamon Farrell who showed a loyalty to his friends you couldn't possibly understand.'

David said nothing but the light in his eyes said it all. He was pure hatred, she thought and she suddenly felt sorry for him. He really did not know what it meant to love. He had no friends. He was a creature of this horrible, hateful world he had helped create. Knowing he meant to kill her, she ought to have been frightened. She ought to have run away or screamed. Instead she felt quite calm as she stood in this strange ice house and thought of that cold, shrivelled heart. How did you talk to a man who did not know how to love, only how to hate? He had dedicated himself to an organization which had dehumanized him. He was to be pitied. Perhaps he saw the pity in her eyes and could not stand it because he grabbed her and, as he did so, he felt the gun in her pocket. Holding her in a vice-like grip with one arm, he extracted the gun and looked at it with contempt before throwing it into a corner.

He laughed. 'That was Casey's, was it not? Well, I shall deal with him next. Is he skulking outside? He is? Good.'

Suddenly, Verity no longer felt fatalistic. Fear flowed through her veins and she shouted, 'Let me go!' She struggled but he held her tight. 'I was going to shoot you but I couldn't bring myself to do it,' she panted. 'Shouldn't one shoot a mad dog?'

At that David laughed again and this time it sounded more genuine. 'How typical! You can't even manage to do something so simple as pull a trigger. Your bourgeois sentimentality stops you doing anything worth doing. You're useless. And you know what we do with the useless?' He raised his hand and the long thin knife glinted against the light from the ice. For a second he was dazzled. His hold on her weakened and, with a huge effort, she wrenched herself out of his grasp and fell to the floor. Putting the knife back in his pocket so that both his hands were free, David took a pace towards her, lifted her to her feet so that she had her back to him and felt for his knife.

At that moment, Casey appeared at the door with his gun in his hand.

'Not so fast, comrade,' he shouted. 'Drop the knife and let Verity go. You know I won't hesitate to kill you if you don't.'

David stared at him as though he hardly recognized him. He hesitated before very reluctantly letting go of Verity, and Casey reached out to her with his free hand. 'I see I was wrong about you, Casey,' he said with a half-smile. 'I told you I would let you run back to America if you didn't interfere. I had an idea I was being too generous. Now you have interfered so you too must die.'

'Oh yes?' Casey replied, almost gaily. 'But who has the gun? It is you who cannot escape. In this beastly world of ideas we have made, what could be more horrible than the fanatical idealist? Instead of people, you care only for ideas and theories. Your utopia – if, God forbid, it ever came into being – would be hell on earth. You may despise America but it stands for freedom – for the fight against your sort of tyranny.'

Verity never knew what would have happened next if Edward had not materialized behind them. Would Casey have shot David? She thought not unless he had sprung at him with his knife. Edward took in the situation and immediately jumped to the wrong conclusion. He saw Casey holding Verity against him, a gun in his hand. He saw David, apparently unarmed, standing in front of them. It all happened in a moment. With a hard blow to Casey's arm, he sent his gun clattering across the floor. Verity screamed and stumbled to one side. David stepped forward and plunged his knife in Casey's chest.

'No, Edward!' Verity's despairing cry came too late. 'It's David. He tried to kill me and Casey . . . oh God!'

Not caring that David had withdrawn the knife and was now standing over Casey as though transfixed, she knelt beside the dying man. 'Casey! Please . . .'

He was trying to say something but blood filled his mouth and silenced him.

Realizing the terrible mistake he had made, Edward went for Casey's gun but, by the time he had picked it up, David had vanished. Edward went to the door and watched helplessly as David threw himself on a toboggan which had been left at the start of the Run. Edward saw him kick off and gather speed down the first steep slope. In seconds he was out of sight but Edward knew that, without spikes on his feet to slow him or a helmet and goggles, he could never survive.

He turned and saw Verity cradling Casey in her arms. 'I'm going after David,' he shouted to her but he knew that there was no hurry. David would reach his journey's end long before he could get to him.

When Edward arrived at Shuttlecock he found, as he had expected, a knot of people staring down at a crumpled body splayed out beside the track. It was a miracle that David had got as far as he had.

Joe Jr happened to be one of those who had witnessed David's final moments.

'Edward! What happened? He came out of nowhere. It was all so quick. For just a second we saw him on the ice. I knew at once he was going too fast. There was nothing he could have done. Do you see, he wasn't even wearing a helmet? His wagon leapt thirty feet in the air before falling back on top of him. I'm afraid his neck's broken. He must have hit the ice bank at seventy miles an hour. Poor guy – do you know him?'

Edward knelt beside David but, as Joe Jr said, there was nothing to be done.

'I knew him, yes,' he said grimly. 'His name is David Griffiths-Jones and he has just murdered Casey Bishop. Will you be a good fellow and go to the hotel and call the police? I've got some unfinished business back at Top.'

He found Verity as he had left her, rocking backwards and forwards with the lifeless body of the young American in her lap. Gently, Edward went to her and dropped down beside her. 'David died on the Run.' He gave the news starkly without trying to spare her.

'No more dying,' she murmured. 'No more death. I can't bear any more death.'

CHAPTER 18

'I guess I owe you an apology, Lord Edward,' Mr Kennedy said, wriggling in his chair with discomfort. He wasn't a man who found it easy to apologize. 'I didn't tell you everything I knew. I guess I muddied the waters. And I should have let that kid, Lulu, alone and maybe she would have been alive today. I guess women have always been my weakness.' He spoke as though he were confessing to liking chocolate too much. 'And when I tumbled to it that you were working for the British secret service, I jumped to the conclusion that you were trying to smear me but I know now I was wrong. I'm sorry.'

Edward was in a forgiving mood. He understood how difficult it must have been for this stubborn man to say 'I'm sorry.'

'Don't mention it, Ambassador. We all make mistakes. I was led to believe that Churchill's would-be assassin had a connection with the American Embassy. He did not, as both you and Casey Bishop told me. I thought Casey was a killer but I was wrong. When I found him with a gun in his hand I jumped to the conclusion that he was about to kill Verity. I was wrong again and, as a result of my foolishness, Casey died and Verity might also have been killed.'

He could not admit that for a few mad moments he had believed Casey was Verity's lover – that was a secret he would take to the grave – but he forced himself to face the fact that his judgement had been affected by his jealousy. He felt compelled to continue his confession.

'I was already half demented at the thought of losing her. She seems to have forgiven me but I can never forgive myself for letting Casey be killed in front of my eyes. I've been wrong all along. I'm so disgusted with myself that I have decided to give up "investigating" crimes. I had an idea I was good at it but now I realize I was fooling myself. Hubris and the gods have punished me.'

'You're too hard on yourself, my boy,' Kennedy said, putting an arm round Edward's shoulders, 'but I don't say it ain't the truth. I suppose it's no comfort but the doctors had given Casey only a few months to live. That durned disease! Even though he looked as good as when I first knew him, it was eating him up inside. They tried everything but I'm told there's no cure for syphilis. He wouldn't have wanted to . . . you know, to deteriorate.'

'Don't try and make excuses for me. I know I got tangled up in a web of lies. Fortunately, Verity saw more clearly than I.'

'And Eamon Farrell?' the Ambassador inquired

sadly. 'I don't really understand why this man Griffiths-Jones – was that his name? – murdered him.'

'None of us guessed that Griffiths-Jones was hidden in Dr Channing's cottage while we were staying at Cliveden. Channing, though not a Communist, was his cat's-paw. Casey told Farrell everything he suspected – that Griffiths-Jones was orchestrating a smear campaign against you with a view to having you recalled to Washington – and Farrell went after him. He was too angry to be careful and I fear he paid the price. He loved you like a father and he died trying to protect you. A noble fellow. Anyway, Griffiths-Jones saw us go off to play golf that afternoon at Huntercombe. I think he must have seen Washington put the clubs in the boot of your car and maybe asked him where we were playing or perhaps he simply followed us.'

'With Eamon's body in the trunk of his car?'

'I'm afraid so. He must have been holding his breath that we wouldn't give up before the eleventh hole. It was a long way from the club-house and perfect for his purposes with a quiet road nearby leading to Nuffield along which he could escape when he knew that we had discovered the body . . .'

'But if we had been better golfers we might never have found Eamon's body!'

'Perhaps he counted on Lord Astor's dog discovering it even if we didn't. We can be sure that, one way or another, he would have made certain that we found the body.'

'Hmm,' Kennedy mused. 'But you solved the mystery in the end.'

'On the contrary,' Edward replied with feeling. 'I ought to have done because Fred Rooth, one of the Cliveden gardeners, telephoned me to say he thought he had identified the car that had carried Tom Wintringham's body to the Blenheim Pavilion.'

'Whose was it?'

'Channing's. As I didn't know that Griffiths-Jones was hiding in Channing's cottage, I jumped to the conclusion that it was Channing who had driven the car that night. Casey was cleverer than me. He worked out who was behind Tom's death. He was suspicious of Verity when she came to interview you. He found out – it was no secret – that she was a member of the Communist Party and suspected she had an ulterior motive for wanting to become friendly with you. He did some digging and identified Griffiths-Jones as her – what shall I say? – her superior in the Party. He marked him down then as a dangerous man. I had long known that Griffiths-Jones was quite unscrupulous but it never occurred to me that he might be a murderer.

'I may say that Verity never did anything that wasn't above board – never betrayed a confidence – but Farrell did not know her as I do. He believed she was out to do you harm. In fact, she consistently refused Griffiths-Jones when he asked her to do anything she thought was wrong. That was what infuriated him – that and the fact that she decided to marry me after all. She was sleeping with the enemy and that he couldn't tolerate. In his view, she was a bad comrade. She'd betrayed Danny O'Rourke. She wouldn't obey orders. In short, he no longer had a use for her.'

'He'd have killed her too?'

'For certain,' Edward said grimly. 'Did I mention that she has resigned from the Party? No? Well, she has, for which I am very grateful.'

'But how did Casey know that Wintringham had anything to do with Griffiths-Jones?'

'Tom went to Cliveden to warn you that Griffiths-Jones planned to blackmail you. He never got to see you but he did see Casey and Casey told Farrell. They discussed most things.'

'I see. And you decided Casey was the killer?'

'I did. I was pretty sure it wasn't Channing even though it was his car at the Blenheim Pavilion. I didn't think he would have the guts for one thing and, as I say, I jumped to the conclusion that Casey must have been driving it. I was quite wrong. It hurts me to admit it but I was jealous. I thought he might try to seduce Verity as he had once, long ago, stolen the first girl I thought I loved. He was very good-looking, very charming. I should have trusted Verity. I *did* trust her but jealousy's an odd thing. It clouds the mind. I could say to myself a hundred times, "I trust Verity absolutely" and mean it but still be jealous. My sympathies lie with Othello. It didn't help that Verity never really believed Casey was a murderer. I just thought she was protecting him.'

'So Eamon, Casey and Miss Browne all worked it out before you did?'

'They did. That's why I am now going to retire from sleuthing and devote myself to something less demanding.'

'Like?'

'Sir Robert Vansittart thinks I may be some use in the Foreign Office . . . some sort of trouble-shooter. I don't quite know yet what he has in mind. I have an appointment with him after my nephew's wedding.'

'Well, I guess, Lord Edward, we may see each other again. I hope so. I'm not an admirer of English aristocrats as a rule – arrogant and stupid I find most of them, but I'm prepared to make an exception of you.'

'Before I go, may I ask you one more thing?'

'Shoot. I owe you.'

'Did you know Danny O'Rourke?'

'I did. I knew him for what he was – a man of violence. I had some dealings with him in Boston a few years ago but he was never in my employ. I told the police everything I knew about him.'

'Ah! I'm glad of that. I didn't think you would support the IRA.'

'I support Irish independence but not through violence on the streets of London. By the way, talking of the aristocracy, my daughter Kick seems to think she's in love with young Billy Cavendish. I've told her, he's a nice boy but she can't marry him, For one thing, his family wouldn't allow him to marry an Irish Catholic with no "pedigree", I think they call it, so I'm not too worried. She says if I won't give my permission she'll elope. I think she's nuts but she won't listen to me. She has an idea that you might be able to help her. She wants to come and talk to you. Would you do me a favour and knock some sense into the girl? She seems to think highly of your common sense but I can't see it myself – specially not after what you have just told me.'

There was just a suspicion of a twinkle in the old man's eyes.

'I'd be delighted. I have a high opinion of all your children – those whom I have been privileged to meet, I mean – but Kick is very special.'

'I'm glad you think so, Lord Edward,' Kennedy said, getting up from his desk. 'I would echo your sentiments in regard to my daughter. Miss Browne – Verity – is also a very special person. I don't say I would care to be married to her. I have had all the adventure I want in my life.' He winked. 'Gloria Swanson was a firebrand but that's one hell of a girl you've got yourself. I just hope you know what you have let yourself in for.'

The wedding was all pomp and magnificence. Winchester Cathedral was ablaze with candlelight and the assembled gathering of friends and relations of both families filled the nave. As the bride processed to the altar on the arm of her tiny, rotund father, the Maharaja of Batiala, who was almost bursting with pride, Edward shook his head in wonderment at the ways of fate. Just a couple of years back, when he had introduced Frank to Sunita at Lord Louis Mountbatten's house, Broadlands, he could never have imagined that the daughter of his old friend would one day marry his nephew and that the future Duke of Mersham would be half-Indian. Watching Sunita process up the aisle, her long train afloat in a cloud of children – bridesmaids and pages – he was struck by her tranquil beauty and the way she carried herself, proudly but with the supple grace of an athlete.

He had no doubt that she would make an ideal Duchess and lead Frank along the right path to true happiness if the good Lord allowed him to survive the coming conflict. Indeed, there was an unspoken feeling among those who had received the coveted invitations that this was probably the last grand society wedding before the war and who could say whether there would be any such when it was over. As the congregation craned to catch a glimpse of the bride, gold and silver saris glimmered and glistened among black morning coats and the less subtle confections of Bond Street dressmakers.

Edward and Verity watched Sunita take her

place beside Frank at the altar, her beauty a fragile beam of light in the darkness at the heart of the great church. To Verity, it seemed unbearably poignant – as though she was watching some ancient sacrificial ritual. It was not what *she* had wanted but she understood that Frank saw it as his duty to his father and his ancestors and a public statement of his love for Sunita. At least, she thought, this was no arranged marriage. Sunita had entered into this elaborate ceremony in love with Frank. Verity had no doubt that she would do her duty and bring forth heirs to the dukedom, that the Duke would love and cherish her and the Duchess would protect her against the unreasonable demands made upon her by society.

Edward had knelt before the service, his face in his hands, and prayed fervently that his nephew would survive the coming storm. He had seen the tragedy of the many thousands widowed by the last war with Germany and the many thousands more who never married because the men they might have loved lay dead in Flanders' fields. And yet he did not pray that Frank be spared the trial before him. He would prove himself in the fire as so many of his ancestors had done. No man could escape his fate. He could only face it with courage and hope, in the knowledge that he was doing his duty and offering his country his life. Edward prayed, as he always prayed when he prayed at all, for the soul of his brother – another Frank – who had died in the first days of the Great War. Frank had made the sacrifice he had never been required to make and the knowledge humbled him.

When she reached the altar, Sunita let go her father's arm with a loving smile and passed her bouquet to one of her bridesmaids. She raised her veil and it was as though the whole congregation held its breath. She turned to Frank and gave him a smile that left him speechless. Then she caught sight of Edward and Verity just a few feet away in the choir stalls and smiled at them as though to say that this was also their marriage. Verity's eyes filled with tears and she gripped Edward's hand fiercely as though she would never let him go.

Sunita's voice was strong enough to echo down the nave as she repeated her vows. When the bishop had declared them man and wife, Frank kissed her gently and respectfully on the lips and the congregation rustled its approval. Then, at last, it was over and the bride and groom walked slowly down the aisle to the West Door to the triumphant trumpeting of the thunderous organ. Verity, who normally hated churches and religious pageants, was little more than a pool of tears. As she and Edward slowly followed after the Duke and Duchess and the Maharaja and Maharani, she could not help but recall that she could have had all of this had she wanted and she hoped Edward did not feel cheated.

Mersham Castle was at its most splendid for the

party that followed. The Great Hall was decorated with branches of evergreen and blue cedar, and orchids from Mersham's hothouses. As it was still cold, a fire blazed at one end of the hall, huge logs sending flames high into the great chimney. Torchères on every ledge and three huge chandeliers hanging from the rafters bathed the guests in soft candlelight. Much hilarity was engendered by the children from the *Kindertransport* as they ran joyfully among the guests, upsetting champagne glasses and chasing after Basil who seemed to take pleasure in this friendly persecution.

After the bride and groom, Verity and Edward were the most sought-after as friends congratulated them on their marriage. Verity had, with Connie's blessing, invited several comrades who survived remarkably well the sacrilege of being guests of one of England's premier dukes. George and Mary Castle had come, even though they had been shocked and horrified by David Griffiths-Jones' death and Verity's decision to leave the Party. Alice Paling was there, happily pregnant even if she were – at least for a little while longer – short of a husband. Leonard Baskin stood shyly beside her and Verity hoped he would not mind being a father to another man's child.

Verity had also invited Tom Wintringham's widow, Sheila, but she would not come without Jimmy Friel and, though he sent Verity a cartoon he had drawn of her as a wedding present, he could not bring himself to come to Mersham

Castle. Verity respected his principles and did not press him.

Guy Liddell had been invited and, to Edward's surprise and pleasure, had appeared at Mersham – despite the international situation – about an hour after the party started. Edward took him to the gunroom for a private conversation and, when they had discussed other matters for a few minutes, asked what he had decided to do with Fernando Ruffino.

'It's all been rather satisfactory,' Liddell told him, sounding almost smug. 'As you know, our most important task is to identify every German agent in this country so that, when war breaks out, we can put them behind bars or turn them into double agents. Ruffino is ideal material. We sent him back to Italy last week with instructions to give himself up to OVRA immediately and confess to being a British agent. He will tell them he only agreed to spy for the British in order to get out of prison but that, in reality, he's an Italian patriot and had no intention of doing so.

'I heard today, as a matter of fact, from my man in the embassy in Rome, that it seems to have worked – so far at least. The Italian authorities have hailed him as a hero and he's even met Mussolini who attached a medal to his chest. His wife and son have been restored to him so he's a happy man. Now I'm hoping that the Abwehr will step in and decide to train him as one of their agents and then return him to England. We know very little about how the Abwehr train their agents so anything Ruffino can tell us will be most useful. They have a secret training camp at the Villa de la Bretonnière outside Nantes but we don't know much about what goes on there.'

'Well, I hope he's not as confused as I am as to whether he's on our side or not,' Edward remarked. 'Der Adler had, after all, nothing to do with Kennedy or the American Embassy.'

'No, that was a false trail.'

'So it was pure luck that we hit upon his identity?'

'I hate to admit it but it does so often comes down to luck in our business. It was certainly lucky that you were courting Miss Browne and told her enough about your mission for her to recognize him.'

'We owe her a lot, don't we?'

'We do, and England has every reason to be grateful to her.'

'Can I tell Verity that?'

'I will tell her myself.'

'But surely . . . ?'

'I can let her into a few secrets now she's no longer a member of the CP.'

'So, she's one of us now?' Edward put in, sarcastically.

'Precisely!' Liddell said, smiling. 'I like your girl, Corinth, but – if you haven't realized it already – let me tell you she's going to lead you a hell of a dance.'

'Why does everyone tell me that? She's just a

strong-minded girl when it comes down to it, not a Gorgon.'

'Of course!' Liddell said, taken aback by this spurt of anger. 'I only meant . . .'

As they lay in bed after the party, exhausted but happy, Edward asked Verity what she thought of Liddell.

'I liked him,' Verity confessed. 'He said I was to be congratulated for finding out what Fernando was planning and putting a spoke in his wheel. By the way, do you tell him absolutely everything about us? I'd like to think that you at least keep our sex life secret.'

'I don't tell him everything – only what he needs to know,' Edward responded guiltily, wondering if Liddell did indeed know about their sex life.

'Well,' she said, pinching him, 'I'll forgive you this time but no more secrets. You promised, remember?'

'I promise.' Edward hesitated but he had to ask. 'What do you feel about David?'

'I'm glad he's dead,' she said flatly. 'A great weight has fallen away from me. I never knew how much I feared him. Do you think it was suicide?'

'How would I know? I don't think so. It wasn't in his nature. I think he just took one risk too many. He sacrificed himself for the Party. It wasn't an ignoble death.'

'And it was quick.'

'Yes, I hope my end will be that sudden.'

'Don't talk about that.' She shivered. 'We're just beginning aren't we?'

'A pact then,' he said, taking her hand. 'No gloomy thoughts and no secrets.'

'No more secrets, husband,' she agreed, kissing him.

Frank and Sunita were married on Saturday, 11th March, and on 15th March Hitler entered Prague as conqueror and raised his standard over Hradzin Castle, the ancient palace of the Bohemian kings, and the republic of Czechoslovakia ceased to exist. In Britain, all leave for the armed forces was cancelled and Frank had to join his ship after the briefest of honeymoons.

Verity went to see Lord Weaver at the *New Gazette*. As many of his reporters were about to be called up – unlike in the previous war, conscription was brought in even before war broke out – he welcomed his star foreign correspondent back with open arms.

'I was sorry I couldn't come to Mersham for the great party. The Prime Minister wanted me at Chequers,' he bragged, 'but Van said it was a great event. I hear you are no longer a member of the Communist Party?'

'I'm still a Communist,' Verity said, rather too aggressively. 'In fact, I think it's the Party which has left me.'

'Well, be that as it may, it makes my life easier. I'll be able to send you to places where you might not be too welcome as a Party member. I'll be in touch.'

As they shook hands, he added wickedly, 'How's that *husband* of yours?' but she did not rise.

'He's going to join the Foreign Office. Van thinks he has a job for him.'

'It sounds as though your married life will mostly be spent apart?'

'It seems like that – at least for a year or two – but we think we've found a house, somewhere to call home. I can't move into Edward's "set" in Albany and my flat is much too small.'

'That's good. Where is it?'

'Sussex – near our friends the Hassels.'

'Well, you'll be safe there,' Weaver said comfortably. 'No dead bodies in Sussex, so I would imagine.'

HISTORICAL NOTE

Adam von Trott did visit Cliveden in February 1939 and Nancy Astor introduced him to a number of British politicians but his final attempt to prevent the two countries he loved going to war was doomed to failure.

Joe Kennedy was never forgiven for his support for appeasement. When war broke out Churchill preferred to deal with President Roosevelt's personal representative, Harry Hopkins. Kennedy did his best to persuade Americans that 'this is not our fight' and to stay out of the war. He resigned in 1940 and died in 1969.

His daughter Kathleen, 'Kick', married William 'Billy' Hartington on 6 May 1944 against the wishes of both their families. Billy was killed by a German sniper four months later. Kick was killed with her lover, Peter Wentworth-Fitzwilliam, in a plane crash in May 1948.

Joe Jr – who really did ride the Cresta Run in February 1939 – died on active service on

12 August 1944. Jack Kennedy became the first Roman Catholic President of the United States and was assassinated in Dallas, Texas, on 22 November 1963.